Amid concer's
new case involves a dead Catholic bishop in Chicago. The intrigue and scandal swirling around the bishop while he was alive are nothing compared to the danger and deception that follow his murder. Paul Turner has to balance his familial devotion with the expectations and pressures surrounding the murder of the prominent cleric. Local politicians and priests compete as they add risk and menace to an already difficult case. A smart, tough detective and a good, loving dad, Turner plunges into the slew of crises that confront him.

Featuring a roll call of some of the best writers of gay erotica and mysteries today!

Derek Adams

Simone Anderson

Helen Beattie

Barry Brennessel

James Buchanan

Karenna Colcroft

Ethan Day

Taylor V. Donovan

Kaje Harper

Jambrea Jo Jones

Sasha Keegan

Geoffrey Knight

J.L. Langley

Anna Lee

William Maltese

Kendall McKenna

Jet Mykles

Gregory L. Norris

Neil S. Plakcy

Rob Rosen

Jardonn Smith

Christopher Stone

Lex Valentine

Lynley Wayne

Stevie Woods

Mark Zubro

Z. Allora

Victor J. Banis

Ally Blue

Nowell Briscoe

TA Chase

Michael G. Cornelius

Diana DeRicci

S.J. Frost

Alex Ironrod

AC Katt

Kiernan Kelly

Christopher Koehler

Vincent Lardo

Elizabeth Lister

Z.A. Maxfield

AKM Miles

N.J. Nielsen

Willa Okati

Rick R. Reed

George Seaton

DH Starr

Liz Strange

Haley Walsh

Missy Welsh

Sara York

Maura Anderson

Laura Baumbach

J.P. Bowie

Jade Buchanan

Charlie Cochrane

Jamie Craig

Vivien Dean

Kimberly Gardner

DC Juris

Thomas Kearnes

K-lee Klein

Matthew Lang

Cameron Lawton

Clare London

Timothy McGivney

Robert Moore

Cherie Noel

Erica Pike

AJ Rose

Riley Shane

Richard Stevenson

Marshall Thornton

Mia Watts

Ryal Woods

Lance Zarimba

Check out titles, both available and forthcoming, at
www.mlrpress.com

PAWN OF

SATAN

MARK ZUBRO

mlrpress

www.mlrpress.com

Published by
MLR Press, LLC
3052 Gaines Waterport Rd.
Albion, NY 14411

Visit ManLoveRomance Press, LLC on the Internet:
www.mlrpress.com

Cover Art by Deana Jamroz
Editing by Neil Plakcy

Print format: ISBN# 978-1-60820-903-3
ebook format also available

Issued 2013

I wish to thank Bob Beran, Barb D'Amato, and Jamie Michel for their kind help and assistance.

ONE

Saturday 9:03 A.M.

Brian Turner thudded into the kitchen in the way only an athletic teenager can. He clumped to the refrigerator, yanked open the door, and gazed into the interior as if looking for the secrets of the universe. He spoke into the coolness. "You better talk to your other son."

Paul Turner and his husband, Ben Vargas, looked up.

Ben said, "You're wearing a pair of my black boxer briefs because?"

"All of mine are in the laundry."

Paul said, "You make a huge deal about wearing only white silk boxers, and you're parading around the house in those? Close the refrigerator door."

Brian said, "I'm not parading." He leaned into the refrigerator and selected a quart bottle of what looked to Paul like green, living, organic slime. Brian shut the door, unscrewed the cap, and guzzled straight from the bottle. Neither Paul nor Ben reminded him to get a glass. No one else would touch the health-conscious teen's odd concoctions.

"Why should we talk to Jeff?" Ben asked.

Paul and Ben wore jeans and T-shirts. They'd been sitting at the kitchen table and drinking coffee. They were reading early editions of the Sunday Chicago papers, which were delivered to their corner grocery store on Saturdays before nine A.M.

Brian wiped his lips with the back of his right wrist, pulled out a chair, turned it around, spread his legs wide, and straddled it. He said, "You know how relentlessly cheerful he is, and how he loves to do his homework with his nerdy Homework Club?"

Ben said, "Don't say nerdy."

"Sorry."

Jeff and the Homework Club conferenced over the Internet every Saturday morning before holding their online Chess Club meeting, another highlight of Jeff's week.

As the boys' grandfather had said last Christmas time when he visited, "At least he isn't into drugs and heroin."

Brian guzzled again. His parents watched his Adam's apple undulate in awed fascination as half the bottle's contents disappeared in a fifteen-second performance. More face wiping with the back of his wrist, then Brian said, "Well, he's sitting in his wheelchair not moving. Not reading. Not playing games. Not texting. I asked him what was wrong. He told me to go to hell."

Paul said, "What did you say?"

"You first."

The two men exchanged a look. Ben said, "He was fine last night when I picked him up from the Junior Science League meeting at nine."

Paul added, "When I got home and looked in his room, he was asleep. I put a bookmark in his book, closed it, kissed his forehead, shut off his light, and left. Nothing odd."

"Did you have a fight with your brother?" Ben asked. Squabbles between the two boys did happen, verbal sparring mostly.

"I was at Monica's and got home last night after he was asleep."

"Did he eat breakfast?" Ben asked.

"I haven't seen him so far this morning," Paul replied.

Brian said, "He's upset about something."

Ben said, "Thanks for letting us know. We'll check it out."

"Don't you have some kind of athletic practice to be at?" Paul asked.

Brian glanced at the time on the microwave. "Not for a couple hours. Plenty of time." But he got up, shrugged his broad shoulders, stretched his torso, and put the nearly empty juice bottle back in the fridge. As he strode out the door, Ben said, "And do your laundry. Stop borrowing my clothes."

Paul said, "And that does not mean you have permission to start wearing mine." Paul knew his older son's penchant for attempting to circumvent rules and directives with teenage legalese, as in you-didn't-say-I-couldn't-specifically do whatever he wanted permission to do or that he wished to get out of. They'd attempted to put an end to these Perry Masonish wranglings with varied degrees of success.

Since Paul had taught him to do the chore himself when he was in fifth grade, doing his laundry as little as possible was a skill Brian had honed to an art form, past the point of expertise. The first app the boy downloaded from the Internet might have been "The Teenager's Guide to Not Doing Laundry." If Brian didn't need clean clothes for dates, Paul didn't know if their older son would ever do a load of wash. They kept the door of his odiferous room closed.

After Brian was out of earshot, Ben said, "Something's bothering him too."

Paul gazed at his husband. "How can you tell?"

"He rarely slips and refers to Jeff or the things he does as nerdy. And that glop he drank?"

Paul nodded.

"It's the stuff he's most likely to drink when he's down."

"How can you tell which color goes with which mood?"

"I know he's got two jars of the red-looking stuff in there, plus a blue one, and the green one he drank from just now. He goes for the green stuff whenever he's down. It's not always true." He shrugged.

Paul sighed. "I haven't noticed anything." Brian was a pretty even-keeled teenager. He seldom appeared as a moody, depressed kid, more often pretty upbeat and willing to deal with the world on a sane basis, except when he begged for a tattoo for months on end when he turned fifteen. That phase seemed to have safely passed.

Ben said, "I haven't seen any signs other than that, and it isn't a totally reliable indicator."

"We'll have to pay a bit more attention to him as well. What do red and blue mean?"

"This isn't a perfect system, but red usually means he's got a date, blue for an important sports event. When it's orange or yellow or purple or other colors, I have no idea. I just happened to notice those three."

Paul walked down the hall toward Jeff's room. When he was a few steps from the door, he heard a loud crash. He turned the corner.

In his left hand Jeff held half of a newly-splintered trophy. Paul saw the empty space in Jeff's trophy shelf. He'd won several junior league chess championships. He held a still intact trophy in his right hand.

"Jeff!"

The boy looked at his dad. Jeff took the remnants of the trophy and banged them against his desktop. "It won't break." The remains of the top half were scattered on the floor. Jeff kept banging the bottom half of the trophy on the desk.

Paul crossed the room and stood next to his son. "You going to smash them all?" Paul looked back to the doorway. Ben and Brian stood there.

"All of them." But Jeff ceased banging the trophy bottom against his desk. Paul saw that there was now a significant groove ground into the desktop.

Paul sat down on the edge of the bed. Jeff looked at him. The boy lowered both hands and put the still-intact trophy and the half-broken one in his lap. Paul saw streaks of tears on his cheeks.

The nearly thirteen-year-old rarely cried. He claimed he didn't like to show emotion. Paul presumed it was because Jeff thought crying would show people he was weak. As a child who had dealt with spina bifida every instant of his existence, Jeff was sensitive to showing any sign of weakness, no matter how often his dads told him how proud they were of him, that physical strength wasn't the only kind of strength, and that there were lots of ways to be strong and brave.

Paul said, "Smashing things is serious."

Jeff said, "I know."

"Do you want to tell me what's wrong?"

Jeff hung his head for a few moments then looked up at his dad, then to the doorway, then down again.

Paul looked at Ben and Brian. He guessed his son wanted to talk to him without an audience. He said, "Could you guys leave us alone for a couple minutes?"

After he heard the bedroom door click shut, Paul turned his attention back to Jeff.

The boy kept his head down. Paul put his hand on Jeff's shoulder. "If you don't want to talk about what's wrong, it's okay. If it's something I can help with, I will. I won't know what to do or say until you tell me."

Jeff muttered, "There's nothing you can do. You won't understand."

Paul massaged Jeff's shoulder and said, "I can try my best. That's what I expect you to do. That's what I expect of myself. We'll talk as long as it takes for me to understand."

Jeff's head still hung down. Breaking things was usually the result of his attempting dangerous maneuvers with his wheelchair or mucking about with science experiments without his dads' supervision. Deliberately smashing something was new and told Paul that whatever was bothering Jeff was serious indeed.

Violence may have been part of Paul's job as a Chicago police detective, but it was not part of their home lives. Paul had never hit either of his boys. He'd always felt that talking and example and using other forms of punishment were more effective.

Brian had said once when he was thirteen, "Sometimes I wish you did hit."

Paul had asked why he felt that. Brian had said, "Because these long talks can be really boring."

Paul did what his parental and detective training told him to do at crisis moments. He waited. Son or suspect, usually they wanted to talk. Jeff's smashing his favorite trophy meant he very much wanted attention for something.

"You're not gonna leave and go to work?" Jeff asked.

"I'll always be here for you no matter how long it takes."

His son finally looked up. He muttered, "I want to have kids like you and Ben." His face turned crimson.

Paul had had the sex talk with each of his boys. Explaining mechanics had been easy. Answering questions about him and Ben had involved long, complex, detailed discussions of love centering on, "We love and care for each other and you kids like other moms and dads."

His intuition told him that Jeff's concerns might very well involve the mechanics or level of success someone with spina bifida could achieve in actual intercourse. He'd expected the boy would deal with this someday. As far as Paul was concerned, whether or not Jeff involved his dads in how, what, and when he learned specifics, was up to him. If the boy wanted help in dealing with something this personal, he would find a way to help his son. He hadn't expected violence.

"Did you talk to your doctor about this?"

"No, she's a woman. I can't say this stuff to her."

"Would you like a different doctor?"

"No, she's nice. And a new doctor would be a stranger."

Paul said, "You've looked on the Internet, right?"

Jeff nodded.

"And what did it say?"

"I'm kinda not sure."

"You want to go over some Web sites together?"

Jeff's eyes brightened and there was a bit of a smile at the edge of his lips, but the boy hid his eagerness behind a shrug. "Okay, I guess."

"You'll miss your Chess Club meeting."

"That's okay." His fingers flew over the keyboard and the computer screen changed rapidly. A few mouse clicks later, he nodded and said, "The other kids will take care of it."

They looked at the different sites, which gave information about people with spina bifida and sexual activity. They went over them and the information they gave for quite some time, discussing details and possibilities. If Paul felt that Jeff was becoming uncomfortable with specifics that were too intimate, he let the boy take the lead.

Near the end Paul suggested, "You should go over all this with your doctor to be certain. We're both pretty smart, but she's a professional. And don't worry about discussing this stuff with her because she's a woman. She's got lots of spina bifida patients. My guess is she's heard these questions a thousand times."

"Okay."

They turned from the computer.

"Why was this a problem this morning, and why were you smashing things?"

"I was mad because…"

Paul watched his son's eyes.

"Arvin teases me about it."

Arvin was Jeff's best friend. They'd known each other since kindergarten. Arvin was a short, scrawny kid with masses of freckles and curly brown hair.

"What does Arvin care about you having kids?"

"Uhh… It's not exactly that."

Paul waited.

Jeff looked up, looked down, stared at a poster of a chess game in progress on the wall, waited a few more moments and then met his dad's eyes. "We like the same girl."

"Do you want to tell me who that is?"

"Ardis."

"The girl in your Homework Club?"

"Yeah."

Paul remembered Ardis as slightly overweight with a tendency to giggle when she found out Brian would be chauffeuring the kids to an event.

"Does she like either of you?"

Jeff shrugged. "I haven't talked to her."

"Did Arvin?"

"He didn't come out and say it, but he kind of insinuated." His voice lowered to a whisper. "He says he did it." His son's emphasis on the word "it" left no doubt in Paul's mind that the boy meant sex. Jeff continued. "He tried to make it sound like he was a big deal expert." He shook his head. "I think maybe he was lying."

Paul nodded. "A lot of kids brag."

"He knew a lot of details."

Paul said, "Lots of kids know details because of the Internet."

"He was mean about it. He said I was a cripple, and I'd never have kids."

"I'll talk to his parents."

"No, Dad, please. I'd like to handle it myself."

Paul pointed to the smashed trophies. "I'm not sure that was a good way to handle it."

Jeff drew a shuddering breath. After the longest pause so far, he whispered, "Some days I hate this wheelchair and my life."

As the tears flowed, Paul embraced his son. This was the first time in several years that the boy's frustration had erupted so dramatically. They'd often talked about his life shuffling between crutches and a wheelchair, but Jeff hadn't mentioned it for a while. The contrast with his very athletic older brother had on occasion been the spark that led to greater frustration.

With the near onset of his teen years and desire for greater independence and autonomy, Paul expected this wouldn't be the first time they would deal with sexuality.

After a few minutes, Jeff's tears subsided. He moved from his dad's embrace. Jeff said, "I'm sorry, I shouldn't cry."

"You know that's okay."

"Yeah, I guess."

Paul leaned back slightly and looked at him carefully. "You know you could just have asked to talk to me or Ben. And Brian loves you. He would have tried to help. And telling your brother to go to hell is not acceptable. I'll expect you to apologize and mean it."

"I will. I'm sorry I smashed the trophy. It was my favorite."

It was hard to take privileges away from Jeff since most of what he enjoyed were boring intellectual things. How can you tell a super-bright kid, "And for a punishment, don't do your homework?"

Paul said, "And you'll do Brian's chores for two weeks."

"Dad!"

Paul held his son's eyes for a long moment. He said, "Be glad I don't make you do his laundry."

"Euww, gross."

Paul pointed to the desk top. "And you'll need to sand that and revarnish your desk and pay for any materials you need, out of your allowance."

"Okay."

"And if Arvin's teasing is a problem, you let me know." Paul was all too aware of non-special needs kids' willingness to inflict verbal pain on the less fortunate.

"He's not bullying me, Dad."

"Okay, just checking."

He hugged his son. "I love you."

Jeff held him tight for an instant and muttered, "Love you too."

Paul found Ben in the kitchen. It was after eleven. He hadn't been aware of the time while talking to his son. He'd have taken as much time as it took. Ben was putting away the groceries. Paul began helping with the provender. "Sorry I wasn't able to help with the shopping."

"Is he okay?"

Paul explained.

Ben said, "He's going to want to date and have sex."

"And fall in love. And get a driver's license. And be on his own. We're going to have to look into cars that are set up so he can drive. At least that's a few years away."

Ben said, "We'd better monitor him a bit more closely for a while."

Paul shook his head. "It would be easier if he did sneaky things, but mostly he does Chess Club, reads books, plays computer games, and finishes his homework, not quite a delinquent in the making."

"We've been lucky."

Paul said, "We're good dads."

Brian breezed into the kitchen in full baseball uniform. Paul suspected his son enjoyed wearing the tight fitting uniform almost as much as he liked playing the game. Brian tended to go early and stay late, to practice his skill with the sport and flirt with any of the high school girls who happened to stop by. At the moment there was no fairly significant other.

"How's Jeff?" Brian asked.

"Doing better. He'll apologize."

Brian looked at his dads. "That's cool. He's an okay kid."

Paul said, "Thanks for letting us know something was bothering him."

Ben asked, "Did you call to order your corsage?"

"Got it covered."

Planning had been going on for next week's senior prom for months. Brian had put off ordering his tux, making restaurant reservations, and ordering the corsage. Brian could dither about date details with the best of them, but this time his parents had insisted. The corsage had been the last item to be taken care of.

"What kind?" Ben asked.

"A white orchid."

Brian and a bunch of his friends had rented a limousine and were going as a group with each paired into 'close friends' but supposedly no one seriously dating. Paul figured this meant less commitment and less possibility of random sex. At least he hoped so. Brian was off to college in the fall, and he wasn't, as far as Paul knew, leaving any lovelorn young women bereft.

Brian took his slime-juice out of the fridge, finished it, and set the bottle on the edge of the sink.

Both parents frowned at him.

"Okay," Brian mumbled. He took the bottle, washed and rinsed it, then set it in the dish drainer. Paul and Ben didn't have an automatic dishwasher. "See you guys." The teenager grabbed his baseball glove from the kitchen table and dashed out the door.

Ben said, "Jeff's going to Mrs. Talucci's until I'm back from the shop." Ben owned an imported car repair shop in the neighborhood. He often worked on the cars himself. Paul enjoyed the occasional dalliance with Ben while his husband was still in his oil and grease-stained work clothes.

Paul said, "I've got to get to work, but I should be able to finish fixing the screen door on the back porch before I go. I'll bring Jeff over."

"Then I'll head for the shop."

The two men embraced. Paul nuzzled Ben's neck, pulled him close.

The back door slammed, and Brian rushed into the room. "Forgot my cleats." He glanced at his parents. The two men did not unclinch. They had long ago decided it was okay to express non-erotic affection in front of their kids. Brian said, "I can't leave you two alone for five minutes." He pulled the shoes from under the stepstool in the corner and dashed back out.

Ben repeated the universal parental dictum, "Kids are the greatest condoms in the world."

Paul said, "It has ever been so."

They resumed their embrace.

Then they heard Jeff's wheelchair coming down the hall. He had the trophy shards in his lap. Jeff said, "I'm sorry I made a mess. I know it's better to talk when I'm upset. I'm really sorry."

Paul said, "We appreciate the apology."

Ben said, "You want me to help you re-glue those?"

"You got time?"

"Plenty before I walk down to the shop."

The rest of the morning and early afternoon passed quietly. Before he went to work, Paul walked with Jeff to Mrs. Talucci's. The ninety-three-year-old neighbor lived by herself on the ground floor of the house next door. She cared for Jeff every day after school or on weekends depending on the families' schedules. For several years after he started, she refused all offers of payment. Being neighbors, and nearly family, precluded even discussing such things. But one day Mrs. Talucci couldn't fix a broken porch. Paul had offered, and since then he'd done all repairs. He and Ben had even completed several major renovations.

One daughter and several distant female cousins still inhabited the second floor. While Mrs. Talucci ruled this brood, her main concern was to keep them out of her way and to stay independent.

She rarely lost to Jeff when they played chess.

TWO

Saturday 3:12 P.M.

Harold Rodriguez slumped into the squad room. His sad, droopy eyes hunted the corners and alcoves. Then he slouched over to where Paul Turner and Buck Fenwick sat at their desks doing paperwork.

Rodriguez said, "Has anyone seen shit-for-brains?" He planted his skinny butt on Turner's desk.

They knew who he meant, Randy Carruthers, perhaps the most inept detective in the Chicago Police department whose inability to communicate with criminals, victims, suspects, or his colleagues was legendary. Carruthers was Rodriguez's partner.

Even Fenwick didn't have the nerve to ask Commander Molton, their supervisor, what kept Carruthers on the job. Everybody assumed the incompetent cop knew an alderman, a ward committeeman, someone in the mayor's office, or the police superintendent's office, or was a friend of the Cardinal Archbishop of Chicago, or was a close relative of one of the above. Staying power such as Carruthers had, assumed a clout of epic proportions.

Turner thought of clout in the correct Chicago parlance as in, "Who's your clout in City Hall?" Not how much clout did you have in terms of how much influence you had. In Chicago clout was a person first, then possibly a verb describing how much power you had.

Fenwick said, "I heard he's planning to run for office in the Detective's Association." This group served as the Union for Chicago's police detectives.

"What office?" Turner asked.

Rodriguez said, "Probably all of them. What difference does it make?"

"Maybe he died," Fenwick suggested.

"I couldn't be that lucky," Rodriguez replied.

Commander Molton strode into the room with Barb Dams, his secretary. Everyone greeted everyone. Molton began passing out handouts. The department had been undergoing changes and consolidation in the past few years. The most immediate effect being that of almost-daily, thick handouts.

Threats had been made recently that the directives would be sent electronically. While Turner did bring his own laptop from home, and his phone connected to the Internet, there was no assurance that others would have such connectors and, if they did, that they would be networked to the department. If Area Ten and the detectives there could all be guaranteed computers, perhaps that change would have happened already. And Fenwick, while not a Luddite, would consider a shoe-phone as used on the old *Get Smart* television show an upgrade from his "stupid" phone.

So far the new system had meant few immediate alterations in the detectives' work patterns. The most significant new thing was that the Area Ten perimeter had been expanded. With the changes in the department, the Area's boundaries were now Belmont Avenue on the north and Ashland Avenue on the west, but still all along the lakefront south to Fifty-ninth Street. They also got to stay in the old crumbling Area Ten headquarters which was south of the River City complex on Wells Street on the southwest rim of Chicago's Loop.

The building was as old and crumbling as River City was new and gleaming. Fifteen years ago the department purchased a four-story warehouse scheduled for demolition and decreed it would be a new headquarters. To this day, rehabbers put in appearances in fits and starts. The building had changed from an empty hulking wreck to a people-filled hulking wreck. With all the so-called improvements, departmental or structural, crime hadn't decreased, and the number of personnel hired to fight it hadn't increased.

In the Chicago police department, the Areas still took care of homicides and other violent crimes. The Districts took care of all the minor incidents and gave out traffic tickets. There hadn't been Precincts in Chicago since O.W. Wilson was in charge of the department in the 1960s.

Fenwick called the blizzard-like increase in paperwork, "Reinventing the wheel with a badge."

Fenwick glanced at the cover of the new handout. Turner watched him stifle a comment. Molton had long since lost patience with Fenwick's grousing about the changes over which he, Molton, had no control. The Commander had let him know that the complaining was to stop in his presence. Fenwick was no fool. In front of the Commander, he kept his mouth shut.

Fenwick asked, "Anything practical we need to know?"

Molton glared, daring him to bitch about the thing. "Just read it."

Fenwick nodded.

Rodriguez turned to Molton and Dams. "You guys seen Carruthers?"

Molton shook his head. Dams said, "He was upset earlier." She pointed at Fenwick. "I had to listen to him rant about your blaspheming."

"Me?" Fenwick asked.

Dams gave him a mischievous smile. "He doesn't like you referring to visits from your *goddess*."

"People took that goddess shit seriously?" Fenwick asked.

"Carruthers did," Dams said.

"He's an idiot. Nobody with an ounce of sense believes that shit. It was just a joke."

"I don't remember the funny part," Turner said.

Fenwick sulked. "They can't all be gems. I'm doing my best."

Turner said, "Stick to chocolate. You're much better at that than making feeble attempts at satire."

"Or puns," Molton added.

"Or humor of any kind," Dams finished.

Molton sighed. "He complained to me about that goddess stuff, too."

Fenwick said, "He was dumb enough to believe it? It was a joke!"

Rodriguez harrumphed. "As far as I know, Carruthers believes in fairies, sprites, the faces of weeping Madonnas on toast, and things that go bump in the night."

Fenwick got a twisted gleam in his eye. "We've seen one or two semi-clever murders in our time. A few tweaks and turns and voila, Carruthers dies, and we've got a perfect murder. And if I get caught, all we need to have is one person on the jury who's ever known someone like Carruthers. They'll never convict."

Barb Dams laughed. "You're home free. Everyone's known someone like Carruthers."

Turner held up a hand. "Wait!"

"Wait what?" Fenwick demanded.

"I have a solution."

"This I gotta hear," Molton said.

Fenwick cocked an eyebrow.

They all leaned closer to Turner. "Carruthers believes that goddess shit, right?"

Fenwick snorted. "Who cares?"

"No, listen to this. This will work." Paul Turner's eyes sparkled with mischief. "See, we put Carruthers in charge of enforcing anti-blasphemy laws."

Barb Dams said, "There aren't any anti-blasphemy laws, except maybe canon law, and I know for sure Carruthers is not a canon lawyer. And I'm even more sure that canon law is not part of the Chicago municipal code."

"All the better," Turner said. "We put him in charge of

enforcing laws that don't exist. He won't know the difference. He'll be too busy trying to figure it out. The key is, he won't be bothering the rest of us."

"Do I have to help him?" Rodriguez said.

That stopped them for a minute. They all liked Carruthers' long-suffering partner.

"Maybe you'd have more time to get real cop work done," Turner suggested. "Carruthers doesn't get any real cop work done now. How could it hurt?"

"There are so many blasphemers," Barb said, "he'd never get all of them."

"That's even better," Turner said. "We'd have selective enforcement of non-existent laws, a perfect combination."

Sergeant Felix Poindexter from the front desk downstairs interrupted their repartee. He handed Molton a note and retreated. The Commander read the note and snorted, "We've got a dead bishop."

"Chess piece or person?" Fenwick asked. "Or is there a difference?"

"The body is on the banks of the Chicago River at the foot of Willow Street, just north of Goose Island."

"What's it doing there?" Fenwick asked.

Molton frowned at him. The Commander wasn't about to become part of one of Fenwick's gag lines. Besides this one was getting pretty old. Everybody else ignored Fenwick too.

Molton slapped the note down on Turner's desk. "Have a good time, gentlemen."

He left.

THREE

Saturday 3:48 P.M.

Fenwick settled his ever expanding bulk into the driver's seat of their unmarked police department wreck. He ran his hand over his still-thinning blond hair, and struggled to get the extended-length seat belt around his gut. Today they were lucky as they needed neither the heat nor the air-conditioning in the car. They drove with the windows down and let the calm spring air replace the normal interior reek of vomit, piss, and blood. No matter how often the back seats of the department issued cars were vacuumed, sprayed, and scrubbed, the noxious odors never really came out.

They took Harrison Street over to Halsted then drove through Greek Town up to North Avenue, turned left to Sheffield, made a right, and took another left on Willow. The street dead-ended at a junkyard that bordered the river. Fifty feet to their right they saw a patrol car. They pulled up behind it. There was only one other vehicle. It was parked at the dead-end.

This was another part of the city on its way up and down. A few super trendy restaurants and art galleries had encroached on the shuttered and dingy warehouses a few blocks away. On this street all the store fronts here to the river were empty. A long abandoned rail line ran down the middle of the street.

Between the river with its struggling bits of greenery and the dead-end, was a junkyard. The chain link fence facing the street had razor wire at the top. Brick walls lined the two sides. The gate was open. Inside Turner saw twelve-foot piles: one of gravel, another of metallic junk, and a third with twisted metal rods.

A tall, skinny beat cop, Mike Sanchez, emerged from the patrol car ahead of them. His uniform pants fit tightly on his lanky frame, his bulletproof vest barely bulged out his shirt front, and his regulation hat was pulled low almost to the top of his mirrored sunglasses. The hat had two rows of Sillitoe Tartan blue and white checkered bands.

Turner and Fenwick had worked with Sanchez before. He was an efficient, no-nonsense beat cop, who had the unfortunate habit of finding Fenwick's comments funny.

Sanchez said, "The call came in about half an hour ago. We contacted the owner, he got here and opened up. We confirmed the dead body and called it in."

"How'd you know he was a bishop?"

He pointed to the dark gray Mercedes at the end of the street. "See that car?"

The detectives nodded.

"It was here when we got here. Nobody was inside. It wasn't the caller's. We did a little assuming, and it was unlocked, so we looked inside. Stuff in the glove compartment had the name of Bishop Timothy Kappel."

"Nobody noticed a car sitting here?" Fenwick asked.

"Wasn't reported," Sanchez said. "The owner of the junkyard is Darryl Dalrymple. He's…" A short squat man emerged from the opened gate. He rushed up to the detectives. "I got taken away from my family. My kid's got a sports thing tonight. How long is this going to take?"

Turner responded, "In a murder investigation, things take as long as they take."

Dalrymple gasped. "Murder! The beat cops didn't say nothing about no murder, just that I had to open the place up so they could look around. I don't know nothin' about no murder."

Dalrymple subsided from belligerence to compliance as he gave them not an iota of useful information. He'd gone to work the day before, locked up, went home. He had no awareness of any activity outside the perimeter of his property. Turner didn't get any indication of evasion or dissembling in his answers. When the detectives were done with their questions, the junkyard owner stumbled off.

Fenwick gave a sour look to the man's retreating back and said, "I'm not sure I like him."

Turner said, "If we arrested all the people you don't like, we'd have to bring in all the Cubs' losing pitchers for the past one hundred years."

Fenwick grumbled. "Well, probably not the dead ones." He sighed. "Unpleasant people make the best fodder for suspect lists, but he doesn't strike me as our killer."

While Turner agreed with that assessment, he said, "We'll have Sanchez and the beat cops check with all the other employees and keep him on the suspect list."

"We keep everyone on our suspect lists." Fenwick turned to Sanchez. "Who's our corpse catcher?"

"Some guy in a row boat who was going by on the river. Says he was fishing."

"In Chicago? On the river?" Fenwick asked.

Sanchez said, "You gotta ask him." He pointed to the patrol car. Sanchez's partner, Alex Deveneaux, got out of the front passenger side and opened the back door of the patrol car. An athletic man in his mid-twenties emerged. He must have been six-feet-five and weighed two hundred fifty pounds. His logo-less gray sweatshirt with torn-off sleeves and his tight, black basketball shorts revealed rippling muscles.

As Deveneaux and the witness walked over, Sanchez said, "I notified the ME's office. I told them to bring extra lights. Even though it's still daylight, it's kind of gloomy and hidden in there. We'll get started with the preliminaries on the neighbors as well." He glanced around at the vacant buildings. "Not a lot of neighbors on this one, but we'll check."

Turner liked working with competent cops who didn't have to be told exactly what to do at each stage.

They thanked them. Sanchez and Deveneaux left to set up crime scene tape, make sure the area was secure, and begin their canvass. So far no curious onlookers had appeared.

The witness was Don Miezina. For all his musculature, Miezina's hands shook. He spoke in a baritone voice that trembled.

The detectives stood in the middle of the quiet street to talk to him.

Miezina wiped his hand across his eyes. "I couldn't believe it. I still can't believe it."

Turner said, "Why don't you start at the beginning, Mr. Miezina? What were you doing on the river?"

"Fishing. I told the beat cops that."

Turner trusted Sanchez completely, but he always verified everything. He needed to hear the witness tell his story and then confirm later that it was exactly what he'd said to Sanchez.

Turner gave the usual bland assurance. "Thanks, if you go over everything, it'll help us reconstruct what happened."

"I guess. This is so weird. I've only ever seen dead people in funeral homes."

"What kind of fishing can you do on the Chicago River?" Fenwick asked.

"I fish for bass. I start up around Ashland Avenue. You can go east all the way to the locks on the other side of Lake Shore Drive."

"The noise of the city doesn't scare the fish?" Fenwick asked.

Turner knew neither he nor Fenwick gave much of a rat's ass about the fish at this moment, but if it helped the witness feel a bit more normal, he was willing to listen.

"I've never asked." He shrugged. "It doesn't seem to bother them. Nah, you find little corners where there isn't much current. The bass like to hang around in places like that waiting for food to come to them."

"Do you eat them?" Fenwick asked.

"Nah. I release what I catch. I figure if they can survive being in this water, who am I to deny them a full fish life?"

Turner wanted to say to Fenwick, "He sounds kind of like you." Instead, he asked, "So what happened today?"

"Well, I exercise as well as fish. I row quite a ways and then do a little fishing. It's fun to watch the noise and hurry on the bridges overhead while I'm in the quiet down below." He drew a deep breath. "So I got to this point just north of Goose Island, and I saw something odd on this bank." He waved his arm toward the river. "It seemed out of place, you know. Kind of a flash of light and pink. I figured maybe it was just a bit of shiny trash some fool had tossed away. I got closer and I saw it was somebody's glasses on the ground. The sun was reflecting off part of a lens that wasn't smashed. By that time I could figure out what the pink was." He gulped and shuddered. "It was someone. I called out. He didn't answer. I got up to the shore, but he didn't move. I saw a lot of blood. I got scared. I used my cell phone to call the police."

"Did you go up to the body?"

"No. The 9-1-1 person said to stay where I was so I could direct the police to my location. I rowed a little away. I didn't want to be too near to…that."

"Did you see anyone, anything suspicious?" Fenwick asked.

"No, for a Saturday afternoon in May, it was pretty quiet. Most of the boats that would be going out to the lake would've gone by in the morning."

They thanked him and asked him to wait. Deveneaux would take charge of him, get his information.

Fenwick let out one of his gargantuan sighs. "Once we establish the time of death, we're going to have to find out which boats passed through here. All of the people on them will have to be interviewed."

"And if there were sight-seeing boats that go up this far."

Fenwick added a grumble to another sigh.

While they'd been talking to the witness, the Crime Scene

vehicles had arrived. Sanchez came up to the detectives as they neared the stand of vegetation along the riverbank. "I checked on the computer in the car."

The more modern police cars came with electronic devices which connected to various criminal data bases, so technically they were computers, but they only connected to those data bases and not to anything else.

Sanchez was continuing, "Our witness has no record, no wants or warrants."

He led them to the edge of the trees and brush that stood along the river. "They're about twenty feet in and slightly to the left of the path. Follow the stench and the flies."

The detectives pulled on gloves and donned booties to avoid contaminating the crime scene and any footprints that might have led to or from it. As they walked in, they kept their eyes on the ground and the vegetation along the path.

Fenwick said, "At times like this I want signs along the road, like those old Burma-Shave signs."

"I vaguely remember them."

"I want them to say the killer is Fred or whoever."

"Good luck with that."

Fenwick asked, "How'd they get through the fence, and why here?"

"Check your Burma-Shave sign. Maybe that will tell you."

Sanchez's hints for corpse-finding were quite correct. They smelled it before they saw the Crime Scene tape.

"Been here for a while," Fenwick said.

The fully clothed body lay on the ground. He wore black pants, a black shirt with a Roman collar, and an unzipped black, nylon, moto jacket. The pants were stained and torn at the knees, the shirt partially untucked. Turner got a view of bloody skin through the rents in the knees of the pants. Bits of cloth protruded from his mouth.

The corpse's glasses were broken. A vast dark smear had gathered on the dirt and mushed-down weeds on the right side of his head. Your normal wounds to the exterior of the head caused extensive bleeding. Blood, bones, and brains oozed or extruded from that side of the head. Flies feasted. His eyes were closed.

Fenwick stated the obvious. "That much blood next to the head, he must have died here. With that head wound, gotta be a heavy weapon. Do bishops die violently?"

Turner shrugged. "This one sure did."

In their regulation blue notebooks, they made sketches of the placement of the body and of the surrounding area. Yes, the crime scene people would have pictures and video of the scene. That didn't stop Turner and Fenwick from keeping a written record of their own, filled with details and impressions. They wanted their own memories, thoughts, and observations. After noting numerous details that may or may not have been crime related, they backed off to wait for the Medical Examiner to finish.

They walked up to a fire pit, which was fifteen feet from the body. Fenwick held his hand a few inches above blackened ashes. "I don't feel any heat. Probably not lit last night."

"We'll get the Crime Scene people to check."

FOUR

Saturday 4:16 P.M.

The Medical Examiner, Darryl Jones, pointed at the shattered skull. "Somebody was really pissed off." He took a pointer from his pocket and extended it towards the victim's knees. "And they wanted it to hurt. He could have suffered a while. His kneecaps are smashed. Somebody was very pissed at him." The ME was in his early forties, stood maybe five-feet-six, and had slicked-down black hair.

"Knees capped while he was alive?" Fenwick asked.

"Yep."

"Ouch."

"Big ouch."

Turner said, "Somebody either wanted information or hated him a lot."

"Or both," Fenwick added.

Turner said, "Since that was the order the wounds were inflicted, it had to be more than one person. Or the killer said would you please hold still while I kneecap you and then afterwards bash your head until you die."

"More than one is logical," Fenwick said.

"Nobody found a weapon so far," the ME said, "but if it wasn't a baseball bat, it was something very much like a baseball bat."

Turner said, "They could just toss the murder weapon in the river."

"Do baseball bats float?" Fenwick asked.

"Wooden or aluminum?" the ME asked.

"Wood floats," Fenwick said. "Does aluminum foil? Is

aluminum foil the same as an aluminum bat? And a piece of wood floats but does a baseball bat?"

Turner said, "They both float."

Fenwick and the ME turned to him. "Brian left his baseball equipment out in one of those small backyard pools when he was ten. It poured rain that night. In the morning his wooden and aluminum bats were floating."

Fenwick said, "So if we don't find them in this underbrush, we have to hunt along the river for wooden or aluminum bats?"

"Pretty much," Turner said. He clapped his heavily built buddy on the shoulder. "We won't make you don a bathing suit and go swimming up and down the river looking for them."

"Got that right."

The ME said, "And I'll let you know if I find traces of wood or aluminum or splitzfizzle on the corpse so you can have an idea of which you're looking for."

"I hate when you find splitzfizzle," Fenwick said. "There's just too much splitzfizzle on this planet."

Turner said, "Didn't you have splitzfizzle fried for dinner last night?"

The ME said, "You should try it with a red sauce, garlic, mushrooms, and a robust red wine."

Turner said, "The killers could have come by boat."

Fenwick looked doubtful. "One guy in a car, the others by boat. The bishop was willingly going to a meeting where he was going to die?"

"Maybe he didn't know he was going to die."

"I got nothing on that," the ME said.

"Any signs of a struggle?" Turner asked.

"No obvious defensive wounds. No evident traces under his fingernails. We'll check under the microscope."

Turner glanced at the area around the body. "I don't see

evidence that there was a struggle."

Fenwick said, "Somebody had to be holding him. He just stood still for what was happening to him?"

"Or he was tied up or drugged."

The ME used his pointer to lift the sleeves from around the wrists. "I have no obvious ligature marks on here. They could have tied him on the outside of his jacket and the outside of his pants around his ankles. I would presume with the method of death, they'd have to have bound him in some way, duct tape, held his arms. If he was held, it would have to be one very, very strong person or several. Unless he was drugged. We'll look for trace elements on the outside of the clothes."

Turner added, "Or it was a surprise attack. He didn't see it coming."

Fenwick shook his head. "Someone walks in carrying a baseball bat to an assignation in the middle of the night, and you don't get suspicious?"

"So, planted here," Turner said, "gotta be premeditated." Then he asked, "How strong do you have to be to break a guy's leg with one swing of a bat?"

The ME chose to be picky. Turner actually preferred him that way. Better a persnickety investigator willing to be exact in getting things right. "I didn't say the knee was broken. How strong do you have to be to incapacitate him? Depends on how pissed off you are. My grandmother could, if she had enough time and no one was fighting her off. As for the death blows to the head, if that was indeed what killed him, although that seems obvious, if he's on the ground incapacitated, then you've got all the time in the world to keep on bashing."

"Any notion on time of death?" Turner asked.

The ME said, "The bishop died at midnight."

"You can be that accurate?" Fenwick asked.

With his gloved hand, the ME bent over to the corpse and picked up the lifeless arm. He used his flashlight to shed extra illumination on the watch on the wrist.

Fenwick said, "Is it time for the wrist joke?" Fenwick was referring to an ancient bit of humor that he still found so funny he couldn't tell the joke without bursting into his own fits of hysterical laughter. Turner thought it was one of the dumbest bits of attempted humor Fenwick ever indulged in. Worse, Turner still laughed every time Fenwick told it.

The ME intervened in his most severe and officious tone. "You will not now, or ever, tell that joke again in my presence. At the trial, we will play a tape of you telling that joke. If the jury itself doesn't decide to lynch you on the spot, they will most certainly come in with a verdict of justifiable homicide."

Fenwick grumbled. "Your trial or mine?"

The ME said, "If you tell the wrist joke, you will be deader than the corpse."

"How can you be deader than the corpse?"

"Watch me."

Turner pointed to the wrist. "What does the watch prove?"

"The thing is smashed. The time is precisely twelve. I would presume it stopped when the other hitting and beating occurred. Or you have two separate crimes. One where someone attacked his watch for who knows what reason and the other when someone beat him to death."

Fenwick asked, "Why attack an innocent watch?"

The ME asked, "Or why attack a guilty one?"

Turner groaned. "If you two don't stop it, I will tell the wrist joke."

They gaped at him for a moment. The ME recovered first. "I calculate he's been dead around sixteen, seventeen hours."

"He died at midnight for real?" Turner asked, "or the beating started at that moment and continued on, or it began before that, and they just happened to hit the watch at the random moment of midnight?"

"Probably, yes." The ME smiled. "Lots of possibilities."

"Why not noon?" Turner asked.

"The body's been here. Maggots in the wounds."

Fenwick sighed. "Or maybe he somehow got the watch smashed at midnight or noon some other day, and the beating had nothing to do with the watch being smashed. Or maybe the watch was stopped at the twelve position and just happened to be smashed at some later time, which may or may not have been connected to him being killed. Or even better, the watch was smashed long ago, and he wore a broken watch for sentimental reasons."

The ME said, "That's what you guys get the big bucks to figure out."

"He still wore a watch?" Fenwick asked.

"Lots of people still do," Turner said. "Did he have a cell phone?"

The ME pointed to an eight-inch-by-nine-inch plastic bag at the top of his open Crime Scene satchel. "That's what's left of it." Inside Turner could see plastic shards.

Turner said, "We'll get it to our computer people. Besides the watch, what do the forensics say about the time of death?"

"The corpse never lies," the ME said.

Fenwick said, "I hate chatty corpses."

Turner frowned at him. "You got nothing on lying corpses? You're slipping."

"It's a Saturday PM shift. Gimme time."

The ME said, "I'll know more after I cut him open, but for now the midnight time strikes me as about right."

Turner said, "I see blood on him and dark smears on the ground. He did for sure die here, right?"

"Yep."

"Must have made a lot of noise," Fenwick said.

The ME said, "What looks like a rag protruding from his mouth looks to have been bitten through at several points. It would most likely have muffled any screams."

"He choke on it?"

"Not as far as I can see. It looks like a very wet, very bloody, ordinary hanky. Wet from saliva and blood, I presume. As always, I'll know more at the lab."

"Anything else?" Turner asked.

"That's what I've got here. You can process the scene now."

"Thanks."

With his gloves on, Turner took the wallet out of the back pants pocket. He checked the driver's license. "This confirms the stuff in the car back there on the street. The address he lives in is one of those buildings on Lake Shore Drive just north of Oak Street."

"Bishops can afford to live in high rises?" Fenwick asked.

Turner said, "I have no idea what they can afford or where they usually live." He held out the ID. "This says he lived there." He checked the rest. "Odd," he said.

"What?"

"His voter ID says he lives on North Avenue, at an address which, I think, is a little west of Milwaukee Avenue at a place called the Sacred Heart of Bleeding Jesus Order abbey."

"Bishops can afford two places?"

"I don't think he'd own a whole abbey. We'll have to try both."

Turner shuffled through the rest of the items. "No emergency notification number or person to contact."

"He wasn't expecting to die? Are bishops immortal?"

"Not this one," Turner said. He counted the cash. "Still a hundred twenty-seven dollars here."

"Not a robbery."

They placed each bit from the pockets in evidence bags.

When they stood up from that work, Turner said, "Nobody missed him in all that time? You'd think somebody would miss a bishop gone for that long, then again, I don't know any bishops."

"It would have made the news," Fenwick said. "Missing bishop or kidnapped bishop. Bishops don't just disappear, do they?"

"I don't know. I've never been a bishop."

A couple members of the ME's staff began removing the corpse.

A short, young guy wearing a flat gray, cotton driving cap, jeans, long-sleeve blue shirt, and black tie led a team of three Crime Scene workers going over the ground. They'd boxed it in squares. One was taking photographs. One was on his hands and knees near the riverbank. Turner knew the heavy-five-o'clock shadowed, short guy's name was Milo.

"What do you have so far?" Turner asked.

"Your corpse finder wore running shoes with a distinct bottom. He let me take a picture of them." He showed it to them on his phone. "Those shoes came up to here." He pointed to a spot about twelve feet from the corpse. "The ground within around six feet of the corpse in pretty messed up. There's a ton of footprints, some of which, presumably, are from last night. My guess is at that time, you had at least two guys, plus the corpse, but maybe more. We're going to need to get some lights in here, and probably come back in the morning as well. It's fairly clear the footprints come from the direction of where that driverless car is parked back there on the street. Whether he drove himself, or they all came in the same car, or there were two cars or sixteen cars." He shrugged. "We'll check the ground all around back here. We'll also check for footprints and blood traces in all directions."

"At the least they must have gotten blood on their shoes."

"I would presume so, but I don't know so. After we're done, you can have your guys hunt for the weapon."

"Somebody left carrying a bat covered in blood, brains, and

gore?" Fenwick asked.

"Unless," Turner added, "he washed it off or cleaned it off in the river. Dipped it in the river. Or the killer or killers came and left by boat. Anybody can sneak up on someone and clobber them in the head with a baseball bat, but if you're torturing them ahead of time..."

"I dunno," Fenwick said. "If the first shot is one good pop on the knee, you're guy is crippled, at least down, and you can do pretty much what you want."

Milo said, "If you find the killer and the weapon, if it was a baseball bat, presumably there'd still be traces of Bishop Kappel on it."

"Or he tossed it in the river and it floated away into forever. Or they weighted it down and we'll have to drag the river."

"It'll take hours to look through all this undergrowth for blood traces. And that's when we'd be lucky to find your weapon."

"Anything that tells us how long they were here?" Turner asked.

"Not so far." Milo bent over and touched the glasses with the tip of his gloved hand. "These are in the exact position they were in when we got here."

"The dead guy walked in?" Fenwick asked.

"I have no evidence of a person or thing being dragged in. He most likely walked or was carried. It doesn't look like your killers bothered to try and obliterate footprints. We'll do the usual forensic analysis, which might or might not tell us something. I know with a dead bishop, you guys will be under a lot of pressure. I'll push my team."

Turner said, "You know we appreciate what you do. Your usual excellent job in your own time will be great."

Fenwick asked, "Could they have been on a boat and brought him in from the river?"

Milo looked down at the ground again. "I sure don't see evidence of that, and you've got that car back there. I'll email you a preliminary report on any of this crap here."

"Anything about the fire pit?" Fenwick asked.

Milo said, "Nothing so far. I don't think it's been lit for at least a week, but as usual we'll check."

"Thanks."

Milo went off to organize his people to hunt for any traces around the immediate area, throughout the vegetation, back through the junkyard, and out onto the street.

Turner said, "If they brought him here in a boat, why not kill him while they were on the river? Plus they could have just dumped him in the river at any point. For that matter, why'd they leave the body here? Why not just heave it into the river?"

"Was it kind of hidden here? In the river it might float around and be discovered sooner?"

"But dumping it in the river would make finding the actual crime scene that much harder. As it was, the body and the crime scene were only found by accident. And if it happened to rain, would any evidence at the scene be even more compromised?"

"So they cared if we found the body, but they didn't care if we found the crime scene? This isn't making sense."

Turner said, "Well, if it was making sense, it wouldn't be much of a mystery, and we'd be out of a job. It could be as simple as they didn't plan all that well, but that would mean we've got professional killers who don't plan well."

"Doesn't sound right when you put it that way."

The corpse had been removed so they could observe the ground underneath clearly.

Turner and Fenwick stepped closer to the glasses. Turner squatted down, "The glasses wouldn't have caught the reflection of the sun until about the time of day our corpse finder saw them." He looked up at the overhanging trees. "But they'd only be seen from the river." He stood back up and glanced up and down the river. The new wave of riverside high-rises and rehabs hadn't reached this far north. Mostly there were tree, brush, and weed-grown riverbanks, strewn with trash: cans, popsicle sticks, used condoms, crumpled cigarette packs, cigarette butts both filtered and unfiltered. All that would be picked up by the crime scene people as well. The sun was low in the sky. The buildings on the opposite bank were two and three story warehouses with few windows.

"Lots of cover on this side, not likely to be seen."

Turner asked, "Did they want the corpse never to be found, or they didn't really give a shit? And why'd they kill him here or leave him here? Any significance to this spot?"

They both examined the surrounding area.

"I get no sense of place," Fenwick said. "Convenient body dump or significant meaning? Not a clue."

"I agree." Turner gazed at the softly lapping water. "Why didn't they dump him in the river? Throw him in. He drifts away and it makes it infinitely harder to find the spot where they killed him."

"Could be they didn't care."

"Then why not kill him in the car, next to the car. You get out the door, swing the bat, and kafooey, dead."

"Is kafooey dead a new kind of dead?"

"Can be if you want it to be."

Fenwick sighed, "I hate too many questions."

"How many is too many?"

"If it's any number divisible by one, it can't be right." Fenwick added, "The knee cap shit sure gives the impression that it was a professional job, and there was some kind of torturing, talking to, that had to be done."

"Bishops need to be offed next to deserted river banks by professional killers?"

"Very angry, very professional, and very dangerous. Who knows what shit this guy was up to?"

They left the Crime Scene people to their work. They stopped at Sanchez's more modern patrol car to check to see if anyone had called in Kappel as missing. They got nothing.

The two of them looked up and down the deserted, empty street.

They took off their gloves and booties and placed them in evidence bags. Probably a useless activity, but they weren't about to risk headlines in the paper about "Cops Lose Case Because of Forensic Failure."

Turner said, "Killers picked a perfect venue."

"Killers?"

"Had to be at least two cars."

"They could have had a caravan in here, nobody would have noticed."

"So the killers knew the area? This wasn't random chance?"

"Unlikely."

As Fenwick drove, Turner called up the Internet on his phone and Googled Kappel. As he tapped at the screen, he gave a grumble equal to any that Fenwick could emit.

"What?"

"If the damn screen wasn't so small, it would help." When the tiny screen came up, Turner moved to enlarge the bits that would help him scroll through the list of sites. "Lots of articles on this guy." He peered more closely at the tiny letters. "And by this guy." He moved the screen back to the first entry. He enlarged the print and read a few sentences. "This says he was some kind of investigator. I'll have to go through all these on my laptop at the station. This screen is too small." Fenwick's bumps, starts, abrupt stops, and floored acceleration over the ruts and potholes in this part of town caused Turner's hand to sway. The nearly constant movement didn't make it any easier to read the tiny letters on the screen.

FIVE

Saturday 5:31 P.M.

Turner and Fenwick arrived at the luxury high-rise on Lake Shore Drive just north of Oak Street.

Fenwick said, "I thought they took a vow of poverty."

"I'm pretty sure that's just monks in abbeys and nuns in convents."

Fenwick gazed at the multi-story edifice that towered above them. "This don't look like no convent to me." It was one of the most exclusive residential addresses in Chicago. "Will the goddess be pissed if I'm working with Catholic bishops?"

Turner put his hands on the dashboard and looked at his partner.

"What?" Fenwick demanded.

Turner said, "Dear, sweet partner, friend, my gargantuan buddy, shut the fuck up about that goddess shit."

Fenwick gaped.

Turner said, "Precisely." He opened his door and got out of the car. Fenwick followed.

The lobby was modern chrome, with gray steel accents and marble floors. They identified themselves to the doorman and asked to speak to whoever was in charge. The head of security was Harold Waldin. He walked with a slight limp and had an unlit pipe clamped between his lips. He wore a dark gray suit, shirt, and tie.

"We have one of your tenants dead, a Bishop Kappel. His driver's license gave this address, said he lived in 65A."

Waldin said, "Let me check my computer." He led them to his office. He sat behind his desk. "I've got the files on all the owners here. What's the name again?"

Fenwick told him.

A few seconds later Waldin said, "Yep, here he is."

Turner said, "We'd like to see the place. He's dead and there may be clues to the killing."

"He was murdered?"

"Got his head bashed in," Fenwick said.

"Wow. Sure, I can bring you guys up since the tenant is dead."

As they rose in the elevator, Turner asked, "Did you know Bishop Kappel?"

"I mostly handle complaints and problems. He never complained that I know of, and those records I was looking at didn't say there were any."

They arrived at the sixty-fifth floor and stepped off the elevator and stopped in the hallway. Before entering the condo, Turner asked, "He live with anyone?"

"No one is listed in the registry. I don't know of anyone. We don't ask about their private lives. You'll want to ask the regular doormen."

"Anybody friendly with him?"

Waldin shrugged. "You'd have to ask the neighbors."

"We'll try to talk to them after we're done in the condo."

"No problem."

"What do these places run?" Fenwick asked.

"They start at a million and a half. The view of the lake or of downtown is unparalleled."

Using a universal key card, Waldin let them in. He moved to follow, but Turner said, "While we look around, could you assemble as many of the door personnel, maintenance, and garage people as you can?"

"Hard to get them to come in on a Saturday night."

"Anything you can do will be a help. Or get us their names

and addresses. Try not to tell them why we want them."

"That'll be tough."

"We appreciate anything you can do. And if you could assemble any video footage that you've got."

Waldin said, "We've only got lobby footage. It's a twenty-four hour loop. We only save them for the past week."

"Nothing from the parking garage?" Fenwick asked.

"They need a key to access the garage."

"Whatever you've got would be great," Turner said.

Waldin left.

Once again they donned gloves and booties. The front door opened onto a small vestibule with a coat closet to their left. A few feet farther on, they entered into a thirty-by-forty-foot living room.

To their right was a kitchen. Turner saw no dishes in the sink, only a toaster on the wide counters, a glass-front refrigerator that showed a well-stocked interior.

The living room had a Bryce coffee table with an ebony colored base, and a burl wood top that gleamed. Behind it sat an eight-foot, brown-plush chaise lounge. Two over-stuffed pillows with designs of autumnal leaves on the cover sat on either end. On each side were two brass lamps. Behind the chaise was an ashless fireplace flanked by solid brass urn andirons. The five-piece tool set had burnished bronze handles. Two comfy chairs with leather upholstery flanked the chaise on either side. A Soho bookcase filled the wall opposite the fireplace.

Fenwick said, "Nothing in the place is disturbed."

Turner nodded. "Expensive condo at an exclusive address with very pricey furnishings."

The bathroom was to the left. They found neatly hung towels and pristine porcelain fixtures, shower, and toilet. They opened both of the mirror-covered doors of the vanity.

Fenwick said, "The left side has a couple of prescriptions for

Timothy Kappel."

Turner held up a bottle from the right side. "This one's made out to Joshua Tresca." He pointed to the toothbrush holder. "Two different toothbrushes."

Fenwick asked, "Can we presume two guys lived here?"

"Beginning to look that way."

They entered the bedroom. A Parnian furniture bed sat against one wall. It had a curly maple eye-like headboard. The iPod holder/charging station and television were built in. It had a gray-with-white-bands, Grande Hotel Egyptian cotton percale duvet cover. The antique oak dresser on the opposite wall was six drawers high.

Turner said, "There's only one bedroom with one bed."

"Big feet means…"

"Big shoes," Turner finished Fenwick's gag line for him, shook his head, and added, "I'm finishing your punch lines."

"You can be taught." Fenwick nodded at the bed. "They didn't stint on the basics. Nice if you can afford it."

Turner checked the iPod for music. It was fully charged and had over a thousand playlists all listed as classical music. They ranged from ones he recognized such as Beethoven and Bach to Steve Reich, James Dillon, and Arvo Part.

After checking the closet, Fenwick said, "Two different sizes of clothes here too including black suits, black shirts, and religious collars for both."

Turner moved the clothes in each dresser drawer. After he was done with the top two drawers, he said, "Two sizes here." When he moved the boxer brief underwear in the bottom one to the side, he found a framed photo and took it over to Fenwick.

The picture was of two men when they must have been in their early twenties. They were on some beach with palm trees in the background. They wore tight skimpy bathing suits and had their arms around each other but their hips were turned slightly toward the camera. They stood far enough apart that the prominent bulges in the fronts of their Speedos revealed that one was cut and the other was uncut. The cut one had a flat ass while the other sported a nearly round bubble butt. Turner knew that many men who wore Speedos shouldn't, but when these two were young, their suits fit as well as a model's in a porn display.

In the photo their heads were turned so they could gaze into each other's eyes. An inscription read, "To Tim with all my love forever."

Turner said, "They were in love at one time. I wonder if they still were." He pointed to the taller, thinner one who had blond hair. "My guess is that's Kappel, our corpse. The dead guy sort of resembles him. Plus he's wearing glasses and the other guy is not. If the prescription bottles in the medicine cabinet tell a true story as well as reflect the past, the other guy is Joshua Tresca."

"And why hide the photo in the bottom drawer?" Fenwick asked.

"Fear? Shame? But it's odd."

"What is?"

"That this is the only personal thing. I mean, where are the monthly bills, tax records, or if they have them, personal papers, personal letters? Was this just a love nest? It's a hell of an expensive place for a love nest."

"So there must be another place for all that stuff. The only other address we've found is that abbey. We'll have to try there."

They returned to the living room. The lights of the city to the south began twinkling in the twilight of a late May sunset behind them.

The view out the windows east and south was phenomenal. Turner walked up to them and gazed out the east vista. Far below he could see Oak Street Beach and in the distance the gigantic Ferris Wheel on Navy Pier.

Turner said, "Only one name on the lease, but two people living here. If one's a bishop, then it might be safe to assume some kind of intrigue or at least need for secrecy."

"We only know clothes, pill bottles, and tooth brushes." He paused as they looked at each other. "No," Fenwick said, "I don't believe in coincidences either."

They stood at the entrance to the vestibule as they got ready to leave. Turner glanced around. He hesitated.

"What?" Fenwick asked.

"Something is not right."

"No women's underwear hidden in the back of the closet?"

Turner said, "The lack of or presence of kinky underwear is not a crime."

"No clues pointing to the killer?"

"Well that, but, no, it's something else."

Fenwick waited.

Turner swept his arm around the room facing them. "There's nothing personal here. Sure, the furniture is all expensive, but not a knickknack or a calendar. Almost as if it were a showcase. There are no displays of personal things. Clothes and prescription bottles for two different guys. And that photo. But…" He peered around. "Wait a second." He stepped to the other rooms and came back a few moments later. "Kappel was a bishop. Why the hell aren't there any religious things in this condo?"

"Do they have to have religious stuff?"

"They don't have to have anything, but you'd think a bishop would have a crucifix, something."

"The clothes are clerical stuff."

"But that's like official uniforms. I mean personal stuff."

"We found the picture."

"Hidden as if they were ashamed or frightened."

Fenwick repeated what they knew for sure. "Clothes and stuff in the dresser. Two different sizes for two different guys. Two different sized sets of clothes in the closet. They lived here."

Turner nodded. "There's that and they must have had a

cleaning service. There isn't a speck of dust. The place doesn't look lived in."

"Is that suspicious?"

"I don't know. It's just odd. I don't like odd things in a mystery."

"But it's explainable."

"I guess."

Fenwick said, "And no computer although maybe they just used their phones for access. No office space here. We'll have to find out where they worked."

The front door banged open. Instinct took over. The detectives whirled around, moved apart, hunched into crouches, and reached for their guns.

A man rushed into the room. He wore a black cassock with red buttons from collar to bottom hem and a red sash around his waist. Turner recognized the cassock accoutrements that indicated he was a bishop. He was in his early or middle fifties. His black curling hair was uncombed. Small splotches of unshaven beard showed on his chin. He addressed Turner and Fenwick, "What are you doing here?"

His voice was imperious and demanding. He brandished no weapon. The detectives lowered theirs. Years older and much heftier, but still there was little doubt this was the other man in the photo hidden in the dresser.

Fenwick used one of his favorite lines, "And who might you be?"

Turner knew Fenwick desperately wanted the suspect, witness, or arrested criminal to say, "Who would you like me to be?"

Fortunately for Turner and the rules that governed humor in the universe, none had responded so yet, much to Fenwick's dismay. Didn't stop his bulky partner from trying. Turner suppressed a smile. He would be loath to admit the amount of enjoyment he took in his partner's attempts at mirth. The attempts often being funnier than the jokes, puns, limericks, and salacious tall tales that actually emerged.

"I'm Bishop Joshua Tresca. What's going on? What's happened? You have no right to be in here."

Turner said, "Bishop Tresca, we're sorry to have to tell you this, but the man you lived with here, Bishop Timothy Kappel, is dead."

The man threw his hands up in the air, let out a shriek, turned deathly pale, and collapsed.

They holstered their guns and hurried to him. Fenwick asked, "Stroke? Heart attack? Fainted?"

Fenwick checked the man's pulse and breathing. The Bishop was doing both. Turner took out his phone, punched 9-1-1, identified himself as a police officer, and requested assistance. Then he got a glass of water and a damp washcloth from the kitchen.

Fenwick found a wallet in a pair of pants under the cassock. He riffled through it quickly. "Definitely says he's a bishop and his driver's license lists this as his address." He replaced the wallet as the man began to come around.

Tresca groaned and sat up. "What's happened?"

They helped him to his feet and to the nearest chair. He was a roly-poly man and moving him required a bit of maneuvering. For a few moments he sat with his head in his hands. Turner put the glass of water and washcloth within his reach.

Fenwick plunked himself onto the chaise but there was nothing for him to rest his back against. Turner watched his partner squirm for a minute then get up and move to the other comfy chair. Turner sat on the chaise in the space Fenwick had vacated.

After a minute, Tresca lifted his head and asked, "Is what you said true?" He had a disproportionately small head with ears that protruded outward in deformed twists. He'd have been teased about them as a child.

Turner thought, I'd lie to you about something so horrible

because? What he said was, "Yes, I'm afraid so. We're sorry for your loss."

The bishop wiped at his eyes with a starched, white handkerchief. Tresca said, "I can't believe he's dead. How did he… What happened?"

Fenwick said, "He was murdered."

Tresca clutched the arms of the chair. His eyes looked wildly around the apartment.

"Who did it? Why? How?"

"We're investigating," Turner said. "We're hoping you could help us."

"I guess. I suppose." He drew several deep breaths. "This is such a shock. Are you sure?" He gazed from one to the other of them.

The detectives waited. If this was the murderer, they needed to be extremely careful. If this was someone with information, they wanted to give him time. If this was someone who just lost a loved one, they wanted to proceed as gently as decency, courtesy, and caring required.

"I loved him. He wasn't the easiest man in the world to be in a relationship with, but I loved him." Tears fell. He used his hanky and wiped at them.

When he'd composed himself, Turner asked, "How long had you known him?"

"Since we were twelve. We were altar boys together at Saint Cathari's on the far north side of the city."

"And you both lived here?" Turner asked. "You didn't need to keep up appearances?"

"We didn't both live here."

Fenwick said, "We saw two used tooth brushes in the bathroom. Two sets of clothes in the dresser and closet. You had a key." He didn't reveal he'd gone through his wallet.

"It was someone else."

Turner thought this was kind of an absurd lie. A few seconds earlier he'd admitted to a relationship with Kappel. Turner said, "We found two sets of prescription bottles in the medicine cabinet. One set had your name on it."

"Well, I…"

The detectives waited. Turner wondered why he was bothering to lie.

Tresca moaned. "This is a nightmare."

A phone in the bishop's pocket rang. Tresca fumbled it out. He glanced at the caller ID, turned even paler, and answered it. He listened a moment, turned paler still, and stood up. Turner thought he might faint again.

Tresca gave the detectives a wary look and walked with the phone into the kitchen. The detectives instantly went into protection mode, standing up, Fenwick moving left, Turner right, hands near their guns, alert for the most minuscule sounds or actions. Turner made sure he could see far enough into the kitchen so he could observe both of Tresca's hands. Bishop or gangbanger, he and Fenwick took no chances.

All they heard for several minutes were occasional murmurs, but they couldn't hear actual words. Five minutes later when Tresca came back into the room, his ashen face was streaked with sweat. The hand with the phone trembled as he put it back in his pocket. He said, "You have to go."

"We had a few more questions."

Tresca gulped and shook his head. "I'll have to ask you to leave. Now."

"Is something wrong?" Turner asked. "We called paramedics. They should be here any second."

In a clipped, cold voice Tresca said, "I don't need them. I don't want them. Get out. You have to go. Now." The detectives rose but hesitated in front of the chaise. Tresca's voice was now a snarl. "Get out. You had no right to be here. I shouldn't be talking to you. Get out."

Turner said, "If there's something wrong, maybe we can help."

Tresca marched to the door and opened it. His cold, staring eyes did not meet theirs as they left.

Out in the hall Fenwick asked, "Should we cancel the paramedics?"

Turner shook his head. "Let them come. Let him refuse treatment. Then if there is a medical problem, it's on him, not us."

Fenwick said, "That phone call frightened the hell out of him."

"The guy faints when he hears his lover is dead, that's care, concern, passion, monumental upset. If you'd have said 'boo' to him, he might have had a stroke, but that phone call. That was fear, command, obedience, something strong enough to triumph over the news that his lover was dead."

Fenwick said, "We'll have to check on background on both of these guys. Since they're bishops, half the clergy in the city will want to butt in."

Six

Saturday 6:37 P.M.

They glanced up and down the hall. Turner said, "We might as well start with the neighbors."

Fenwick said, "We can see how they felt about our bishop buddies."

They took off their gloves and booties.

There were only two other units on this floor. At the first, no one was home. Fenwick paused with his finger an inch from the doorbell of the second. "Only three condos per floor. You need real money to live in this place."

"As opposed to fake money?"

"That's my line."

"Ring the damn bell."

A short, bird like woman with skinny arms sticking out of a heavy housecoat answered the door. She blinked at them several times. "You must be the police," she said. "I'm Loretta Eisenberg. Mr. Waldin called and said there might be officers in the building. What's happened?"

"May we come in?" Turner asked.

She demanded their identification. They showed their IDs. Satisfied, she led them inside. Turner guessed she was in her seventies. The apartment ran heavily to pink: rugs, walls, and seat cushions. In contrast white Empress Style round doilies covered every headrest and chair arm. A solid white cat sat on top of a black grand piano. The over-fed creature gave them an indifferent look and shut its eyes.

They sat on a pink, velvet-covered settee. She offered tea. They declined.

She eased herself onto a comfy chair that matched the settee, pulled her knees up under her, tucked the ends of her pink housecoat around her legs, and asked, "What's going on?"

Turner said, "We're asking questions about your neighbors on this floor, Kappel and Tresca."

She nodded. "The two bishops with one bed? None of us are supposed to know they're clerics or that they live together. Or at least share this place. I'd say they're here about half the time."

"Where are they the rest of the time?"

"I don't know."

"They cause problems?"

"Very, very quiet. Rarely had visitors that I know of."

"They never wore their Roman collars here?"

"Once in a great while."

"How'd you know they were bishops with one bed?"

"I'm not stupid. My place is three times as big as theirs. I was one of the first tenants in the building. Been here for years. I knew the two gentlemen who used to live there. Good, quiet, sweet men. Andy was a wonderful cook. Had me over for excellent gourmet meals. His lover died quite a number of years ago. Andy followed some years later. They were older, in their eighties. When Andy died, he left the place to the church. He was a very devout Catholic. I'd been in their home. I know there's only one bedroom." She leaned forward. "Andy left the whole condo to the church including the furnishings. No one ever moved in a second bed."

"Maybe you just weren't here when it was delivered."

"Oh, my, no. We all talk. We all tip the doormen well. We know."

The detectives chose not to challenge her certainty. No need to risk turning a willingly chatting, nosy neighbor hostile.

She was continuing. "Andy had given all his clothes and personal things to relatives and charities before he died. But the

Church got all the furniture." The cat jumped onto her lap. She stroked its fur with a languid hand with pink-painted fingernails as she went on. "So the place was vacant a month or two and then those two started showing up."

"When was this?" Turner asked.

"About a year after the new Cardinal was installed. I know. I went to the installation. Beautiful ceremony."

Fenwick asked, "And this was?"

"Eight years ago."

"How'd you know they were clergymen?"

"Well, when I hear elevators at three in the morning, I look out my security device in the front door. That's when I'd see them in Roman collars." She gave them what Turner thought she must think was a clever grin. "Plus, I checked their names on the Internet. You can't be too careful these days." She leaned forward with a frown. "What's happened? Why are you asking all these questions?"

Fenwick said, "Bishop Kappel was found murdered."

She gasped. "No." Her hand flew to her mouth. The cat leapt off her lap.

"Unfortunately, yes," Fenwick said.

"Was it here? In the condo? Are there killers on the loose in the building?"

"No, Ma'am," Turner said. "The body wasn't found here."

"Well, something to be thankful for."

"Yes, Ma'am," Turner said. "How well did you know them?"

"Not real well. We talked once in a while."

"Did they have visitors?"

"Not often. I can hear the elevator. I like to check to make sure no one's gotten up here who shouldn't. I don't think I'm supposed to tell, but the Cardinal has been here. It was such a thrill. Of course, I wasn't introduced. I just saw him in the hall."

"Was the Cardinal in cleric's clothes?"

"No, he wasn't."

Fenwick asked, "Did the Cardinal stay the night?"

Mrs. Eisenberg frowned and looked at both of them before answering. "I can't imagine he did."

"Did Bishop Kappel have brothers or sisters, maybe his mother or father is still alive?"

"Not that they ever mentioned to me."

"Did you ever see or hear Bishops Kappel and Tresca argue, fight?"

She said, "Listen."

They did.

"Hear that?"

They shook their heads.

"Precisely. We don't get city noise or tenants upstairs or downstairs or next door neighbor noise. This building is very solid. You don't even hear Lake Shore Drive. The windows are very thick and the place is very well insulated. The only thing I ever hear is the elevator arriving on this floor because the shaft is right next to my bed. But when was it? Let me think. It must have been about a week ago."

"What was that, Ma'am?"

"A large man, white."

"As big as my partner?"

She eyed Fenwick. "Much bigger. I was frightened."

"Why was that?"

"He was such a huge man. He kept banging on their door and shouting. I called downstairs. He left before help came. He was furtive."

"How so?" Turner asked.

The cat was now snaking his way between Fenwick's legs.

"He wore sunglasses in the building. I saw the man sitting in a parked car down the street a day or so later. He was there when I went out for groceries. He still had those big sunglasses on. He was there when I came back. I mentioned it to the doorman, but when he looked out, the car was gone."

"Did you ask the bishops about him?"

"I never got the chance."

"How'd he get into the building?"

"I asked the doorman. He said that large man must have had a key to the parking garage and got in and left that way."

She knew no more.

SEVEN

Saturday 7:15 P.M.

In the elevator down Fenwick said, "A furtive guy bigger than me. That's pretty damn big."

"And way more furtive. He knew enough to use the parking garage where there was no surveillance. And somehow he got a key. Unless maybe he also lives in the building, or used to live in the building, or knows someone who does or did, or one of the doormen is bribable."

Fenwick said, "They didn't often wear their collars around here, but Tresca showed up today in a cassock?"

Turner quoted, "Curiouser and curiouser."

Fenwick said, "Maybe when they knew she was watching they'd take off their clerics stuff to drive her nuts."

"Criminals after your own heart."

Fenwick asked, "How do you install a cardinal?"

Turner said, "Very carefully?"

"I knew that."

Turner said, "Gotta be some big deal ceremony with lots of ritual. If you care enough, you can Google it."

"I'll care if it leads to a solution to the mystery."

Downstairs Waldin had assembled the staff. He said, "Some paramedics arrived, but whoever's up in that condo told them to leave. What happened up there?"

They told him. When they finished, Waldin asked, "This Tresca lived there?"

"Says he did. He had a key."

Waldin called over an older man in a gray suit. "This is Sam

Koet, the doorman on duty now. These are detectives Turner and Fenwick from the Chicago police."

Waldin led them to an office which was more in line with an executive suite, with lush chairs, thick rugs, and better than usual hotel paintings on the walls. Waldin left them. They sat in the plush chairs around a glass top coffee table.

Fenwick asked, "Did someone go up to 65A about a half hour ago?"

"Sure, Bishop Tresca."

"He lived there?" Fenwick asked.

"Him and Bishop Kappel. When the paramedics arrived, I called up. He told me to tell them to leave. A few minutes ago, he ran out the front door. I hailed him a cab. Is something wrong?"

Fenwick said, "Bishop Kappel is dead."

"Up there? Mr. Waldin didn't say anything."

"It happened off site. How was he the last time you saw him?"

"He looked perfectly healthy yesterday about seven."

"Was he coming in or going out?"

"Out. Some big, hefty guy opened the back door of a limousine for him."

There was nothing special about the man or the limo that Koet remembered.

"Kappel and Tresca cause any problems?"

"No."

"You knew they were clerics?"

"Sure. I'm Catholic, go to mass on Sundays. I've seen pictures of them in the church bulletin and in the papers."

"Did they ever wear cleric's clothes?" Fenwick asked.

"Not usually. Priests don't as often as they used to. Lots of them just walk around in regular clothes and only put on official stuff when they have official things to do."

"Do you remember what Bishop Kappel was wearing the last

time you saw him?"

"Cleric stuff, I guess. I didn't notice anything odd."

"Were they here every night?"

"They travelled a lot, but usually."

"How often were they gone traveling?"

"It varied. Sometimes a few weeks at a time. Mostly just a day or two."

"Anything recently?"

"No, as far as I know they've been around pretty much. I don't see them every day, but we weren't saving their mail recently."

"Ever notice anything unusual about the mail?" Turner asked.

"No, but I'm not sure this was either one's primary residence. They were very quiet. There were no complaints from them or about them."

"Any particular visitors you remember?"

The man shifted from foot to foot. "Takeout food deliveries sometimes. Late at night, they had kind of a parade of visitors."

"Anything special about them?"

"Well, I've been a doorman for a long time, and we kind of notice things. Sometimes there's not much to do in a place like this. Mostly we're just supposed to keep the tenants happy."

"What did you notice about Bishops Kappel and Tresca?"

He cleared his throat. "Like I said, I'm Catholic and these guys are bishops, but I think they were doing something wrong. I'd never say something about religious people. They do lots of good, but these guys. Maybe they did good, but something was, well, odd."

"What was odd?" Turner asked.

He cleared his throat again and continued. "There were frequent visitors, young men, who came by themselves and stayed for an hour or two and then left."

"When they were both home?"

"I only met them when Bishop Kappel was here alone."

"How often did these young men show up?"

"Usually once a month and then on holidays as well."

"Same ones?"

"I don't remember any repeats."

"Any of the visitors look underage to you?" In this day with Catholic priests, if you didn't ask such a question, you were negligent.

"No, pretty much twenties, sometimes thirties."

They went through six more members of the staff from cleaning people to doormen to garage attendants. No one noticed anything unusual about the bishops in 65A. They tipped okay. No burly strangers had tried to get in to see them or had been noticed coming in with them. Turner and Fenwick would have to come back later and interview others on the day staff who Waldin hadn't managed to get in.

The detectives were finishing their notes when Waldin brought in a young man with taut muscles who wore tight, faded jeans, a torso-clinging black shirt, sleek, black running shoes, and thin wrap-around sunglasses.

He was introduced as Jose Gravis. Once the door was shut behind Waldin, Gravis took off his sunglasses and said in a deep voice, "Man, I got places to be. You can't make me come in on a Saturday night. This ain't right. I didn't steal nothin'."

Turner could see now that he had dark brown eyes that had a vulnerable, sad droop to them.

"Please sit down, Mr. Gravis."

He slouched into a chair with his legs spread wide emphasizing his slenderness, the tightness of his clothes, and the bulge in the front of his jeans.

"I gotta go quick."

"Mr. Gravis," Turner said, "Bishop Kappel is dead."

"Huh?" He sat up, glanced at each of them, leaned forward

his elbows on his knees. His eyes got a wary look.

"What shift do you work?" Turner asked.

"I'm on midnights. What happened to him?"

"He was murdered."

The detectives watched his look of incredulity. Neither of them was of the school that believed you could intuit what a person had for breakfast three weeks ago from a twitch in their left eye. That kind of body language intuition they left to writers of bad television shows. On the other hand, they noticed Gravis did not shift his eyes or twist his body. A neon sign did not appear on his chest, flashing guilty or innocent.

"The Bishop? Got murdered?"

"Yes. What can you tell us about him?"

"Not much."

"Whatever you know might help us catch his killer."

Gravis squirmed in his chair. "Are you supposed to tell stuff about bishops?"

"Did they go to you for confession?" Fenwick asked.

Gravis shook his head. "Not like that."

Turner asked, "How much did they pay you to have sex with them?"

Gravis turned his now worry-filled dark brown eyes on Turner. He hesitated, wrung his hands together, cleared his throat. He stood up, paced the room for a few seconds, glanced at them, looked away. "I don't want to get in trouble."

"We're not looking to bring trouble to you," Turner said. "We just want to solve a murder."

He nodded, cleared his throat. "It was only Bishop Kappel. Wait. Who told you?"

"You just did."

"Oh. I thought maybe it was that neighbor, Mrs. Eisenberg. She's a racist bitch. She doesn't like immigrants, people with my skin color. I was born right here in Chicago."

Turner said, "We're not trying to arrest you because somebody paid you for sex. We don't care about that. We just need to know about Bishop Kappel."

"I'm not gay."

"We don't care about that either. We just need to know about him. When did he first approach you?"

"About a year and a half ago."

"How long have you worked here?" Turner asked.

"About that long. It started a few weeks after I got hired."

"How did it come about?"

"Well, he was always real friendly, Kappel was. I was hired just before Thanksgiving. He'd talk to me. I told him about my wife and kids."

"You're married?" Fenwick asked.

"Well, yeah."

"What happened?" Turner asked.

"He'd tip me ten bucks every time I got him a cab. One time I told him I really appreciated it because things were tight. He said he wished he could help more, and a week before Christmas, he'd had a few people over. He came down after they were all gone. We talked. Somehow I mentioned not being able to afford much for the kids' Christmas presents. He told me he could tip me a bit more, if I was willing to do a bit more. I'm not stupid. I knew what he wanted. He said he was just offering. The more I was willing to do, the more he would pay."

"Anything unusual about what he wanted you to do?"

Gravis shrugged. "I don't know what's usual. I'd never done that before. It wasn't so bad, really." He blushed. "Pretty much he'd touch me, blow me, and that was that. He offered me a lot of money to kiss him." Another shrug. "So I did. It was his money."

"Did he ever talk about his life?"

"No. He'd ask about mine. He was nice like that. A lot of the time he'd want me to talk about when I had straight sex, or even descriptions of when I beat off."

"One of the other employees told us they had young male visitors."

"I only work midnights to eight A.M. five days a week. I never noticed any others."

"How'd you get into his place without his nosy neighbor noticing you?"

"I always went to the floor above and took the emergency stairs. That way she wouldn't hear the elevator stop on her floor."

"He ever ask you to find other willing guys?"

"No. I think that first time, I was sort of his Christmas present to himself."

"Why do you think that?" Turner asked.

"He told me at that time of the year, he liked to treat himself, but it became a regular thing when Tresca was gone."

"You never went with Tresca?"

"He never asked. Tresca, he was kinda nasty and snarky."

"Because of what you were doing with Kappel?"

"I don't know what he knew." He shrugged. "I think he was just that way. I suppose if he offered enough money." Another shrug. "As it was, an extra thousand a month really helped with my bills at home."

"Sounds like a lot of money," Turner said.

"For me it was. After the first couple times, I didn't mind what he wanted me to do. The cash was great."

"When was the last time you were with him?"

"Last Saturday night. I came in on my night off."

"Anything unusual?"

"He wanted to kiss and make out and hug a lot. I didn't even have to take my clothes off. He clung to me for a long time. It was a little different, but he paid me, so I didn't care."

He knew no more.

As they sat in the office for a few minutes finishing up notes on the conversations, Fenwick asked, "How did you know Kappel was paying him?"

"We had the one doorman talking about visitors. We've got a very good looking younger man. It would be unusual if he wasn't asked."

"So, it was a lucky guess."

"An educated insight."

"Same thing."

Turner said, "For all that, it shows us Kappel was human, had needs, and could afford to fill them outside of his primary relationship. Maybe he just got lonely and needed a friend."

"Yeah, well, I'd like to talk to Tresca about the nature of their primary relationship."

Turner asked, "Is it significant, him wanting only to hug, hold, and kiss Gravis the last time?"

Fenwick shrugged. "Beats the hell out of me."

Turner said, "Maybe he ran into a hustler who beat the hell out of him. Or a group of hustlers. Hunting on the Internet would be logical, but we don't have his computer to check."

"Want to try the address of the abbey?"

"It's not that late, and we've got a corpse."

"The Cardinal has been to their place. He must have known them."

"Presumably."

"We're never going to be able to interview the cardinal archbishop of the diocese of Chicago."

"Not in this lifetime."

EIGHT

Saturday 8:10 P.M.

They headed west on North Avenue. As they drove, Turner used his phone to look up information on the Order. He read the opening of the article out loud to Fenwick, "The members of Sacred Heart of Bleeding Jesus Order are known as the Pope's Commandos."

"I thought the Pope didn't have divisions."

Turner shrugged. He read several moments then summarized. "They were started at the time of the Avignon papacy. The Italian pope needed loyal defenders. Charles of Avignon got some followers, had a vision, and poof, he was a religious order."

"Good for him."

Just past Milwaukee Avenue, a seven-foot stone wall on their right ran for half a block. It ended at an open wrought-iron gate. Two snarling gargoyles sat on pillars at either end of the opening. A brass sign with raised letters said they were at St. Pachomius Abbey of the Sacred Heart of Bleeding Jesus Order.

They pulled into the well-lit, tree-shrouded driveway, which led to the front steps of a medieval fortress. A five-story tower rose above the center portion. The drive continued on to the right around the building. They could see the back end of a car peeking out from around the edge of the building. Turner walked a few steps over. He said, "It's a stretch limo."

"Anybody big, burly, and dangerous in it?"

"Not that I can see." He took down the license plate number.

From what they could see in the darkness beyond the well-lit drive, there were at least two substantial buildings on the grounds. The vast, medieval fortress they stood in front of, and then an immense five-story dormitory building that had an 1890's look, dark red brick, white window treatments, the top floor sloped to flat peaks. The dormitory stretched back toward Milwaukee Avenue.

They rang the bell. The only thing missing when the door opened was the creak from a 1930's horror movie. Somebody must have oiled the hinges. A row of motorcycles across the front, and it would have fit in with the entrance to Dr. Frank-N-Furter's castle in the *Rocky Horror Picture Show*.

An elderly man in a full cassock looked out at them from the doorway. They held out their IDs. With a halting gait, he led them into a vestibule.

"You're here about Bishop Kappel." The man must have been at least in his eighties. He had a crepey neck with wrinkled, saggy, loose, blotched skin, and with only wisps of feathery white hair on his head.

"Why would you guess that?" Fenwick asked.

The man gave him a thin-lipped smile. "I'm Brother Graffius. I don't get out any more. One of my few hobbies as I monitor the entrance is listening to the police scanner." He held up the currently silent instrument in his hand. "Plus it's on CLTV News already." CLTV was the local all-news television station. "They only let me answer the door at night when they think no one will knock. If they were the least bit Christian, they'd put me out in the first snowstorm next winter and let me die. If I last that long. Although God said fire not flood next time. A dream come true."

Turner found the despair in the old man's voice disturbing. "Is there something I can do to help?" he asked.

The old man reached out a hand and patted the detective's arm. "Thank you, no."

Fenwick cleared his throat. "Is there someone we can talk to about Bishop Kappel?"

The old man flashed his thin-lipped smile again. "It won't do you any good. They won't give you any real information."

"How do you know that?" Fenwick asked.

The old man gave a brief hint of a smile. "I've been around this religious organization a long time."

Hurrying footsteps interrupted their repartee.

Fenwick said, "Maybe we'll see you on our way out."

"Maybe so."

A portly gentleman in his late sixties or early seventies approached them down the wainscoted hall. His voice boomed, "I'm Abbot Bruchard. May I help you gentlemen?"

Turner and Fenwick introduced themselves and showed ID. Turner said, "We're here about Bishop Kappel."

"Of course. Please follow me." Bruchard wore black shoes, black pants, and a black shirt with a Roman collar. He led them through the vestibule, opened a set of ten-foot-wide dark-oak double doors, and into what looked most like a half-size nave of a medieval cathedral. Three tiered rows of chairs faced each other across the center aisle they now traversed. Oak beams in the ceiling, oak wood halfway up the walls, white plaster above.

Paintings filled the walls. They showed clerics in various period garb. They ran all the way back in time to what looked to be a woman radiating beams of light as she flew through the sky. Below her was a crucified Jesus who had phenomenal pecs and incredible abs and who was bleeding profusely. In this last, at the left-hand side at the bottom of the painting was a man in a suit of armor looking up in worshipful adoration at the woman and the bleeding Jesus.

Bruchard waved at the man in armor. "That's the founder of the Sacred Heart of Bleeding Jesus Order, Saint Charles of Avignon."

Fenwick held back a moment, leaned toward his partner, and whispered, "That can't be a boner in the front of his crotch?"

Turner looked at the protruding bulge. "Or he's hiding a ten-inch dick."

"Or the artist had a sense of humor."

Turner said, "Or in the international gay conspiracy of the

day it was a signal to others that he was one of them."

"The painter or the subject?"

"Both?"

"There was an international gay conspiracy?"

"No."

Bruchard turned back to them, "Gentlemen?"

The detectives hustled forward.

When they caught up, Fenwick said, "Hell of a place you got here."

Bruchard said, "Meyer Danforth, the great meat-packing baron, built what we call the home complex in the 1880s. It consists of the castle, the cathedral, and the old monastery. They were renovated several times. The last in the 1950s when the dormitory was built."

The three of them arrived in a room that seemed to be a mix of armory and office. Suits of armor stood every three feet against two of the walls. One wall was hung with battle axes: starting at the top, a Valkyrie's battle axe, then a double edged axe, a black dragon axe, a knight's battle axe, and nearest the ground a warlock's double axe. The rug, woven with a replica of the St. Charles of Avignon painting, covered much of the hardwood floor. A vast teak desk took up about a quarter of the room. A six-foot in diameter stained-glass rose window loomed behind the desk.

The detectives took the indicated high-back leather chairs in front of the desk. The bishop sat in a maroon swivel chair behind the desk. On it was a computer monitor, keyboard, and mouse.

Bruchard settled himself and said, "Bishop Kappel's death is a great tragedy. All who knew him cared for him and loved him. He did great, good work for Holy Mother Church."

Fenwick said, "All who knew and loved him except one, probably more than one."

Turner asked, "How well did you know Bishop Kappel?"

"All of us in the Chicago province knew each other. He and I were dear friends. His loss is most grievous."

"Did he have enemies?" Fenwick asked. "Someone who wished him ill?"

"We are a prayerful, monastic order of men dedicated to God."

Which didn't answer the question.

Fenwick said, "We'd like to examine his room."

"I'm afraid that's not possible. I'm sure there's nothing there that would help in your investigation."

Fenwick said, "We'd like to make that decision ourselves."

"I'm afraid as this is church property, that won't be possible."

Turner said, "He lived here and in a condo in one of the most expensive addresses in the city with his lover Bishop Tresca."

Bruchard frowned. "I'm aware of the condo."

And that's all he said.

Fenwick said, "Bishop Kappel's name is listed as the owner. If he took a vow of poverty, how could he afford that?"

"I'm sure you're aware that church finances are not the purview of the Chicago police department."

Fenwick asked, "Is Bishop Tresca here right now?"

"We're all adults here. We don't do bed checks."

"Would you check?"

"I don't remember him being here." He made no move to ascertain Tresca's whereabouts. If there was an intercom system, he was not going to use it. If there was a room to visit, he was not going to go there or send someone there. No search of the premises seemed to be in the offing.

After several moments of silence during which the Abbot eyed them with bland indifference, Turner asked, "Were they lovers?"

"The church has said that homosexuality is an intrinsic disorder that is grounds for not being admitted to the priesthood."

"Did anyone report or notice that Kappel was missing?"

"Again, we are all adults. We don't do bed checks."

"Did they have any friends or enemies, especially someone who wished them ill?"

"I'm sure we all have friends and enemies who wish us ill, even detectives on the Chicago police department."

Fenwick asked, "It doesn't worry you that one of your priests was murdered?"

"Are you sure it was murder?"

Fenwick said, "Unless he broke his own knees and then bashed his own head in with a baseball bat, which was not at the scene, yeah, it was murder."

"Are you attempting to be amusing, Detective? Do you treat everything as a joke?"

"Just you."

The Abbot frowned and gave him a look drenched in pity. "Someday you're going to laugh or make a joke at the wrong moment."

"And this is that?" Fenwick asked. He returned the Abbot's look of pity with a bemused condescension worthy of the most hardened Vatican bureaucrat or Chicago gangbanger. He said, "It won't be my first or last opportune or inopportune moment. How about you? I think you're pretty funny."

The Abbot said, "I think you're sad."

"I think you're ahead on pathetic points so far," Fenwick retorted. "And no, murder is rarely funny, but you are."

Turner knew that showing this amount of hostility this quickly meant that Fenwick hated the guy.

The Abbot said, "I sense hostility, Detective."

"I sense obfuscation, Abbot," Fenwick replied.

They glared at each other. After a few moments, the Abbot

spoke first. "Are you saying there's a killer targeting bishops? Priests? Members of the Sacred Heart of Bleeding Jesus Order? I'd say that was more your problem as an inability to protect the faithful from persecution, an attack on religious freedom."

Turner asked, "Did Bishop Kappel have any family that needs to be notified?"

This question brought the first break in the Abbot's demeanor. He paused for a moment. "I don't know."

"Who would?"

"I'm not sure."

Turner thought this was a crock.

The Abbot said, "We'll need his personal effects, his wallet back."

Turner said, "They're part of a murder investigation. Perhaps when we're done."

"We're eager to follow all procedure."

Fenwick asked, "Do you employ or have any knowledge of a large burly man who was seen banging on the door of Kappel and Tresca's condominium?"

"There are numerous large, burly men in this world, yourself for example. Do you have that large, burly person's name?"

Turner ignored the question. "Bishop Kappel is listed in numerous articles on the Internet as an investigator for the church." Silence from the Abbot. Turner pursued it. "Was he investigating something or someone who might want to kill him?"

"He was investigating internal church matters which I am not at liberty to discuss."

"Where were you last night around midnight?" Fenwick asked.

The Abbot smiled enigmatically and didn't answer.

Turner said, "Cardinal Duggan is a member of your order."

"That's not a secret nor is it a crime."

In ten more minutes of conversation, they got not the slightest bit of information out of him. Turner felt as much rising frustration as Fenwick did. His partner sighed and grumbled. The Abbot ignored him.

Bruchard pressed a button, and after a few minutes Graffius entered the room. He nodded his head to the Abbot who said, "If you would show these gentlemen out?"

Graffius limped ahead of them down the hall. Turner said, "I'm sorry for the way you're forced to live."

Graffius spoke softly, "Hush for a moment."

When they exited the great hall into the vestibule, Graffius cast a haunted look back behind them. He nodded and led them to a door on the right. It opened soundlessly into a short hall. He ushered them through it. The detectives kept their hands near their guns and their senses on high alert. All the medieval elegance and cleric obfuscation didn't dull their awareness of that which might be dangerous.

Graffius led them into a ten-by-twenty foot chapel lit only by rack upon rack of glowing red votive candles near the front. He collapsed into the last pew on the right.

Turner sat next to him and Fenwick leaned against the pew in front of them.

"He didn't tell you anything, did he?" Graffius asked.

"No," Turner said.

"Liars and fools." He breathed deeply as if exhausted. He ran his hand over his pate and disturbed the wisps of white hair barely a whit. "I was Abbot. Forced out years ago by these so-called political priests. I believed in real Christianity. Then God punished me for my pride. I thought I knew best. I thought no one would listen to their palaver about taking up arms against the enemies of Christ."

"Who were they?"

Graffius coughed. "Their greed and their blind ambition." He'd been speaking in a rush. He paused now, breathed deeply, and then began rocking himself back and forth in the pew.

Turner felt sorry for him. "Can we get you something?" he asked.

The aged cleric shook his head, wrapped his arms around his torso, drew a deep breath, and stopped rocking and then resumed. "My greatest sin, my greatest hubris, came in 1968. We thought our little bit of pride could change the world." He shut his eyes, rocked himself again, then gazed mournfully at Turner. "We were driving to Washington D.C. for a protest. We were going to burn draft records. We never got there. Our car went off the highway just the other side of Cleveland. Two of us died, one a dear friend, a priest, the other a seminarian. My spine has been wrong ever since. I've paid for my pride with years of pain." He sighed. "But you don't want to hear that."

Turner said, "You were trying to do good."

"We failed as will all who try to do good. Evil will triumph. It always does." He gave Turner a sad, wan smile. "You want to solve your mystery. As if that would make any difference to the corpse. He's dead. He won't care. And these other bishops and priests and the Cardinal himself, will care even less. Your investigation is a threat to them. You should look to fear for yourselves, to protect yourselves and the ones you love."

"What could they do to us?" Fenwick asked. "They can't excommunicate us or deny us communion."

"You shouldn't be flip. The Catholic Church relies on threats to one's faith when it can. When it has to, it can be a very real and a very serious institution indeed. Be careful. Take note. Kappel is dead. Be afraid."

Fenwick asked, "Are you saying members of the Order conspired to kill him? Or if we're investigating, they'd conspire to kill us?"

He rocked some more then whispered, "I don't know. They are capable of anything."

"Did Kappel or Tresca have specific enemies who would conspire against them?"

"Their enemies were legion, and they had no friends. Although they did have each other. They loved each other, I think, in their way. At least that was something."

A door to the chapel opened. Abbot Bruchard stepped into the room and marched toward them. At his approach Graffius cowered back.

"Ah, Graffius, I didn't see you at your post. I was afraid you'd fallen asleep or perhaps become ill. I assume you're all right." He glared at the officers. "You detectives don't seem to have quite made it to the door."

Turner asked, "Brother Graffius, are you all right?"

"He's fine," Bruchard said.

Fenwick said, "He can answer for himself."

Graffius hung his head. They saw him nod, heard him mumble, "I'm fine, thank you."

"Excellent! Gentleman, I'll see you out myself."

He ushered them to the front door. Moments later the detectives were in their car and on their way back to Area Ten. They stopped at Casa Lenora, a twenty-four hour deli at the corner of North and Elston. It was Fenwick's new favorite stop for artery-clogging sandwiches. Fenwick got the Italian with the works including hot peppers. Turner got an antipasto salad. They ate at a picnic table in the not-that-cool night air. After he chewed and swallowed his first gargantuan bite and guzzled half of his diet soda, Fenwick said, "Bullshit, bullshit, bullshit. And I don't like the Abbot."

Turner said, "I agree. Although, frankly I'm a little disappointed there hasn't been an Abbot and Costello reference from you."

"The fucking Abbot wasn't funny."

"Well, then you have something in common."

Fenwick growled and chewed and then slurped some more from his extra-large diet soda.

Turner ate a forkful of salad then said, "Graffius was a

revelation. I felt sorry for the old guy."

Fenwick said, "Me too."

Turner sighed. "Murder is a First Amendment attack on the Catholic church?"

"Just like contraception isn't."

"We've heard dumber shit."

"Name one."

"We're going to make a list of dumb things criminals have said to us?" Turner asked.

"It'd be a best seller. I can see the title now. *Criminals Say the Darndest Things*, or *Stupidity; the Real Story*, or the *Stupidest Criminals of Cook County*." Fenwick's eyes gleamed. "Or a reality show based on stupid."

Turner said, "Isn't that kind of redundant?"

Fenwick smiled. "I hate when you're right."

Turner remembered last winter when Jeff and a couple of his buddies, including Arvin, had spent several months of Saturday nights obsessing over some television show the name of which Turner vaguely recalled, maybe "Surviving Singer." He wasn't sure. Brian used to tease the younger boys unmercifully. His suggestion was that instead of denying the contestants food and water until they could sing, they deprive the contestants of such necessities until just after the nick of time, when, the older teenager said, he hoped they'd all "Keel over and shut up." Paul and Ben had been forced to intervene and ban Brian from the room while the younger kids obsessed. The ultimate parental question to Brian had been, "What is it to you?"

Brian's response had been, "It's a stupid waste of time."

"And did any of us make comments when you obsessed over activities of questionable use when you were younger?"

When Brian hesitated, Ben had said, "Do not dare to claim that every single one of those video games had intrinsic moral value."

Brian had said, "Every single one of those games had intrinsic moral value." Brian and his dads had laughed. And after that the older teenager left the younger kids alone.

Turner returned to the conversation. "Why'd he ask about the wallet?"

Fenwick shrugged. "So the official line is all was sweetness and light, and we are to butt out, and the unofficial line is they are all threats to each other, willing to cut each other's hearts out."

"Sounds like a lot of organizations we've dealt with."

"More secretive with more protections. And a readily available supply of toadies to hold down people as you're beating them to death with a baseball bat."

Turner said, "And we've got his knees broken before death. A lot of anger or a lot of torture."

"Torture for the hell of it, or torture to get him to tell something he knew, or to punish him? Or maybe all of the above?"

"We'll have to see if we can get Molton to budge those Church people on being more cooperative."

Fenwick shook his head. "I don't hold out much hope. Not because Molton isn't good, but this is the Catholic Church in Chicago. They may not be what they once were, but they still have influence."

Turner said, "Unfortunately, I think you're right, but there's more odd shit."

"What?"

"One of their own was missing and they weren't concerned? Running around frantically looking?"

"Maybe he went missing a lot or was gone for long periods of time. Or they were frantically looking but didn't feel the need to call the police or tell us about it just now. If he lived at the condo, would the people at the Abbey know where he was?"

"Presumably Tresca would."

"Tresca who may or may not exist at the Abbey."

"That's strange, but I still don't get why the Abbot wanted Kappel's stuff?"

"There's a clue in it that leads to the murderer?"

"I didn't see any."

Nine

Saturday 9:20 P.M.

It was just after nine. The temperature had sunk into the lower fifties. Fenwick parked their car in the cop-lot. Ian Hume emerged from the shadow of a building ten feet away.

Ian was a reporter for the *Gay Tribune*, the largest gay newspaper in Chicago. Many years ago he had been Turner's first partner on the police force and his first lover. He wore his trademark slouch fedora, khaki pants, and leather jacket.

"You could come into the station," Turner said.

"As an ex-cop, I'm not real popular around here."

"Does anybody really remember you?"

"I don't want to take the chance," Ian said. "There was a big limo out here earlier. You guys riding in style?"

"You see a big, furtive guy?" Fenwick asked.

"Bigger than you?"

"But more furtive," Turner said.

Ian asked, "Is it more burly than Fenwick or burlier than Fenwick?"

"Who cares?" Turner asked.

Ian sneered. "Philistine." And added, "I don't know about the people inside. It had tinted windows."

"Why are we being graced with a late night visit?" Turner asked.

"I hear you got a bishop for a corpse."

"Not a secret."

"I have news about their secrets."

Fenwick said, "You were dating the dead guy, his lover, and

their pet goldfish."

"They had a goldfish?" Ian asked.

"What do you know?" Turner asked.

"I used to date one of the priests in the Sacred Heart of Bleeding Jesus Order."

"You were dating a priest?" Fenwick asked. "I find that hard to believe."

"Why?"

"You're kind of radically gay, right?"

"What does that mean?" Ian asked.

Turner leaned back to listen to the exchange, slightly fascinated, slightly amused, mostly wanting to get on with their work so he could get home.

Fenwick asked, "You find the church's teachings offensive, right?"

"I kind of think the love-your-neighbor, do-unto-others parts have a lot going for them, maybe even a certain appeal. After that, not so much, and sure, the anti-gay stuff is pretty nuts, among other things."

"And you didn't mind dating a representative of those offensive teachings?"

"I'm not prejudiced. If we could only date people with flawless personalities, how'd you ever get married?"

Fenwick said, "I have hidden perfections."

"Well hidden indeed," Ian murmured.

Fenwick said, "You were willing to date a guy who believed you were an intrinsic disorder?"

"He didn't whisper church doctrines in my ear when we fucked. Mostly he called out, 'Make me daddy.'"

"The point of this?" Turner asked. "I'd like to get home before the end of the month."

Ian said, "I think the guy I used to date would be willing to talk to you about these guys."

"He knew the dead guy?" Fenwick asked.

"All the guys in the Chicago province of the Sacred Heart of Bleeding Jesus Order knew each other, at least peripherally. All of them knew Kappel, Tresca, Abbot Bruchard, and Cardinal Duggan."

"Intimately?" Fenwick asked.

"That's what I'm hoping he'd be willing to tell you."

"Have you talked to him?" Turner asked.

"I thought I'd check with you first."

Turner said, "If you can get him to talk to us, that would be great."

Ian added, "I also know, professionally, the reporter, Tyrone Bruno, who writes for the liberal national Catholic newspaper, *American Church News*. I was doing a series on gay Catholics for our paper last year, and he and I met a few times. I could get you an intro to him. He might know stuff."

"Thanks," Turner said. Ian promised to call the next day after he'd set up meetings.

TEN

Saturday 9:41 P.M.

The first thing they did when they got inside the station was find Steve Fong, the late night electronics expert at Area Ten. Fong inhabited an office in the deepest sub-basement of the decrepit old building. Naked pipes clanged and gurgled in the hall. The linoleum on the floor had long since faded to yellowish gray and begun to curl at the edges. His office had been part of the coal bin back when someone actually had to stoke coal into a furnace to heat the place. The LED displays from all the electronic equipment added to the dim light from a forest of small lamps. Fong had tried to install stronger lamps, but if he plugged in too many even slightly high-powered electronic devices, all the circuits in the building shorted out. He had the largest computer monitor Turner had ever seen, but it was seldom on as it used up too much of Fong's limited power. More wattage in the basement had been promised. Like all promises at Area Ten, it never got fulfilled.

Fong was six-foot-three and rail thin. He had a wicked sense of humor. The detectives presented him with the bag with the remnants of the cell phone. Turner said, "We're hoping you can recover data from that."

Fong took out paperwork to fill out for the chain of custody. They were all used to doing this kind of bureaucratic necessity, and it took only moments. When finished, Fong lay the bag down on the top of his work station. It was a gray metal slab with several lap top computers and microscopes. "I shall work my magic although first look says this thing is pretty well kaput."

"That a technical term?" Fenwick asked.

"It's a new computer language."

"Whatever you can get," Turner said. "We've also got credit

cards." He handed them over. "Can you run his financials?"

"I'll do what I can. I can at least get his cell phone records from the phone company, but there's no computer stuff to go through? Everybody's got a computer."

Fenwick said, "We haven't found it yet. It wasn't at his apartment. The killer or killers took it, or it's in his office, presumably on this planet, if it hasn't been destroyed."

Fong smiled. "I'm reasonably certain this planet hasn't been destroyed. At least last I looked. Although I do interplanetary investigations but for an extra fee. If you've got a destroyed planet that can be a bummer, and there isn't a whole lot I can do about that. However, if you get the computer for me, I can do the usual. I'll get to work on the cell phone remnants and see what I can retrieve, and I'll do some financials on these cards."

"I wonder if he has a Facebook account."

"For what?" Fenwick asked.

"Why does anyone?" Fong asked.

"To prove they can live as pointlessly as anyone else?" Fenwick asked.

Turner said, "That's a little harsh."

Fong began typing as the detectives reparteed.

"Maybe he tweets," Turner suggested.

"A bishop tweeting?" Fenwick retorted.

Fong said, "The Pope tweets."

"Who cares?" Fenwick asked.

"I presume the Pope," Turner said.

Fong said, "He has neither a Facebook account nor does he tweet."

"I don't tweet therefore I am not?" Fenwick asked.

"A mantra in reverse for the modern world," Turner finished.

Fong promised to get back to them as soon as he had any information.

Back at their desks, Turner went through Kappel's wallet again. He found nothing he thought might be suspicious. He included it in the packet for forensics.

Turner used his laptop to connect to the Internet. His wireless service was pretty good from this location. Fenwick was stubbornly holding out. If the department wanted to get in touch with him electronically, he was determined to wait until they supplied him with an appropriate device invented less than twenty years ago.

While Fenwick began writing up reports, Turner got to work electronically.

He ran the license plate for the limousine parked in the drive at the Abbey. It came back clean, as owned by the Sacred Heart of Bleeding Jesus Order.

Then he Googled Kappel and then Tresca. He clicked on several sites. He found this larger screen much easier to navigate. As he read, he reported highlights to Fenwick. "I got more stuff on Kappel than Tresca. Kappel was involved with investigating the diocese finances."

"Current or former?"

"Former, although according to this, there were also rumors of irregularities in the current finances." He read for a few moments then said, "This says there was a huge scandal under the previous cardinal."

"I sort of remember it. Didn't the Church try to cover it up?"

Turner said, "It all came out after the new cardinal was appointed. This says one of the problems in the diocese was financial mismanagement, supposed dirty dealings in collusion with one or more banks. A parish priest somehow got hold of a thread to the malfeasance, and his information prompted the investigation."

"Lots of motive for murder."

Turner wrote down the name of the priest in his notebook then clicked on the next article. This came from the paper that

Ian told them about.

Turner peered at the screen, read for several minutes, and then reported. "This is from the *American Church News*, which claims on its masthead to be a liberal Catholic newspaper."

"Such a thing exists?"

"Must be. It's got the name Tyrone Bruno on a couple of the articles. That's the guy Ian mentioned. This claims the old cardinal died before his monetary malfeasance got revealed."

"It really says 'monetary malfeasance'?"

"It does. You're not the only poetry pretender on the planet."

"I'd never do that kind of cheap alliteration."

"Good for you."

Fenwick said, "I still find it hard to believe a liberal Catholic paper exists."

"Because of censorship from the church itself?"

"Well, not censorship really. Even the church can't make the First Amendment disappear. No, I meant it would be hard for it to exist more because of such a small interest, such a small circulation. How can they afford to be in business?"

"I have no idea." Turner returned to his perusal of the screen. "And supposedly years ago the cardinal was involved in shuffling priests around and might possibly have been indicted from when he was a monsignor in Amarillo, Texas."

"Might possibly?"

Turner said, "The accuser was in a car accident and died. Says here it was an awfully convenient death for the future cardinal. Is death ever convenient?"

"Not on this job. I sort of remember that financial crap, but I didn't pay much attention because I don't give a shit about the Church."

Turner went on to the next article and reported again. "This one has Kappel as one of those who was investigating those nuns."

"Which nuns?"

"You heard about it. The ones who were taking care of the sick, the meek, the poor, and the downtrodden instead of playing abortion politics."

"Oh, yeah. How'd he wind up doing both?"

"This is in an article in that same liberal Catholic newspaper. The writer accuses Kappel and Tresca of being the hit men and enforcers of the Sacred Heart of Bleeding Jesus Order."

Fenwick asked, "What kind of name is that for a religious order?"

"What do you want them to name it?"

Fenwick thought a moment then said, "Steve."

"You want to name a religious order Steve?"

"Or Frank. Why not Frank? Or Pat? Maybe Otto?"

"I'm not sure you've quite got the whole religious order notion."

"Do I need to?"

"Not as far as I'm concerned, but if you really care about the names, you could complain to the Vatican."

Fenwick snorted. "What other shit is on the Internet about them?"

Turner peered at a side bar on the page he was on. "This next one is written about a guy, Theodore Keerkins, who wrote a book on the Sacred Heart of Bleeding Jesus Order."

"What kind of book?"

"Doesn't say." Turner called up Amazon.com and checked for the book. In a few seconds it came up. He read the summary and then several of the reviews. "This is something."

Fenwick leaned back in his chair.

"The reviews are all over the place. I'm guessing the reviewers are from different sides of the political spectrum. They go from raves about the book revealing the truth about a religious Order still stuck in the days of the Inquisition."

Fenwick interrupted. "No one expects the Spanish Inquisition."

Turner couldn't help himself. He laughed remembering one of his favorite bits from the old Monty Python television show. He also knew this was a moment of triumph for his partner. As much as any gay man caught in a Bette Davis time warp, Fenwick lived to quote lines from old movies or television shows that he thought were funny. Turner knew Fenwick lived for the moment he could use the line, "Don't call me Shirley." Turner suspected that saying that phrase was not as enjoyable as an orgasm for Fenwick, but it was in the same ballpark.

Turner read on and then summarized. "Some other reviews viciously attack the book for being part of attempts to crush religious freedom in this country."

"The author from around here?"

Turner checked the author profile. "Says he's from Chicago. We'll have to talk to him." He added the name to his growing list.

Turner returned to the Internet and began noting more references in the articles on Kappel and Tresca. He reported his findings to Fenwick. "Tresca I don't get so much on. He wasn't as newsworthy, or he heavily edited where he could on sites that mentioned him on the Internet. Kappel is another matter. Besides finances and nuns, he was investigating doctrinal purity at Pope Saint Agatho University on the south side."

"They really do that in this day and age?"

"I guess so. We've got lots of places to try tomorrow."

After he scanned each article, he printed it out. He'd brought an extra cable and multi-head connector from home months before so he could send print commands to a machine that with a week's worth of repairs might rival Gutenberg's in speed and efficiency.

Next Turner again looked up more articles on the Sacred Heart of Bleeding Jesus Order. In the history section, the first thing that appeared was a replica of the painting they'd seen in the great hall at the Abbey. He found that the person with the bulge in his pants adoring the flying, emanating woman was, as the Abbot had said, Charles of Avignon.

He skimmed the history to the most recent sections. The Order was very big in attempting to influence American politicians especially in terms of abortion and contraception.

After he reported to him, Fenwick said, "I could appreciate a woman being pissed off enough to get even."

"You're always pretty pro-revenge."

"I'm not sure I'm pro-revenge, but I understand it."

"Angry women, angry nuns, angry people who were molested. Although I get nothing on Kappel himself being accused of touching anybody."

"Except Tresca and the midnight to eight doorman in that building."

"And other anonymous escorts."

ELEVEN

Saturday 10:00 P.M.

Commander Molton strode to their work stations. "We have a meeting."

Fenwick grumbled.

Molton said, "This will be fun."

Fenwick asked, "At ten at night on a Saturday? Are you sure we have the same definition of fun?"

"With whom?" Turner asked.

"Bishop Pelagius the Papal Nuncio from the Vatican and Vern Drake."

Fenwick said, "The head of the Cook County Board, Vern Drake?"

"They came together."

"What the fuck?" Fenwick asked.

Molton said, "That seems to be the correct medical question."

"What do they want?" Turner asked.

"They want to give their input on your murder investigation."

Turner raised an eyebrow. Usually Molton headed off direct contact between interfering politicians and the detectives. That they were meeting had to mean something.

Molton replied to the raised eyebrow. "I think their presence here makes them great suspects. You are welcome to treat them as such."

This was pretty strong for Molton, a good boss and a great commander who they respected, but who was seldom likely to openly antagonize an official.

Fenwick grumbled all the way to Molton's office. The deep

rumbling was like being accompanied down the stairs by an unhappy circa 1890s steam engine that intermixed profanities with its huffing, puffing, gurgling, and whistling.

At the door to Molton's office, Turner asked, "What the hell is someone from the Vatican doing here? The murder was only discovered a few hours ago."

Molton said, "Precisely."

The Papal Nuncio and the head of the Cook County Board remained seated as they entered. Molton did introductions. Nobody extended hands to shake. Turner and Fenwick sat in chairs flanking either side of the Commander's desk. They faced the interlopers. The Papal Nuncio, Bishop Antonio Pelagius, was a short, stout man, with gray hair, and hands that tapered to well-manicured nails. He had the movements, demeanor, and charm of a foreman on a work crew on the side of the road, him being the guy who stood leaning against the nearest solid object while the others worked.

Vern Drake was notorious in Cook county government for tying his star to right wing Catholic causes. He was tall and thin with black hair. He ran in marathons and tended to lie about how well he had done in them.

Drake began the conversation. "We need to know what's going on with the investigation on Bishop Kappel's death." He spoke in an oily voice in the alto range.

Fenwick burst out laughing. Molton kept a placid look on his face.

Drake said, "I demand respect from a public employee."

Fenwick asked, "Where were you at midnight, twenty-three hours ago?"

"How dare you!"

Pelagius waved his hand in a dismissive gesture. "Thank you, Commissioner. You are most kind to take an interest. I'm here to help protect the good name of Holy Mother Church." He spoke in a gravelly voice, too many cigarettes and perhaps too much whiskey. He had a slight accent.

Fenwick turned to Pelagius, met his eyes and didn't look away. "Where were you at midnight, twenty-three hours ago?"

"Is this really necessary?" Pelagius asked.

Turner said, "It's a murder investigation. Those who are too interested are immediately suspects. You qualify." Turner referred to this as the Jessica Fletcher syndrome. In real life, an amateur sleuth such as Jessica would have immediately raised the suspicions of every competent cop with whom she came in contact.

Pelagius turned to Molton. "Really, Commander, couldn't we be spending our time better here?"

Molton said, "They're great questions, which neither of you have answered."

Pelagius said, "We're concerned that someone is trying to smear Holy Mother Church."

Fenwick asked, "When is the last time you saw Bishop Kappel?"

Pelagius said, "In Rome last winter."

Drake said, "I never met the man."

"Bishop Pelagius, do you know anyone who would be really angry with him?"

"Why would anyone necessarily be angry?" Drake asked.

"Because murder is a violent crime," Fenwick said, "and his death was extremely violent. Someone must have been very angry."

Drake huffed. "I don't know anything about angry."

Turner said, "A number of articles on the Internet talked about him doing a lot of investigating for the Church."

The Papal Nuncio pulled himself up. "No member of the Church would commit such a crime. His investigations were all connected with high Church matters and were conducted discreetly and with professionalism."

"Tell us about them," Fenwick said.

The Papal Nuncio sniffed. "I'm afraid that's Church business."

"When you say you know he handled them discreetly and professionally, that implies you knew something about the investigations. Knowing about them could help us catch his killer."

"I know no details that could help you."

Turner asked, "You guys familiar with Abbot Bruchard?"

Pelagius kept his mouth shut. Drake said, "No."

"We were meeting with him a little while ago," Fenwick said. "You guys talk to him, get your stories straight?"

Pelagius said, "This is getting more and more absurd."

And yet you sit here, Turner thought, *what is it you want or need or are trying to cover up?*

Fenwick asked, "Since Bishop Kappel was involved in those investigations, did he have enemies, people who were angry at him, hated him because of them?"

Pelagius waved his hand. Turner suspected the man thought it was a suave, conciliatory gesture, with a bit of authority and command behind it. Turner thought of it as a kind of effeminate gesture from a man used to commanding minions and being obeyed. "As I said, those investigations are internal Church matters."

"Seems like a lot of money might have been involved in at least some of them," Fenwick said. "Money can be a great motive for murder."

"The finances of the Diocese of Chicago are not the purview of the Chicago police department."

Fenwick asked, "How'd you find out about the murder and get here so fast?"

Drake said, "You need to remember your place."

Fenwick said, "I know exactly where my place is, arresting criminals, which you both strike me as being."

Drake turned to Molton. "Really, Commander, can't you control your people?"

"Their level of control is of no concern of yours, and you haven't answered the question."

This comment was met with silence from Drake and Pelagius.

Fenwick said, "Kappel hired call boys and had them up to his condo on Lake Shore Drive. We need to check his computer to find information about how he found them and who they might be."

"See, this is what I mean," Pelagius said. "You're deliberately smearing him."

Fenwick snarled. "Reality is reality. We've got solid evidence he hired call boys. It isn't a great stretch to investigate his connection to them. Violence can happen."

"You have no proof."

"We have at least one of the men involved."

"What's his name?"

Fenwick asked, "Are you insane? Why would we give you that name?"

Drake said, "We have a right to know what's going on in the investigation."

"No, you don't," Molton said. He turned to Pelagius. "Why are you here in Chicago, and why did you come here tonight?"

The Bishop said, "I was already here on a visit."

"Convenient," Fenwick said. "What was the visit about?"

"Apostolic work for the Holy See."

"What does that mean?" Fenwick asked.

Drake said, "We'd like to know where the investigation is headed."

Molton replied, "It's heading to finding a killer. And you didn't answer the second half of my question. Why are you here in this office now?"

Pelagius said, "I already answered that. I'm here to protect the name of Holy Mother Church."

Drake said, "We want to make sure prejudice against the Church isn't coloring the investigation."

Molton said, "Prejudice against the Church is not coloring the investigation."

Drake said, "We really need more than that."

This time all three police officials laughed.

Drake turned very red, stood up, and smashed his fist on Molton's desk. "You will be sorry you didn't treat us better."

Pelagius had a look on his face as if he'd been annoyed by a recalcitrant child. Turner couldn't tell if it was meant for them or Drake or both.

Molton stood up as well. Very quietly, he said, "Get the hell out of my office."

Drake stormed out. Pelagius stood, bowed his head an inch toward Molton, and strode after his companion.

The three officers looked at each other. Molton sighed. "That won't be the end of that."

Turner and Fenwick nodded. Fenwick said, "We got stonewalled at the Abbey." They explained what happened and what they'd found so far.

When they were done, Molton smiled.

"What?" Fenwick asked.

"I got a call from some third assistant to the mayor. The Abbot tattled."

"Third assistant?" Turner asked. "The Abbot's a nobody? Pelagius and Drake didn't seem to be from him, didn't mention him or defend him."

Molton said, "If the Abbot had complained to them, they'd have brought it up. Or at least they left the impression they hadn't spoken tonight. My guess is he would have mentioned your treatment of the Abbot among your sins."

Fenwick snorted. "They don't know sin until I get really started."

Turner was pretty sure he didn't want to know what that meant beyond an obvious bluster. He asked, "So who sent them?"

Molton said, "They came on their own?"

Fenwick said, "All who believe that raise their hands."

No one did.

Fenwick said, "The next best guess is the Cardinal sent them, but for what? To influence us? What's the point?"

Molton added, "Maybe we'll find that out when we catch the killer."

Turner said, "Finances might be the key. We found all kinds of stuff on the Internet about Kappel investigating. Supposedly he was in the middle of looking into the diocese's financial doings past and present. We need the diocese's records under the old cardinal and under the new guy. It's easy to imagine Kappel and this Tresca guy being up to something. Maybe the Cardinal, too. Maybe all of them."

"You want to examine the finances of the diocese?" Molton asked.

Fenwick pushed. "How are we going to get them to give in? We going to be able to get a warrant or a subpoena?"

Turner added, "You heard the answers from Pelagius. And remember, we got the same nothing from the Abbot, and Tresca for the short time he was talking to us."

Molton shook his head. "I'll make some calls about this church stuff. I'll do what I can. My best guess is that you are not going to be able to interview the Cardinal Archbishop of Chicago."

Fenwick asked, "Do the higher ups expect this case to be cleared by hamstringing the investigation?"

"You know the answer to that. To them, protecting the Catholic church is more important than catching a murderer.

This is Chicago. But this is my command and catching whoever the son of a bitch who did this is my and your priority. Just like it always is."

Fenwick said, "You know, one thing I don't get about this."

"What?" Molton asked.

"Nobody listens to the bishops and cardinals. Their congregations ignore them. One example, isn't it over ninety percent of Catholic women use contraception?"

"So?" Molton asked.

"So, how do they have so much power?"

Molton said, "Do we really have the time to debate the nature of power and influence in the history of politics, in the history of the United States, or in the shit-hole microcosm that is Chicago politics?"

Fenwick shrugged.

Molton said, "And no matter how much the right-wing shrieks about how awful Chicago politics is, I'm afraid it's the same story as everywhere else. Pathetic, petty men desperately trying to hold on to their vestiges of power and influence. Petty men in a colossal bureaucracy. Doesn't change from Podunk to Chicago. There's just more media here than where ever there is."

Fenwick growled but the detectives left without further comment.

While climbing the stairs back up to their floor, Fenwick finished a string of invectives with, "Numb nuts, triple fuck assholes."

Turner said, "Once again you have the correct medical description."

Fenwick had categories for people and events he didn't like. He'd gone back to triple-fuck-numb-nuts as the most egregious category, saved often for Cubs pitchers who walked in winning runs or Bears quarterbacks who threw interceptions during drives in the last two minutes of a fourth quarter.

Fenwick added, "Lying shits."

Turner said, "But who were they lying for? Themselves? Covering for the murderer? Which means they know who it is? And why cover for an escort?"

"If there is an escort involved."

"Can't rule it out. And why is the head of the County Board here?" To all that neither of them had the answer.

Fenwick said, "Those two could afford to hire burly guys in limousines to hurt people."

Turner said, "I want to know where the hell Kappel was from when the doorman saw him yesterday until the time of death. And what was Tresca doing in a cassock when Mrs. Eisenberg said he and Kappel seldom wore cleric's clothes in and out of the condominium."

"The cassock problem doesn't seem as serious to me."

"Unless it leads to finding out who the killer was."

Upstairs in the squad room, two other detectives on their shift, Joe Roosevelt and Judy Wilson sat at work stations. Two beat cops led away from them a man with his arm in a cast and two black eyes.

Roosevelt and Wilson had been detectives since the year one. Joe, red-nosed, with short, brush-cut gray hair and crooked teeth, and Judy, an African-American woman with a pleasant smile, had a well-deserved reputation as one of the most successful pairs of detectives on the force. Despite this, they averaged a major squabble about a senseless issue at least once a week. It usually started with something minor and stupid and ended with them in pouty silence. Turner noted their current pouty silence. He'd known them long enough to know this also meant they just solved a case. As soon as they started a new case, they shrugged off the problem. Anyone observing that stage of their relationship would have thought they were best friends, which in fact they were.

Roosevelt and Wilson looked up from their paper work.

Wilson asked, "What did you guys do to Carruthers?"

Fenwick said, "We haven't seen him all day. He's not dead?"

Wilson said, "I've never seen him happier. He was running around here earlier, beaming and smiling."

"But not pestering us," Roosevelt said.

Fenwick asked, "Where was Rodriguez?"

Roosevelt said, "When he showed up, Carruthers kind of deflated. He followed his partner out of here like a whipped puppy."

"What was he happy about?" Turner asked.

Wilson said, "He kept blathering on about arresting blasphemers. He was pleased with himself. He had a copy of the Chicago municipal code, several law books, and about a six-inch thick stack of printouts."

Turner filled them in on his suggestion from that afternoon. He finished, "Who told him? It was just a joke."

"You know how things fly around this station," Roosevelt said. "And Carruthers believes every rumor or even rumors of rumors."

Wilson said, "I heard two beat cops laughing about it when we were having dinner at Montini's over on Dearborn." According to Fenwick, Montini's made the best Reuben sandwiches in the city. They also had brownies made with Oreos in the middle, Fenwick's latest food-crush.

"It is funny," Roosevelt said.

"Until he arrests some poor schmuck," Turner said.

"You guys got the dead bishop case?" Wilson asked.

Fenwick said, "And what would you do with a case of dead bishops?"

Wilson said, "We should petition to have them give you Carruthers for a partner. That would be justifiable punishment."

"Cruel and unusual punishment," Roosevelt said, "but

appropriate for you."

They told them about the case then trudged back to their own desks. Turner Googled Vern Drake and Bishop Pelagius. Among the political palaver about Drake, he found that he was a member of Opus Dei, the conservative Catholic group. Looking up Pelagius, he found the bishop was a member of that organization as well as belonging to the Sacred Heart of Bleeding Jesus Order. Besides being Papal Nuncio to the United States, the next biggest thing about Pelagius was that he was a major force in the drive to canonize Pope Pius XII.

Turner reported this to Fenwick who asked, "Opus Dei? Why do I care? Are they sending a self-flagellating blond to attack us?"

"Not that I know of. It's just another piece in the puzzle."

"Why does he want a former Pope canonized? Why does he care?"

"After you become best friends, you can ask him." Turner continued, "Pelagius has been a full time Vatican nunciature."

"Huh?"

"Diplomat."

"Oh."

"And our buddy Vern Drake is a Knight Crusader of the Pontificate Medieval Guard of Saint Aloysius the Great with a gold star upgrade."

That got another, "Huh?" from Fenwick.

"They get a uniform and have ceremonies." He turned his monitor so Fenwick could see a picture of Drake in a group of other men similarly dressed. Turner said, "I'd call them Medieval drag queens but I think a drag queen would have more taste." The men wore red sashes over sparkly, pink balloon pants, and vast purple capes longer than the longest bridal train Turner had ever seen.

Fenwick took one look and said, "I wouldn't wear that dead." He peered closer for a second or two. "What's with the really big, really long, ugly capes?"

Turner read from the screen. "*Cappa magna* which I think is Latin for really big, really long, ugly capes."

An hour or so later, having finished a good chunk of the paperwork on the case, they looked at each other. They looked at the remaining paperwork on their desks. Turner checked the clock on the wall. Of all incongruities in Area Ten headquarters that timepiece was one of the oddest. Maybe older than the station, maybe the first electric clock ever put together, and the damn thing kept working, its red, sweep hand, going round and round and round. Turner knew how it felt.

Fenwick said, "I'm going home."

Turner said, "Me too."

On their way out, Molton accosted them just outside his office. He said, "I'm getting absolutely zero cooperation from higher ups about getting you information or interviews with any person or thing connected to the Catholic church. Maybe I'll have better luck in the morning."

With few other words other than goodbye and see you tomorrow, Turner and Fenwick left.

TWELVE

Sunday 12:21 A.M.

The night was warm for May, the temperature still at least in the mid 60's. As he parked the car in his driveway, Paul saw that Rose Talucci was still in her rocking chair on her front porch. She wore a dark blue shawl she had knitted. Paul strolled over.

He sat on the top step and leaned his back against the pillar on the left. He looked up at Mrs. Talucci. She often said she couldn't sleep well. On warm nights when she wasn't in the mood to read and especially when the full moon was rising, she often sat on the front porch in her favorite rocking chair. When Paul was on evening shifts on warm nights, he often strolled over, and they would talk as the stars and moon twirled overhead.

They discussed minor gossip and the neighborhood and his sons and Ben and then she asked about his case. When he finished, she asked, "The Church giving you a pain in the ass?"

"Yeah." He told her about his frustration with getting financial information about the Church or being able to interview personnel.

She agreed. "It's a closed system, rife for abuse. They are answerable only to Rome."

"But they go broke in bankruptcy court here."

"You know that's as big a joke as I do. You ever see a priest hauled away to a poor house? You ever see all the church property sold off to pay the bills? You saw how that diocese transferred millions from one fund to another to avoid having to pay."

"There's nothing we can do."

"That's often the case with the ways of the world. Maybe I can talk to some people."

Turner was never quite sure about Mrs. Talucci's connections.

Her "talking to people" could mean anything from being connected to the most powerful mafia don in the country to gossiping with the neighbors. Often amazing things seemed to get done when Mrs. Talucci talked to people. Several years ago a gang of street kids had been harassing older women returning from the neighborhood grocery store on Harrison Street. One of the kids had been found hanging naked upside down from the front of the store the day after Mrs. Talucci had "talked to someone." The problems at the store never recurred. The kid was fine, but never said a word about who attacked him. Turner also knew that the local alderman had Mrs. Talucci on speed dial. Politicians tended to recognize real power when they saw it.

Mrs. Talucci took off her glasses and massaged the bridge of her nose with two fingers. Paul knew she was tired. She still hadn't recovered from her trip up the Amazon, and she'd been back a week. Sometimes Paul forgot how frail his ninety something neighbor was. For a woman her age, she was remarkable, but nevertheless, she was that age, and time was nibbling at the edges of her life. When she took her hand away, Paul saw the indentions that the glasses made on each side of her eyes. He said, "Anything you can do, I'd appreciate."

THIRTEEN

Sunday 12:45 A.M.

At home he found Brian still in his baseball uniform. The boy was asleep on the couch, his shoes on the floor, headphones attached to his iPod, listening to music, a book open, spine up, on his chest. Turner noted the readout on the iPod. Brian was listening to a classic blues compilation. Paul remembered that Brian liked to listen to that set when he was depressed.

He touched the boy's shoulder. Brian wakened. Paul said, "Time to go to bed."

Brian nodded.

Paul asked, "You okay?"

"Sure, Dad."

Paul wasn't sure, but until the boy was ready to talk, there wasn't much he could do. The son-or-suspect-being-ready-to-talk rule didn't readily apply to reluctant or recalcitrant teenagers. If he could solve the communicating-with-your-teenager conundrum, Paul figured he could write a book and get very, very rich. No one else had yet solved that problem, so he didn't hold out much hope.

Quiet as he was when he came in from a late shift, Ben always wakened when he crawled into bed.

He gave his husband a light kiss. "The boys okay?"

"No blood, no broken bones."

Paul smiled. It was their shorthand for the world was right.

FOURTEEN

Sunday 8:47 A.M.

The next morning Brian wore a pair of his fitted, pristine clean white silk boxers as he clumped about making an orange version of his extra-lean protein glop. He got out vegetables, fruit, and raw eggs from the refrigerator and began chopping and stuffing things into a blender. Paul finished dumping the ground beans into the coffee maker and pressed on. He sat down across from his son.

"You okay?" Paul asked.

Brian didn't look his dad in the eye. He said, "Sure."

"You were listening to Blues music on your iPod, and you were drinking from the blue bottle. Sometimes you're down when that happens. Anything you're down about?"

Brian finally caught his dad's eye for a second or two then looked down. "I'm okay."

Paul let it go. If it were a teenage secret or a teen tragedy or a teen love affair or some other storm in his son's life, he'd have to wait to hear about it.

"Did your brother apologize?"

"Yeah. I feel bad for him lots of times."

"You know he doesn't like pity."

"I know. I don't show it to him. I don't say it to him, but I feel bad for him. I wish I could make it so he wouldn't have to be in a wheelchair."

Every day since the boy was born, Paul had felt the same thing.

Sunday mornings were quiet newspaper reading time. Brian read the *New York Times* Sunday sports section as well as going out and buying the final editions of the Chicago papers so he'd have the most up to date articles and in depth coverage especially of local high school teams.

Jeff did the *New York Times* crossword puzzle. In ink. Much to his brother's annoyance. Although this Sunday before starting on the puzzle, Jeff completed one of Brian's weekly chores. The youngster dusted all the downstairs, then vacuumed. Paul was glad to see that Brian, without being asked, helped his younger brother by moving the larger pieces of furniture so he could vacuum under them. He liked watching the boys work together.

Ben concentrated on the Week in Review section and the front page. Paul started with the Style and Travel sections. He still read the entirety of all the same-sex marriage announcements every week. Eventually, he and Ben and Brian would switch sections of the paper. Jeff clutched onto the puzzle and stayed close to his Internet connection sometimes for hours in his quest for completion.

They'd resolved the going to church issue a few years before. The two boys had asked to speak with Paul and Ben together. They'd presented theological, philosophical, and logistical arguments.

Paul wound up chatting with Mrs. Talucci about her attendance. She'd been feuding with various parish priests and pastors for years. She was too liberal for them. But on that bright, humid, July, Sunday morning, she'd patted his cheek and said, "I don't go because I don't believe in imaginary invisible beings in the sky who can angrily or benevolently influence our lives."

"The boys talked to you."

"Some time ago. Jeff especially expressed lack of belief. He was looking for an excuse for years to stop going to church. When Brian stopped going, he saw his opening. Brian is a sweet, smart boy. Jeff is smart and sensitive." Her smile widened. "But you know that."

"Why didn't they tell me they talked to you?"

"You could ask them that." She smiled. "I'm afraid I corrupted your sons."

"Who better?" Paul said. "At least you were there for them. Thank you."

"My dear, that was just religion. You're there for them as their dad. So is Ben. They love you both."

When he was younger, Paul himself hadn't made the break with the church he'd grown up with. As an adult, he decided it wasn't an issue worth fighting his kids about. And the need for belief in a supreme being, he now found childish.

So they spent Sunday mornings quietly.

Before he left for work just after noon, Paul and Ben met in their bedroom.

Ben said, "Kids seem normal. Has Brian been into his secret stash?" Several years ago, Paul had found the box with Brian's old baseball gloves, souvenirs, baseballs, and trophies in the garage. At the bottom in an old cigar box was Brian's secret stash.

Of candy bars.

Brian never mentioned their existence. If the boy felt a need to cheat on his self-imposed health food regimen, Paul and Ben agreed they didn't need to bring it up. They both knew that the supply got depleted when the boy was under stress.

Paul said, "I checked a few minutes ago. Nothing in it has passed its expiration date so it's reasonably fresh like it always is. It looked the same as it did after he got over the break up with Mary Ann what's-her-name a few months ago."

"That was serious."

"I know the supply was down a lot then, and way down after they lost the baseball championship last year. Last time I looked it was full. I haven't checked it in a while."

"Me either."

Ben said, "It's down a lot now."

"So he could have been munching for months."

"He's pretty faithful on his health food diet. I just don't check it that often."

"I never felt the need."

"Level of candy as a sign of a teenager's state of mind?"

"Good as any. Better than some."

"If it's accurate."

"It's another indicator that tells us we need to be watchful."

"So what do we do?"

"Worry."

Ben sighed. "Like every parent ever."

Fifteen

Sunday 1:30 P.M.

Outside the front of the station, they saw television trucks from every local and national television network and a clot of bored reporters. Inside they ran into Molton. Fenwick said, "I thought this was your day off."

"The command structure never gets days or nights off. This should not be a surprise to anyone. I've been inundated with shit on this Bishop case. Odd shit has hit the fan."

"Odd shit?" Fenwick asked.

"Do you really want to know?"

"Kind of not," Fenwick admitted.

"Besides the usual, the word I have is that your buddy, Bishop Pelagius, and his minion, Vern Drake, had a meeting with the mayor."

"That quick?" Turner asked. "They were only here last night."

Molton shrugged. "Shit happens."

Fenwick said, "I thought Drake and the mayor hated each other."

"They do." Molton chuckled. "It might have been kind of funny to be at that meeting. No, the problem is too many idiot politicians in this city, this time mixed with demented clergymen. I'll handle it. Do your jobs although it would help a lot if you caught a murderer sooner rather than later." He grinned. "But I guess that's true of all these cases."

Fenwick asked, "What about getting a subpoena for church records or talking to the Cardinal?"

Molton sighed. "Both are hopeless."

Fenwick emitted an angry growl.

Molton said, "You can growl. You can turn into a grizzly bear. You can bring a pride of lions or an angry polar bear in here and destroy the place. You are not going to interview the Cardinal Archbishop of Chicago. You can rage about it. You can fight about it. And yes, I've raged and fought about it already. Do you really want to question my ability to fight on your behalf?"

Head shakes from Turner and Fenwick.

Molton continued, "Don't worry about those assholes. You'll solve it. You know I have total faith in you guys. There's always obstacles in cases. You can beat the Cardinal and the Church if you have to."

After talking with Molton and despite his assurances, they knew the pressure was on, the media was going nuts, and there wasn't a hurricane, national tragedy, or international incident to distract the media from a dead bishop.

At their desks both Fenwick and Turner had phone messages that told them the Crime Scene personnel would meet them at two at the site of the murder and give them the results of what they had.

Before they left, Turner called the Amarillo, Texas, police department about the accuser who had died in the car accident. The detective he spoke to said there had been nothing suspicious about the death.

Turner also called the Medical Examiner. "He was not drugged. The cloth in his mouth was a hanky of the kind that is sold in a thousand stores around the country. It had only the victim's DNA. I found traces of foreign residue on his jacket cuffs and on the legs of his pants. He was bound with tape which the killers took with them, possibly to avoid leaving fingerprints or some other thing that would be on the tape which would lead to identifying the killer or killers."

Turner thanked him.

They got into their decrepit unmarked car and headed to Willow Street. They parked at the dead end next to the Crime Scene van. Milo, the same hot, youngish guy, exited his vehicle.

He said, "I have secret forensic evidence that shows who the killer is."

"Really?" Fenwick asked.

"No. I save that for poorly written cop shows on television."

"Asshole."

"I'm the asshole who has the forensics degree and training and you're the asshole who doesn't. So we're even."

"Does that make sense?"

"Who cares?"

Milo looked satisfied, as if he'd won a round of one-up-man-ship with Fenwick. Turner wasn't interested in keeping score.

Turner asked Milo, "What have you got?"

Milo said, "It took us quite a while to get all this sorted. The actual site where the body was found is a little hard to get to. That said, it has been used as a trysting place for all kinds of illicit stuff probably for many years. We got traces of drugs. We got condoms. We got sexual residue. The usual shit you'd find in a hidden urban area. And no, none of the residue we found so far related to your case. Or at least probably not much help."

He pointed to the yet-to-be towed victim's vehicle.

"First, we examined that. We have the victim's prints on the steering wheel. His are clear. The others in the car are mostly blurred or partials. We ran what we got through the system. No matches."

Fenwick said, "So he came here in it willingly."

Milo said, "I got nothing on that either way. The registration in the glove compartment said the car belonged to something called the Sacred Heart of Bleeding Jesus Order. Your bishop was not cavorting with someone in the criminal justice system who was also a passenger in this car. The back seat had some prints, none of which were the Bishop's or of anyone on file."

Milo swept the ground on the street with a laser pointer. "We have numerous indistinct prints from numerous automobiles.

Nothing that we found seemed useful."

He led the way down the quiet street toward the junkyard. "You know who actually owns this land?" Milo asked.

The detectives shook their heads.

Milo smiled. "Well, I'm a step ahead of you guys on that. The archdiocese of Chicago owns everything for a hundred yards in either direction up and down the river and up to the end of the junkyard property line. The actual junkyard property, however, a narrow strip of land, is owned by the Sacred Heart of Bleeding Jesus Order."

Fenwick said, "Some entity of the Catholic church owns this side of the river?"

"I had my guys check the records this morning. Wasn't hard to find. It's public knowledge. This much real estate in this area would be worth a great deal."

The detectives nodded. Fenwick said, "They sell this land to developers, we're talking millions, tens of millions, hundreds of millions."

Turner said, "But does that knowledge get us closer to the killer?"

The other two shrugged. They all knew that proximity did not necessarily point to a criminal or mean a conviction.

Milo continued to explain as they arrived where the body had been found. "We don't have an access point. We don't know how they got in. There are certainly places where they could have climbed over, but again, we've got no evidence that your corpse was at any of them. And if you go far enough up or down the river, there are places that show evidence that people have used them to gain entrance, but none of that evidence relates to your case, so far."

Turner said, "So one person could have climbed over or gotten in somewhere up or down the river then gone back and unlocked the gate, but you've got no forensics on that?"

"Nope. Same with the undergrowth leading to the scene. So

far we haven't found evidence that shows what your corpse did or didn't do before he became a corpse. We haven't found anything new at the crime scene itself. And half the planet could have used this area for trysting. We've got all kinds of deteriorated DNA and semen. What little we could get from the small bits that were still viable was not from anyone in the system or your victim."

Fenwick let out an enormous belch. "I love no clues."

"Anything on the fire pit?" Turner asked.

"Great news. It's the only thing in here that I can say with reasonable certainty, had absolutely nothing to do with your murder."

Back on the dead end street, Fenwick said, "A depressing lack of forensics."

"Yep."

Turner phoned Sanchez, who said, "We got nothing on the neighborhood canvass. The few people who were even around this morning claim to not have been here at all yesterday or the night before. We started on all the boats in the harbor and the tour boats. Plus we'll talk to all the employees of the businesses up and down the river. Some of that will have to wait until Monday. If we get anything from them, I'll give you a call."

Next they stopped at the condo. As they had asked him to the night before, Waldin had assembled the rest of the staff. This time they already knew about the murder. None was a studly young man like Gravis and none even hinted about, much less admitted to, servicing Kappel. Nor did any of the help admit to noticing strange young men going to the Kappel condo.

The doorman who the neighbor Loretta Eisenberg said was on duty when the "furtive" man appeared was Robin VanSchouwen.

"Furtive? I like Mrs. Eisenberg although she's a little cheap with her tips. She sees the world coming to an end every five minutes. Every stranger is furtive and dangerous to her. I just kind of nod and say yes to anything she says, but I don't pay much attention."

They checked the other neighbors. They could add nothing to what they knew already.

They called forensics. They'd examined the wallet and other personal items and found nothing suspicious.

Back at Area Ten they trudged down to see Fong. He was playing chess on level 19 on his computer. Fong smiled when he saw them. "I managed to get phone records from the number." He handed them a sheaf of papers. "I just got done a few minutes ago. I was waiting for you to come back to deliver them."

The detectives glanced at the list of numbers. "You know who these people are?"

Fong handed him another list of names. They'd go over them at their desks.

Fenwick asked, "You got anything on Kappel's financials?"

Fong handed them a printout of Kappel's credit card purchase records for the last twelve months. He'd made two copies. His printer tended to work more faithfully than the one the detectives had available to them.

"Anything stand out to you?"

"Nothing special, but you'll get some notion of his life from what you've got."

At their desks they perused the phone records first. They glanced back and forth from numbers to names. Fenwick started from the first of April, Turner from the last call made.

Turner said, "The last three calls were to Tresca. One that afternoon at four-seventeen then again at nine-sixteen and the last one at nine-fifty-six. The final two lasted a minute each."

"We gotta talk to Tresca. I think we've got calls to the Abbot, calls to the Cardinal. They were his bosses, friends or enemies, but constant contacts."

"And they aren't talking to us."

"Not yet."

Turner dialed Tresca's number. He got the recording that said the inbox was full. He tried several of the other numbers listed. He got voice mail on all of them. He reported to Fenwick. "I called four numbers connected with religious people, the Abbey, the Cardinal. They aren't answering."

"It's a conspiracy, by members of the Catholic church. Now there's an unusual thought."

They hunted through the credit card statements. Turner said, "We got his travel records and meals. There's a month's worth in Key West for all of January. There's pay-for sites where he could watch porn on the internet." Turner double checked the sites. "These are all just video or picture gallery sites. None of them is an escort site."

"Doesn't tell us who the killer is."

"Nope."

"He watched porn and paid for escorts."

"He was horny a lot?"

"A horny bishop?"

"Bishops don't get horny?"

"No idea."

Sixteen

Sunday 2:30 P.M.

They began interviews from the list Turner had compiled the night before with those who might be most negative about Kappel and/or the Sacred Heart of Bleeding Jesus Order. The first name they had was Xavier Garch. He was the head of the theology department at Pope Saint Agatho University. Like Loyola and DePaul Universities, the other large Catholic institutions of higher learning in the area, it was an urban university. Garch lived on Sheridan Road north of Hollywood.

They parked in the tow zone in front of the high rise at the corner of Granville and Sheridan. Garch's building was forty stories and was your basic glass and steel box with little to distinguish it from other glass and steel boxes.

The doorman called up. Garch was home. They took the elevator to the thirty-fourth floor.

In the elevator Fenwick asked, "Who was Pope Saint Agatho?"

Turner said, "That's why they created Google so you'd have an outlet for your useless questions."

"You could have just said look it up yourself."

"Look it up yourself."

A slender man smoking a cigarette answered the door. Turner thought he was in his late fifties. They showed him identification. He invited them into a room with bookshelves filled with books from floor-to-ceiling on three walls. The fourth wall was floor-to-ceiling windows with a view of the lake.

A large area rug sat in the middle of a hardwood floor. On it were four black leather armchair recliners. Each chair had its own pole reading lamp and small table with a pile of three or four books and an ashtray on each. The place stank of stale cigarette smoke.

Xavier Garch invited them to sit. He spoke in a high, reedy voice. "You're here about Timothy Kappel."

"Why would you presume that?" Fenwick asked.

"I saw the news on the Internet. He was a shit to the university, and he and I had clashes. Why wouldn't you be here?"

"Did you know him?"

"For nearly thirty, forty years."

"You knew him before he was investigating the university."

"Oh, my yes."

"How did you meet?" Turner asked.

Garch leaned back in the chair and with the hand that didn't have a cigarette, pulled the lever on the side of the chair. The footrest swung out, and he rested his feet on it. He crushed out the cigarette in a half-filled cut crystal ashtray. Without checking to see if they objected, he took out another cigarette, but he didn't light it, just held it in his hand.

He said, "Let's go back a little. I knew Kappel and his good buddy Tresca. We were in the seminary together. Those two were inseparable. I got thrown out. The priests in charge told me I wasn't a good fit. They were probably right. I had doubts about God and religion then. I don't believe at all now. Kappel and Tresca? I have no idea if they ever believed. I've always assumed their alliance was part of being in a relationship, although Tresca would go on and on about how he wanted 'a bust in the mouth' before he took his vows."

Fenwick said, "Maybe he was trying to be funny."

"Maybe that's funny to a third grader."

Fenwick had the sense to keep silent.

Garch said, "I've found that those who insist on trumpeting their heterosexual credentials are often the ones most over-compensating."

Turner tended to agree with this analysis. He asked, "Did you have a relationship with either of them?"

Garch snorted. Waved the hand with the still unlit cigarette at them. "I shouldn't tell you this. I very much wanted a relationship with Kappel. He was nice and thin. Below the thorax he was perfect. His face." He shrugged. "Kappel was more intellectual than handsome. I was attracted to how smart he was although they were both pretty smart. Tresca did have a nice bubble butt. His problem is he has a shit personality. Kappel was no prize as a person, but at least he was human. But I never got what I wanted from them, except the last night, the same evening after the afternoon meeting when the priests in charge of the seminary told me I had to leave. It was quite late. We walked down to that spot on the river where Kappel's body was."

"You know that spot?" Fenwick asked.

"All of us did. That spot on the river was a trysting place for young seminarians in any Catholic religious order within fifty miles. It was known the church owned the property. We felt very risqué being there. North Avenue is a mile north of there. Milwaukee Avenue and the Abbey are a mile west, but other seminarians used it as well."

"Why not find a hidden spot at the Abbey?"

"The original parts of the old mansion/castle had all kinds of hidden trysting places, but at the height of the whole thing when I was there, it was like you practically had to take a number to get a spot. And there were homophobic old priests who, if they found you, would get your ass thrown out. It was safer to go to the river."

"A four-mile walk?"

"To not get caught, sure, why not? It was safe."

"How did you get in?"

"You used to be able to follow a path along the river made by trysting couples gay and straight over the years. So we didn't have to walk along North Avenue or down Sheffield. So it really wasn't four miles. We walked the hypotenuse of the triangle not the two sides. At that time for a long way we could go along the river.

Some of us didn't even get as far as the trysting place before we were finished. Sometimes we could check out one of the 'house' cars and drive. Horny guys will find a way. That's where I gave them their blow jobs that last night. One watched the other. I'd wanted to do that for a long time."

"You knew them well," Fenwick said.

Garch snorted. "Far too well." He stared out the windows for a few moments. "I don't know if I sucked them off that night for revenge, pleasure, or desperation. Or all three or none of the above." He shrugged. "I guess it doesn't matter now." He looked back at them.

"And through the years?" Turner asked.

"We lost touch for a long time. I still haven't seen or met Tresca in many years. Kappel, unfortunately, I got to know all too well in the past few years."

Turner said, "We read on the Internet that he led the investigation at the University."

"Investigation! Ha! Inquisition is what it was. Everything except the torture and the rack."

"What was it about?"

"Doctrinal control. Political control."

Fenwick asked, "Was his investigation fair?"

"Fair? You're asking about fair and the Catholic church? Using those words together in a sentence is a criminal offense. Fair! The Catholic church! Not in this city, not on this continent, not on earth, not in this century, not from since before the Inquisition, if even then. The key to his investigations was prudence, or delay, or obfuscation, or secrecy, not justice. Outside the church, anyone was fair game for his whims."

Turner suppressed a sigh of satisfaction. You were more likely to get information from malcontents. A lot of nonsensical belly-aching as well, but that came with the territory.

Fenwick asked, "What about the investigation was unfair?"

"Let me tell you about church and university politics." He stuck the unlit cigarette in his mouth, took it out again. He said, "At a real university what's key is the spirit of inquiry in an atmosphere of academic freedom. That's not what the Vatican wants. They want doctrinal purity. They want marionettes to parrot their bullshit on abortion or contraception or gay marriage or a host of other issues. They don't care who gets in their way or about the notion of a free university."

"A return to the Inquisition," Fenwick suggested.

"Oh, yes. So *fair* is not really an operative word. Fear would be more accurate. The church is frightened and with good reason. But, I stay. I have a very good salary and a great health insurance plan. I run the department, teach a few classes."

"How was Kappel a threat to that?"

"He could destroy it all."

"How?"

"He could get me fired. He could get any professor fired who dared to express independent thought."

Fenwick asked, "But isn't that the nature of a university, to express independent thought?"

"But they don't care about the nature of the university. And really, they don't care about doctrinal purity. They care about obedience to them."

"How'd the investigation come about?"

"In May 2012 the Pope reiterated the mandate that professors at Catholic universities had to be faithful to the teaching of the Church. Canon 218." He got up and dug a book out of the top shelf of the bookcase near a door that led to a kitchen. He leafed through the book for several pages then read, 'Those who are engaged in the sacred disciplines enjoy a lawful freedom of inquiry and of prudently expressing their opinion on matters in which they have expertise, while observing due respect for the magisterium of the Church.'" He closed the book. "Which means do as we say or lose your job."

Fenwick asked, "They can do that to a modern university?"

"They can try. They can get the bishops to try and enforce it. This didn't start just in 2012. They've been cracking down for years. One of my best professors, a good, smart, spiritual, holy man got pushed out."

"When was this?"

"Fifteen years ago, before this most recent investigation. It was my first year as chairman of the department."

"But you stayed."

"I'm a coward. That priest, William Alba, who wrote extensively about recognizing the authority of the church, but still saying he dissented from particular teachings. They got rid of him. A tenured professor! William even took them to court. He lost. No, the church wants strict adherence to their rules. Kappel was the current enforcer. If he decided you were not doctrinally pure enough, you got turned in, and the vast, hidden and not so hidden Catholic church bureaucracy, began to grind you down."

"There's a hidden and an open bureaucracy?" Fenwick asked.

"You bet. And the hidden is far more dangerous."

"But how would anyone know about it if it's secret?" Fenwick asked.

"It's there. Good luck finding it. If it has something to do with the murder, you will never find it, and you will bring danger to you and yours."

Turner asked, "So what did Kappel find out in the university investigation?"

"He called in every single one of the members of the department. He called in over half the students. He asked about what was being said and taught in classes. He and his minions took voluminous notes, tape recorded poor college freshmen. The son of a bitch didn't actually have to find proof. All you need to do is twist a phrase, add innuendo, claim a fact is in dispute or controversial."

Fenwick asked, "But isn't all theology basically someone's

opinion about poetry written hundreds or thousands of years ago?"

"That, my dear detective, is blasphemy."

"Well, I suppose, but doesn't it come down to I think or I believe God said this? Then somebody else stands up and says God said that. There's no way to prove it. God doesn't do a network broadcast."

Garch said, "So we get Holy Wars and Jihad, and millennium upon millennium with bloodshed beyond all reason."

Fenwick said, "But bloodshed within the realm of faith is okay?"

Garch frowned. "You've just described the written history of the planet."

"But what could they threaten a non-church member with? Deny them communion? Who cares?"

Turner had had enough of Fenwick's theological and philosophical banterings with Garch. He got them back to the topic by saying, "Kappel was going to get you fired."

Garch sighed. He flipped the still unlit cigarette across and around the fingers of his left hand in a sort of modified, extended coin walk/nickel roll. One second the cigarette was between his thumb and forefinger, and the next it was between his pinky and index finger. Turner admired the dexterity and nimbleness. He also wished Garch would light the damn thing and stop playing with it.

The professor said, "Probably."

"With him dead, will that stop the process?"

"I don't know. I don't know what stage his investigation was at. I don't know what his reports said, or if he'd even made them yet. That's one of their weapons, uncertainty, the ability to make you anxious."

"But killing him would be likely to put a stop to persecution of you?" Fenwick suggested.

Garch gave him a bitter smile. "Probably not. The Catholic church might not be as openly vicious as during the Inquisition, but trust me, they are still as sneakily vicious." He took out a pack of matches and held them in the opposite hand from the cigarette. "You know Kappel and Tresca were lovers?"

"How'd they get away with having a place for themselves?"

"The intricacies of how they got away with what are unknown to me. I know very little about the actual dynamics of their relationship."

"Were they in love?" Turner asked.

Garch paused and looked thoughtful, put the cigarette in his mouth, and took it out again. He said, "I don't know."

"You heard anything about Kappel hiring escorts?" Fenwick asked.

"I wouldn't know. Nor would I care. He never struck me as the kind who needed any human contact or warmth. I only know about his investigation here."

"What can you tell us about Cardinal Duggan?" Turner asked.

"When the Cardinal was appointed from the Sacred Heart of Bleeding Jesus Order, he brought Kappel and Tresca along with him into his administration from the Order. They have his complete trust."

"Do you know anything about financial scandals in the archdiocese?"

"The diocesan priests are still quaking in their boots and the Cardinal has been in office eight years. Those two were his enforcers. They showed up in your parish, and you never knew what shit was going to hit the fan."

Fenwick asked, "Were there financial irregularities?"

"This all happened internally. There was never a public scandal although there were occasional rumors, but under the previous Cardinal, who was never directly accused of anything, there were allegations of graft, nepotism, cronyism connected to awarding contracts at inflated prices, irregular purchasing procedures. All kinds of shit."

"Any of it true?" Fenwick asked.

He shrugged. "The old Cardinal died. They brought this new guy in, Duggan, and he brought Kappel and Tresca along. The old guard fought back, but the new regime was the master of smear, innuendo, and infighting. People got transferred. People got silenced. The actual truth of who may or may not have done what got lost completely."

Turner asked, "But wouldn't the old guard be just as good at smear, innuendo, and infighting?"

"No one was as good as Kappel and Tresca."

Fenwick asked, "Why wouldn't a silenced priest go to the media, call the police, get a lawyer?"

Garch gave him a condescending smile. "If you've been skimming money and have amassed a fortune, do you want to draw attention to yourself by lavishly spending it on expensive lawyers? And why call a press conference accusing others of what you yourself were doing? Sure, you could accuse, but you'd be accused back, and the diocese has money, tons of it to spend on attorneys. And more than money, influence behind the scenes to start and stop investigations. Probably including yours."

"What if you had documentation?"

"Church documentation? Who's going to be able to prove it? These people are responsible to the Vatican, not to the local Justice of the Peace."

"What if you were an accuser and honest?" Fenwick asked.

Garch let out a bark of a laugh. "Honest? Then you can't afford an attorney. The police? How are they going to get church documents? How hard was it to get documents about priestly sex abuse? Like prying a tooth from an unanaesthetized tiger. And if you're a poor priest, as most of them are, and you go to the media, you've got no standing, no one will back you up. The Church has media experts who will destroy you completely and utterly."

He switched the cigarette and matches from one hand to the other then continued. "And if you're a priest in a position of power, you're older. If you're older, do you have a pension, prospects for a job outside the clergy? No. Do you have health insurance if you get pitched out? No. You don't get Social Security because you've never contributed. You've got nothing. The church protects itself, and very much will hurt, if it can, those who cross it."

"Cheating in the diocese continues?" Fenwick asked.

"I've heard yes and no. The old guard that was replaced certainly has made accusations."

"Do you know any specific enemies?"

"The most public and fiercest was Father Alfred Bernard." Bernard had made headlines at his parish on the west side for decades and was a flamboyant and effective advocate for his parishioners and the community. Numerous cardinals had tried to silence him to little effect.

"Were Kappel and Tresca instrumental in getting Father Bernard thrown out of his parish?"

"He wasn't actually thrown out. Sort of demoted. He still lives there as adjutant, semi-retired assistant. Of course, all of this was done behind the scenes, and sneakily and dishonestly, but it was them." He cleared his throat. "Let me correct myself. I have no proof, but it had to be them. The Cardinal trusts them implicitly."

"And you know this how?" Fenwick asked.

"I work at the largest Catholic university in the diocese. I have friends. Not as powerful or as connected as Kappel and Tresca, of course, but you hear things. You should talk to Bernard. Now there was one pissed off priest."

Turner asked, "Have you seen a large burly man hanging around in a limousine?"

"No, who's he?"

"We don't know."

Fenwick asked, "You ever dealt with Bishop Pelagius the

Papal Nuncio or Vern Drake, the Cook County Commissioner?"

"I've only vaguely heard of either one."

"Where were you on Friday around midnight?" Fenwick asked.

"Home. In bed. By myself."

The detectives left.

In the car Fenwick said, "I wish he was a snarling gangbanger who just murdered some sweet innocent waif."

"Why?"

"Then I could cheerfully shove the damn cigarette down his throat."

"Lit or unlit?"

"Both. What the hell was that act?"

"The cigarette? Beats the shit out of me. If it's longer than it is wide, the old saying is it's gotta be a phallic symbol." Turner put his elbow out the window into the warm May air and settled himself. "The most important thing was that Kappel knew about that place. It wasn't a surprise he was there. It could very well have been that he was meeting someone he knew."

"Lots of possibilities."

"So he walked to his assignation willingly?"

"Maybe he knew what was going to happen and wanted to die."

"Tired of his life and the way he was living it? But we have no proof of that."

Fenwick sighed. "That's you again. Proof."

SEVENTEEN

Sunday 3:30 P.M.

They drove to their next stop, St. Gratian's parish on the far north side, to talk to the priest who'd written the book about the Sacred Heart of Bleeding Jesus Order. He was a member of the Order, but he lived in one of their parishes in the city not at the Abbey.

Fr. Theodore Keerkins, who was most accommodating upon them introducing themselves, used a cane to help himself shuffle to a seat in a living room with lace doilies on the over-stuffed horsehair furniture. He lifted a bottle of Glenfiddich from a table next to him. His hand shook as he poured twelve-year-old Scotch into a glass near at hand. He pointed the bottle at the detectives in turn, but they declined his offer. He settled himself more deeply in his chair, sipped his Scotch, and returned his glass to the center of the small table.

He smiled at them. "Word has gone out not to talk to you two. We all got phone calls."

"Hell of a lot of calls. They weren't afraid we'd find out?"

"Two things. They are confident of their power. And they aren't afraid of two city of Chicago detectives."

"But you're willing to talk to us?" Turner asked.

"Of course. I hate the Abbot and the Order. And those two." He spat. "Kappel and Tresca! Ha! Priests! They didn't believe in prayer or God any more than this cane does."

"Why did they stay?"

"This life is cushy. Why would you give it up? The gullible contribute, and we live easy."

"Aren't you guilty of the same thing?" Fenwick asked.

"What the hell do you think I'm going to do after all these

years? I've got no Social Security. I've just got what the Sacred Heart of Bleeding Jesus Order provides. A roof over my head and a pittance."

Turner realized Keerkins was echoing Garch's view of the financial peril of elderly priests. He said, "They lived in a condo on Lake Shore Drive. Kappel's name is listed as the owner. How could he afford it?"

"Some of us take our vow of poverty more seriously than others."

"That doesn't really answer the question," Turner said.

"Most likely it was given to him, a donation from a rich, guilt-ridden Catholic."

"Wouldn't he have to pay taxes and condo fees?"

"He wrote books, lots of text books. He made a good private income."

Fenwick said, "I'm kind of lost on this vow of poverty stuff. How does that work?"

"They don't promise to be poor, although there are some religious orders that do that. By poverty they more likely mean, and in this case do mean, that everything is held in common."

"So anybody could live in that condo?"

"Oh, my dear, no. Some things are held in common more than others. You don't know what those two were like. They had their little fists deep into financial chicanery on at least two continents, but oh, my, those two and their carrying-on go back a long, long way."

"Were they molesting children?" Fenwick asked.

"Oh, my, no. As far as I know, they were seducing adults starting from an early age. One rumor claims they were quite active before they entered the seminary, but one must be very careful of poisonous rumors in today's Church. No, my guess is a whole lot of people might be afraid of them blabbing about what they'd done. They've had years of practice at being fake. Fake outrage at liberal politicians. You know Kappel helped put out those press releases about the evils of destroying religious freedom? Shock at the immorality of contraception? Kappel and Tresca helped engineer that. They helped with calculated leaks to the media. They worked with politicians. They're up to their armpits in intrigue with that sanctimonious prick, Vern Drake."

"What was the connection there?"

"I'm sure they were of use to each other. Tresca and Kappel never did anything unless it benefited themselves."

Fenwick asked, "Those two could do all those things you claimed?"

"Certainly. They were a perfect pair and had worked their formula for years. Tresca was more gregarious, more political. He could smooth and schmooze, entertain and explain. All that glad-handing Tresca did, it was all hypocrisy, all for show. He was as misanthropic as Kappel, but Kappel was more open about his. They were in the middle of plotting and planning in this diocese, in this religious Order, in this country, and in the Vatican. Be assured, if they weren't in thick with the Cardinal, they'd be much less. But they are in league with him, and that makes them far more dangerous."

"So they weren't harming kids. What were they doing so long ago?" Fenwick asked.

"The two of them screwed every priest in the province they could get their hands on. The key is they did whatever they could get away with. And they seem to have done just that, at least until now." With studied care, he lifted his glass of Scotch, gulped for a second, then replaced it with fussy carefulness on the exact same spot he took it from. The whole process took nearly a minute to achieve. His hand trembled throughout. He resumed, "I heard they started when they were kids. When I knew them back then, they were hot. Tresca wore the tightest pants of any seminarian, and he had a crotch bulge in the front of his pants to make any remotely gay person drool, priest or not. He thought he was funny too. You know he does imitations?"

"Imitations?" Fenwick asked.

"You know, Jimmy Stewart, that stuff. Tresca was the buffoon in that relationship. Kappel was the smart one."

"People knew they were lovers?"

"I assume everyone knew. Who would be willing to admit to having that knowledge, I have no idea."

Turner said, "You had a relationship with them."

Keerkins gave him a vinegary smile. "I never had a 'relationship' with either one although I did screw them both, separately, not together."

Turner only cared who slept with whom if it had a connection to the murder. "Tresca seemed pretty shaken at the news of Kappel's death."

"Maybe they made a life commitment to each other, or in their minds they were married. They had the condo as a household together, or maybe they provided easy sexual gratification for one another? There must have been some reason they stayed together."

Turner reflected that Kappel was going outside whatever the relationship was to get sexual gratification. He wondered if Tresca was doing the same. Could this murder be as simple as a lover's quarrel?

Fenwick asked, "Who were their enemies?"

"The list is long."

"How about a few examples of the most angry enemies?"

"Kappel was leading the investigation into doctrinal purity at a number of universities, Pope St. Agatho's here in Chicago for one. People could lose their jobs and security. He may also have been involved in several Vatican-ordered investigations."

"Into what?" Turner asked.

"That I don't know. Several years back the rumor was the Vatican wanted to rein in the Sacred Heart of Bleeding Jesus Order. Then Duggan got appointed Cardinal here and Bruchard was made Abbot. It was murky and rumors flew throughout the

Order. People took sides. Kappel and Tresca mostly work for the Cardinal now, so assumedly they took his side."

"Isn't it kind of a victory for each, if one gets to be Abbot and the other gets to be Cardinal?"

"My dear man, vast egos are involved. Who knows what drives these men?" He coughed into a hanky. Went through another hand-shaking production of taking a sip of Scotch. "I was not privy to all those intrigues. I didn't want to be. I still heard the rumors."

"Who else might be an enemy?" Fenwick asked.

"Besides the political intrigue with the Vatican and the Order et al, Kappel was appointed to the commissions to investigate nuns in that big crack down on evil nuns last year."

Fenwick asked, "Are you saying that disgruntled, angry nuns killed him?"

"You asked who had reason to dislike him. The nuns ran afoul of the Holy See. That is bad no matter who you are or how much good you do. And those nuns can be tough and vicious."

"How so?" Fenwick asked. He didn't bother to keep the skepticism out of his voice.

"Be careful of the power of those who are actually spiritual and committed. The Vatican knows this and knows it has to be stopped, controlled, made to obey, or ruined. But those nuns, did you see the ones who were on television during the last election? Calm, reasoned, sensible, very powerful enemies against the Roman Catholic church."

"You know of a burly guy in a limousine?" Fenwick asked.

"No, who is he?"

"We've heard him described as someone interested in Kappel."

"I know of no such person."

Turner said, "Kappel had his kneecaps broken before he died. What kind of information would he have that he'd need to be tortured out of?"

"I don't see Timothy as the type who would keep his mouth shut at the first sign of torture. I wouldn't be surprised if whoever did it just didn't like him. He was not a very nice man. He had a degree in psychology as well as ones in canon law from the Pontifical Gregorian University in Rome and his MBA from Harvard and a law degree from Yale. He passed the bar in Illinois."

Fenwick asked, "So lots of people hated Kappel and Tresca?"

"A multitude."

"They had no friends?" Fenwick asked.

"Have you met any?"

Turner asked, "If they were such rotten human beings, how did they rise so far in the church?"

"They knew who to suck up to and when, physically, morally, and for all I know, spiritually. Some of it was competence, some of it was seduction."

"That's all it takes?" Fenwick asked.

"You work in a hierarchically structured bureaucracy, what do you think? None of your brethren are incompetent suckups? These were highly competent, master suckups."

An image of Carruthers flashed in Turner's mind. He ignored it and asked, "What else was he investigating?"

"He was the financial fixer as well. You did not want to come under his scrutiny. If you did, if you were guilty, he'd find it. Even if you weren't guilty, you could be in trouble."

Fenwick said, "But I thought the diocese itself was under scrutiny."

"Kappel could have fixed it either way. He could be involved on either side," he paused to sip Scotch, "or both for that matter."

Fenwick asked, "Whatever happened to the priest who first reported the money problems?"

"I have no idea."

"We need to examine those financial records."

Keerkins choked on his sip of Scotch. "You will never get those records. Not now, not ever. The church will not let you get at them."

Fenwick said, "But all these dioceses have been in court over bankruptcy. Don't they have to reveal all then?"

Keerkins laughed. "A bankrupt diocese! That's a laugh."

"What do you mean?" Fenwick asked.

"Let me give you an example. Who is the biggest land owner in California?"

The detectives shrugged.

"The oil companies. Who is the second biggest land owner in California?"

More shrugs.

"The Roman Catholic church. Another trifling example, you know how much money the Church has tied up in land or art work? You know how much insurance they have? Another example, do you remember *The Godfather II* when Michael Corleone is testifying before that Congressional committee?"

Turner did. It was one of Ben's favorite movies.

"They ask if he has money invested in casinos. Michael adds that he has investments in all kinds of legitimate companies. It's the same with the Church and the Order. They have financial people who rival the biggest hedge-fund managers in the world, and they are accountable only to Rome."

Fenwick asked, "And Kappel was involved in all this?"

"Oh, my yes. Up to his pretty blond eyebrows."

"Who else would know these details?" Turner asked.

"The Cardinal. Good luck even getting to talk to him. And not all the luck in the world will get you the financial records. After the Cardinal, I don't know." He frowned. "The usual plethora of CPAs and financial drones any large, wealthy organization or individual has."

"You don't know anyone on the inside who might be willing to talk?"

Keerkins spent another couple of minutes taking his next sip of Scotch. Then he took his time pouring himself another two fingers then said, "I can make a few calls. I doubt if I'll find anyone."

"You talked," Fenwick pointed out.

"I don't like the Cardinal or the Abbot, and I have nothing much to lose." He drained the entire contents of his newly poured Scotch.

Keerkins knew nothing more. They left.

In the car Turner said, "At least you've never tried doing imitations to your repertoire."

Fenwick started the car. "Give me time."

Turner sighed. "Maybe Kappel was investigating and skimming. What better position to be in, accusator and investigator?"

"Accusator?"

"You're not the only poet around here."

This was a reference to Fenwick's fairly secret profession as a poet of no distinction. Turner had gone to his poetry readings. He was loyal, and when he attended, he always got to see Madge, Fenwick's wife. Turner enjoyed seeing Madge; the poetry readings, not so much.

Fenwick asked, "What exactly is canon law and why should I care?"

Turner called up the Internet and read, "Unchanging rules of discipline."

"What does that mean?"

Between fits and starts of Fenwick's driving, Turner scrolled and read for a few minutes on the Internet about canon law. "Here's a part that might interest you. Seems there's a section of canon law that covers self-castration."

"Why would I care? And why was self-castration a problem

they had to address? Was there an epidemic of it?"

"Must have been a problem to at least one person."

"A painful one. But they made a canon law about it? Carruthers isn't going to start inspecting everyone in Chicago's scrotum?"

"I hope not." Turner held up a finger. "Chicago scrotum? Is that south of the Loop?"

Fenwick harrumphed. "Or the name of a bar in the Forty-third Ward near Willow and Howe during Prohibition." Turner knew Fenwick was referring to a famous old folk song about that era in Chicago. Fenwick was continuing, "We care about canon law if it leads us to a killer. Otherwise, we do not care."

"But lots of people must have."

"And still do. Just not us."

"They had to be afraid that their being gay would come out and cause them problems."

Turner asked, "Which of our glorious suspects do you want to question next?"

"How about the liberal priest they tried to oust?"

Sunday 4:05 P.M.

Fr. Bernard lived in a rectory on the near west side of the city. He was a tall, thin bustling man. He escorted them to a living room done in Salvation Army chic: couches that needed recovering, a rocking chair with runners that had been repaired with duct-tape, a recliner chair with maroon leather cushions with rips that had been mended with thick, bright yellow yarn. One wall had been given over to graffiti.

Bernard offered coffee. They accepted. He returned a few minutes later from the kitchen with a nicked tray upon which sat three mismatched coffee cups, spoons, a bowl of sugar, and a cup of cream.

Bernard began, "You're here about Kappel."

"Why would you think that?" Fenwick asked.

"The son of a bitch tried to destroy me. And he was still investigating me and this parish. He was told to find something wrong."

"He told you that?"

"Right up front. He didn't care what good I'd done in this parish or what the people in the community needed or how much success we've had."

"What exactly was he investigating?"

"He wanted to accuse me of molesting boys. Problem with that, I've never done it. Although, as you know, the accusation would have been enough. Either way, he didn't get around to it."

"Or got stopped by someone with a reason to murder him."

"Or that."

"What else was he investigating?" Fenwick asked.

"The parish finances."

"Was there something wrong with them?"

"No. I've kept perfect books for all these years. Plus he wanted copies of all my sermons and of all the church bulletins I'd put out. He wanted my correspondence. Kappel claimed he was checking for doctrinal purity, but really he was looking for an excuse. He was told to come down here and "clean up this parish." Basically the Cardinal wanted obedience to his dictates. Obedience is real important to John Cardinal Duggan. More important than priests or people." He sipped some coffee. "My demotion wasn't enough. He and they wanted my ruination. He should have been investigating the diocese's finances. He should have been investigating that religious Order he was in. The Pope's commandos. Ha! The Pope's lackeys."

"There were financial irregularities in both?"

"I presume so. No, I have no proof, but even a few vague rumors made it into the local papers. Mostly about the diocese and the banks they supposedly had money in."

"But that was under the last Cardinal. Wasn't Duggan brought in to clean it up?"

"Or profit from it. The financial chicanery can be easily covered up. Who examines these people? Not outside consultants. The Vatican has a CPA police to monitor dioceses. Religious orders? There it gets murky about who is called to account for what. I'm a diocesan priest. I know nothing about those priests in the Order. I have too much to do in my parish to pay attention to gossip and rumors."

"Do you know anyone connected with the old Cardinal's finances?"

"I can make some calls and see if I can get someone to talk to you."

"You can't give us a name or names?"

"No. Although I do have advice for you."

"What?" Fenwick asked.

"Be careful."

Fenwick asked, "You know a big, burly, furtive guy?"

Bernard looked confused. "No."

Turner said, "Please call us if you find someone who will talk."

"If I do, I will call."

In the car Fenwick said, "All these guys are old." Turner's cell phone rang. It was Ian. "I got in touch with Tyron Bruno from that liberal Catholic paper. He's willing to talk."

"When?"

"Now, if you've got time." He gave Turner the address.

Nineteen

Sunday 5:11 P.M.

Bruno lived in a brownstone on LaSalle Street just north of Division Street. When Turner looked him up on the Internet he saw that he was on the board of directors of the Victims Network, a Catholic group helping those who had been molested by priests.

On the stoop just before ringing the bell, Fenwick said, "It isn't condos. No set of bells to ring. He owns the whole place."

"There's money in being a reporter for a small, liberal Catholic newspaper?" Turner let doubt fill his voice.

A short, slender man in blue jeans, a gray T-shirt, and black horned-rimmed glasses answered the door.

The detectives introduced themselves and showed ID.

Bruno said, "Yes, Ian called and said you'd be stopping by." He led them into a room on the immediate left. He shoved aside pocket doors that disappeared into recesses in the wall. Turner thought when the home was built this might have been a parlor.

Up against one wall were two six-foot plywood slabs, set end-to-end, shelves that served as a desk. They stretched the width of the room. Four two-drawer file cabinets supported them. Two Ion chairs sat in front of two work stations. The one on the left had a seventeen-inch MacBook Pro lap top. The other a Dell PC. Both had screen savers with settings that showed distant storms approaching fields still bathed in sunlight.

On a much narrower but equally as long shelf above the desk, Turner saw a collection of books among them *The Cost of Discipleship* by Dietrich Bonheoffer, *The Seven Storey Mountain* by Thomas Merton, *The Phenomenon of Man* by Teilhard de Chardin, and *The Essential Gandhi*, and at least four different versions of the Bible, one of which was a Jerusalem Bible. Those were what he might have expected to find at Kappel's condo. Also on the shelf were dictionaries, atlases, almanacs, and books by P.G Wodehouse and the collected poems of Freddy the Pig.

No other employees were evident.

Turner said, "We're trying to get some background on Kappel. From what you wrote in the paper you seemed to know a lot about him."

"I know everything there is to know publicly about that shit."

"What kind of shit was he?" Fenwick asked.

"The worst kind. Cold, unfeeling, vicious. His kind breeds violence."

Fenwick said, "I don't think of the priestly life as something connected with violence and death."

Bruno snorted. "It's a world of molestation and secrecy. You don't think adults who've been molested aren't angry and upset?"

Turner said, "I'm sorry for what happened to you."

"Who told you?"

"It wasn't hard to figure out," Turner said. "You're on the board of directors of the Victims Network. With that much anger and hatred around there's got to be people who wanted Kappel dead."

"I was molested as a kid. I sued as an adult. I won a ton of money. That's how I can afford the taxes on this place and to keep the paper running. I purchased it from some do-gooders who started it back in the sixties. I didn't have to kill anybody."

Fenwick said, "Did Kappel do molesting himself or was he involved in transferring priests who did?"

"He was part of the universal Church cover-up. We could never get him on anything specific."

"So he wouldn't have been a direct target of haters?" Fenwick asked.

"I guess not. Let me give you an example of their secrecy. You know who owns the land where the body was found?"

The detectives nodded.

"The Church was given a parcel of land many years ago and just kept buying up land on that side of the river until they own nearly half a mile of crumbling buildings. The land is worth a fortune if someone wants to pay to begin to develop it."

"That's what this is all about, land?" Fenwick asked. "But why commit murder about it? Why not just get rich off of it? The church must need money in this day and age."

"The church in no real sense needs money. They've got insurance to cover claims. They own precious art work, jewels, land, companies. They must own stock in every company in the world. And you know how the Milwaukee diocese moved millions into a so-called cemetery fund."

"So his death is about money, not sex?" Fenwick asked.

"That's what this looks like."

Turner said, "We're interested in the internal politics of the Order as well."

"I know a good bit there. The Cardinal and the Abbot hate each other. I wouldn't be surprised to see either of them dead, not Kappel."

"Why don't they like each other?"

"The way I heard it, they've been rivals since their seminary days. When they were young priests they clashed about issues. Duggan was always on what you would call the far right wing on issues."

Fenwick asked, "The Abbot is a liberal?"

"No. He's what I call conservative pragmatist. For example the Sacred Heart of Bleeding Jesus Order used to run an enormous high school on the south side of the city. It was a prestige place, but it lost a ton of money over the years, bleeding the Chicago province dry. Duggan, who I see as a conservative ideologue, fought very hard to keep the place open. Bruchard was on the other side. The Abbot won and the place closed. Over the years, they took different paths and played different kinds of politics. The Abbot got control of the Order. The Cardinal got the archdiocese of Chicago."

"Control of the Order?"

"Yep. Bruchard is the Pontificate of the Sacred Heart of Bleeding Jesus Order."

"What's a pontificate?" Fenwick asked.

"It means he's in charge."

"Why isn't he in Rome?"

"That's where their headquarters is, you're right, but Bruchard made it a condition of his being elected that he'd get to stay here. He flies to Rome frequently. He tried to block Duggan from being appointed Cardinal."

"He has that much power?"

"The Order has powerful friends and even more powerful enemies. They both play the game to win. I can see them murdering each other but not necessarily Kappel, although I wouldn't put anything past either of them."

"But Kappel was on Duggan's side?"

"It was a delicate thing. You'd have to talk with someone directly in the Order. Good luck with that. Could Kappel, and Tresca for that matter, have been double agents, triple agents? Who was loyal to whom could shift and change. Kappel was an ambitious man himself. He'd want to be on the winning side, but what precisely you define as winning can change. Is being Cardinal a win? Being Abbot? Hard to tell sometimes. But both Kappel and Tresca had survived so far. And I only get some information."

"Do you have a contact in the Order we can talk to?"

"If I give you my contacts, they are unlikely to remain my contacts. I can talk to them and get back to you. They only know and/or can tell me so much. I'll do what I can."

"Thanks, we appreciate it," Turner said.

Fenwick asked, "Why still be a Catholic at all?"

"If belief were predicated on the perfections or foibles of the humans running the organization, then no one would belong to any religious institution. They are groups with ideals. Humans, by definition, are not ideal. We're flawed. Because we have flaws does not mean the teachings of Jesus Christ were flawed."

Fenwick said, "If he existed, he was human, so he was flawed, by definition."

Turner was not about to put up with an argument about the divinity of Jesus. He doubted if the resolution of such an argument would lead to the identity of the killer. And he doubted if Fenwick and Bruno would resolve an argument some had been having for two millennia.

Turner asked, "Were you molested by Bishop Kappel?"

"No. I never met him until I was an adult. Like I said Kappel, as far as I know, was only ever peripherally involved in investigating molestations. For me, I use my job here as a reporter to expose any flaws I observe."

Fenwick asked, "Your boss knows your background?"

"I own half the paper. Any small independent newspaper in this day and age is running on a wing and a prayer. I used to have a full staff here on the first floor of the house. I live on the two floors above. This house has been in my family for years. Now most days everybody works from home. We're just all connected from the Internet. Saves the cost of office space."

"Who owns the other half?" Fenwick asked.

"The rest of my family. They don't bother me in the day-to-day operations."

"Have you ever tried to violently harm any of those who attacked you?"

"I've been to the trials of every molester in a five hundred mile radius. I've sat and watched those assholes. I think they're happy with the memories of what they've done, and that makes me angry. They can go to jail for a very long time, but they get to remember the evil they've done and enjoy those memories. I remember the evil they did to me, and it's painful. They need to suffer every instant they take breath."

Turner said, "It must be hard for you to live with those memories."

Bruno cleared his throat. "It will be enough for today if I can help you catch a killer. What else can I tell you?"

Fenwick said, "We heard Kappel investigated finances."

"It was Kappel's finances that should have been investigated."

"How so?"

"He took a month's vacation in Key West every winter. I know the manager of the gay resort he stayed in. A month in winter in Key West is not cheap."

"How could he afford it?"

"You haven't investigated his finances?"

"We can't get into his personal things. The Abbot is stonewalling."

"Where he got his money, I don't know, but it isn't a stretch to see him as making a ton of money off of that which he was investigating."

"That sounds really convoluted," Fenwick said. "We heard he made money from textbooks he wrote."

"I'm sure he did, and that can be lucrative."

"What other things was he investigating?"

"No-bid contracts, bribes to politicians, just about anything. For example, priests who were obstructing justice after being accused of spending church money on their own personal affairs. Many inner city churches are losing money. It's easy to dip a little extra and lose a little more. If there was a crime in the church, he was there."

"Do you know anything about the nuns who were investigated?"

"That was Sister Eliade's group. They've done good work in

this town since the 1890's. The first leader of the order is in the long queue of sainthood possibilities. Maria Eliade should be too, but no, the Holy Roman Catholic church was more concerned with their statements or lack thereof on abortion, contraception, and gay marriage. You should talk to her."

Turner already had her on the list.

Fenwick asked, "Where were you the night of the murder?"

"Upstairs here with my wife like I am every night."

"What can you tell us about the Papal Nuncio?"

"Pelagius? Why do you care about him?"

"He's in town."

"He is?"

"You didn't know?"

"I usually get press releases or know if a Papal visitor is coming to Chicago."

"He seems to be very interested in Bishop Kappel's murder."

Bruno frowned. "How so?"

Turner didn't mind answering questions if it got them more information in the long run. He gave him a very condensed version of the meeting in the hours after the murder.

Bruno's frown deepened as he spoke. He rubbed a hand through his thick, dark hair.

At the end Turner added, "According to the Internet Pelagius and Drake are members of Opus Dei. Was Kappel or Tresca connected to that organization?"

"Not that I know of. Those two didn't believe deeply enough to be involved in an organization that actually involved a level of belief." Bruno shook his head. "Pelagius's interest in this case means if there's a cover up, it has the whole power and might of the Catholic church behind them."

Fenwick snapped, "I give a rat's ass about the Pope."

Bruno's eyes caught Fenwick's and didn't look away. "How

many divisions does the Pope of Rome have?"

Fenwick gave a derisive snort.

Bruno said, "Sneer, snort, and grumble if you wish. But you aren't up against power as you're used to it. This is the wealth and might of the Catholic church. If it is all arrayed against you, you will lose."

"You're still in business."

"I'm a flea speck to them. They must be careful in dealing with me. I beat them once. I'm slightly immune, but I also have no divisions. They and I both know it. You would be ill advised to underestimate their power and influence."

"They can stop a Chicago police department investigation?"

"My dear detective, the Catholic church is one of the largest landowners on the planet if not the largest. They have billions and billions invested in companies all over the world. They have billions in real gold stashed in this country and others. Put that up against two detectives? Fine men as I'm sure you both are, you will lose."

"They'd use all that to protect a murderer?" Fenwick asked.

"They'd use it all any way they please."

Fenwick mixed rage with a snarl. "They didn't use it to stop the Holocaust in Germany."

Turner glanced at his partner. In philosophical, theological, or metaphysical repartee with people they interviewed, he'd seldom heard the fury imbued in this last comment.

After a pause, Bruno said, "I have no answer to that. I'm not trying to influence you. And certainly I'm not trying to justify the Catholic church. I'm just saying be careful."

Turner said, "We appreciate it. But using their power to cover up a murder would imply that someone in the Church would have reason to cover it up. That someone knows who the killer is, but couldn't that killer be a threat to them as well?"

"Or a friend of someone. Or the Cardinal of the Chicago

archdiocese. Or someone of equal stature."

Fenwick said, "If someone's covering it up, then there's another crime."

Turner asked, "Do you know a large burly man connected to any of these people who drives around in a black town car?"

Bruno thought for a moment then said, "Can't say I do."

Out on the street Fenwick said, "These people are fucking with us." He slammed the door as he got into the car. Fenwick seethed. "Again with this be afraid of the Catholic church."

"They've got more money than God, so to speak."

"I don't like any of these people."

"Anything specific?"

"I just get kind of a creepy feeling, like I just crawled through a sewer, and it's going to take a thousand showers to get clean."

"Some of them seem to be trying to do good."

"It just doesn't seem to be very effective or very good."

Turner said, "I feel sorry for them. They were idealistic when they were young and that world is gone. Their world is dying. They are closer to their end than to their beginning and none of them seem to be happy with the world they're part of."

"They could have left the Church, made different decisions."

"So can we all. Theirs just haven't worked out."

"And somebody is dead, and one, some, or all of them were part of it." Fenwick sighed. "That part's not sad. It's criminal."

"You seemed to have hit home with your comment to him about the Church and the Holocaust."

"At the front of the line in 1930's as they were marched off to die, should have been every Catholic prelate, priest, official of any kind. The Jews should not have stood alone. And the Catholic church stood silent."

Turner added, "Their silence and inaction made them complicit in one of the greatest crimes in history." He agreed with Fenwick's fury on this issue. The Pope and the Church in Europe should have acted loudly and actively. Anything less was a crime that should echo through the ages.

TWENTY

Sunday 6:38 P.M.

When they got back to their desks, they began doing paperwork, detailing conversations, filling in Daily Major Incident reports, and completing the blizzard of paperwork involved in a case. Turner actually kind of enjoyed the silence as they worked away. Fenwick could be a garrulous windbag, but he knew his job, worked hard at it, and was an excellent detective and a good friend. The silence surrounding paperwork was a pleasant respite from the ghastly humor.

Just before seven, Molton disturbed their reverie. "You gentlemen have a visitor." After introductions, he left.

Moments later a seventy-year-old nun sat demurely in the chair next to Turner's desk. Fenwick rolled his barely swiveling swivel chair over.

Sister Maria Clarrisa Eliade had begun with, "I thought I'd save you gentlemen a trip." Continued with, "Rose Talucci will be here with cookies. She and I talked. That's why I'm here." Turned out they'd been in classes together at the University of Chicago.

After initial chatting, when the detectives had expressed their dissatisfaction with the case, she said in her soft voice, "Don't you two get it? You must not be very good detectives." It was a comment dealt in sadness. Turner noted no trace of sneer or sarcasm or criticism.

"How so, Sister?" Turner asked.

"Yes, Father Timothy Kappel had his reputation as a vicious enforcer, but see, you had to follow each case to its end. You had to follow each of the recommendations he made very, very carefully."

"I'm afraid I still don't understand," Turner said.

"Let me give you a simple example. You heard about the boy in Maine, a high school boy, who at the time of the referendum on gay rights, put a sign on his lawn in favor of the gay side?"

Turner said, "I read a little about that. It was on a gay news website." Turner checked gay news sites to find out specific gay news of note.

"For putting up a sign, the kid was going to be denied confirmation and then weeks after that, with no publicity whatsoever, the confirmation ceremony happened and the kid was in it. Fr. Kappel was the investigator."

"So he always really tried to help people?" Fenwick asked.

Sister Eliade gave a grim smile. "Well, no. If he didn't like you, you were toast. Or if you made him angry he could really put it to you. That actually made his attempts to help easier to keep secret, or look less like help. He had a vicious reputation. And he never made an issue when something just disappeared. And some things just disappeared and you were never sure whom the disappearing helped. It really looked like most often he was an enforcer because a lot of his biggest cases made news. Plus he was on the Cardinal's side in the wars inside the Sacred Heart of Bleeding Jesus Order. And if you happened to be on the wrong side of a dispute that had any connection with the Order, Kappel would get even."

"The wrong side being the one Kappel was against," Fenwick confirmed.

"Yes, my dear," the placid nun said. "In the Order, you could be in a great deal of trouble. The Abbot won some fights. The Cardinal won some fights. The Cardinal had the ear of the Vatican, obviously, he did get made Cardinal. The Abbot had the power in the Order."

"For what?" Fenwick asked. The fruits of pointless power was one of Fenwick's favorite debating points.

As they discussed the finer points of the morality of power, Molton himself re-entered with a tray of coffee. Turner knew they were the best cups and saucers available in the station. He heard the seldom-used elevator creak in the distance. They looked in that direction. Mrs. Talucci, accompanied by Barb Dams, bore down on them. Turner could hear Mrs. Talucci's cane thumping on the linoleum. Barb bore a tray stacked with Italian cookies. Molton himself poured the coffee and distributed it making sure all had coffee or sugar as needed.

Mrs. Talucci and Sister Eliade hugged. Turner's neighbor said, "I wanted to make sure I got the kind of cookies Fenwick liked from the bakery." Turner saw that indeed, the tray was filled with butter cookies dipped in chocolate and pecan bars slathered in the same liquid.

Molton and Dams retreated. Mrs. Talucci, Sister Eliade, Fenwick, and Turner sat in a circle.

Sister Eliade spoke to Mrs. Talucci. "I was explaining the ways of the world to these nice detectives."

"They are good men," Mrs. Talucci confirmed.

Turner found himself inordinately pleased by the affirmation from his neighbor. He asked, "Do you know if anybody else ever noticed what Kappel was doing?"

"I never discussed it with anyone outside my Order."

"So he may or may not have been confronted about actually helping some people?"

"Not by anyone I'm aware of. It could be very subtle. Did you hear that story about the priest who was ordered by his bishop not to give communion to a lesbian couple?"

"A sad case," Mrs. Talucci said.

Fenwick asked, "How on Earth would the priest or the bishop know they were lesbians or care?"

Sister Eliade said, "Church workers."

"What does that mean?" Fenwick asked.

Mrs. Talucci said, "Homophobic bigots can have their own Internet network. They talk and connive in secret. Somebody in their home parish didn't like them and didn't like the fact that they were raising two children."

Sister Eliade continued the story, "They tattled to the bishop and he got mad. Ordered the priest to take action that next Sunday. The priest didn't. There was a big stink. Kappel was appointed the investigator."

"How'd he get the job?"

"In the Curia in Rome there are various factions. The Order is in with the correct faction for investigating these kinds of things." She sipped coffee. "But if you followed the story all the way, you would have found that after all the news media went away, the priest kept his parish, and the bishop kept his mouth shut."

Fenwick said, "That just sounds nuts."

Mrs. Talucci placed her cup of coffee on Turner's desk, used her hand to pat Fenwick's thigh. "Yes, dear. We know."

Sister Eliade said, "Nuts or not, whatever Kappel was, he was not a monster, or at least not always. He was a complex man."

Turner asked, "How did Kappel get assigned to the investigation? He's connected to this diocese, not that."

Sister Eliade said, "Ah, but you see, Cardinal Duggan is quite a power in the church in America. He is deferred to."

Fenwick guessed. "And it was a church heavily influenced by members of the Sacred Heart of Bleeding Jesus Order."

"Very good, my dear, very good."

Fenwick beamed like a first grader who'd been praised by his favorite teacher.

"As for the boy and his sign," Sister Eliade continued, "there was stink and uproar for a few weeks, and then the issue disappeared from the news, and a few weeks later the boy was confirmed, and a few months later the priest was transferred to one of their missions in India."

Turner smiled. "You're kidding."

The nun took a sip of coffee. "Not about Bishop Kappel.

No, he would work with people, in secret, negotiate quietly. If people were assholes, he screwed the bejesus out of them. If they cooperated in any way, if they were on the side of what I call truth and light, Timothy would find a way to make things easier for the accused. He didn't always succeed. But he was working with us from the inside."

"Us?" Fenwick asked.

"The few liberals left in the church. Most left long ago. And Timothy had to be very, very careful."

"That all seems so arbitrary and capricious."

"Yes," the nun said, "the Church holds dearly to eternal truths and never wavers except when it's convenient."

"They stake their brand on eternal truth," Fenwick said.

"They voted on Papal infallibility," Sister Eliade said. "Voted on an eternal truth. They've done that for centuries. It's the we–got–the–most–votes, and we've–got–eternal–truth–on–our–side theory of theological disputes. That make sense to you?"

"Not really," Fenwick said.

"And you're a detective in Chicago, you should know better."

Fenwick only bristled a little, even he was cowed by this nun's demeanor and presence. He did ask, "How does being a detective make a difference?"

"You see mankind at their worst, and most people, as you know, are a slip of the conscience away from," she paused, "making very poor choices."

They sat in silence. The women sipped coffee. Fenwick wolfed down several cookies.

Turner asked, "Did Tresca know what Kappel was up to?"

"I don't think so."

Turner asked, "Could someone have found out, someone on the opposition side, and killed him for it?"

"So few knew. And it could be hard to figure out which side was the opposition in a case, or which side Kappel was on. I only knew because I follow cases carefully. I try to avoid hysteria. I look things up. I do research in depth. Several of the sisters in my Order kept track on the Internet. We noticed the oddity only after a few years. And then when it came time for him to investigate us, why I just waited patiently for the right signs."

"What were those?" Fenwick asked.

"If it was official corruption from higher ups he didn't like, you were likely to go down. Especially if he didn't like you, and whoever he was working for didn't like you."

"It was politics not corruption."

"Politics and corruption."

"Selective enforcement," Fenwick said. "Based on personal whim. The best kind."

Again Turner thought back to Carruthers. He said, "Could they manufacture evidence?"

"If they really didn't like you or you were really stupid, I would guess so, but I don't know so."

"It sounds like a dangerous game he was playing," Fenwick said.

"How so?"

"Taking sides based on like or dislike instead of evidence could make people very angry."

"Ha! You still don't get it. People dislike you whether you have evidence or not."

Turner said, "But you said sometimes he went easy on some folks. Did they know he was being easy on them?"

"He was very careful."

Turner said, "Or maybe what he found in those cases was bogus and that's what he reported."

She looked uncertain for the first time. "I suppose that's possible. Except with us. There was no question we were helping the poor and the sick instead of preaching doctrine and rigidity."

"Maybe he agreed with what you were doing," Fenwick suggested.

"As far as I know Bishop Kappel always had an agenda or an angle. It had to benefit him."

"How did helping you benefit him?"

"I never knew. A final disposition in our case still hadn't been made." She sighed. "The man was a contradiction."

After they left, Fenwick asked, "Was the nun lying to us?"

"How many people do we meet in this line of work who always tell the truth?" Turner asked.

"Not enough."

"Did whatever she tell us get us closer to the murderer?"

"Not really."

"But it does give us a very different perspective on Kappel. But it doesn't get us closer to a killer."

TWENTY-ONE

Sunday 8:32 P.M.

An hour and a half later, they stopped in Molton's office. "You guys see the evening news?" Molton asked.

They shook their heads.

Molton explained. "Our newest best friends, Pelagius and Drake, managed to get on three newscasts trashing the Chicago police department, sanctifying the dead guy along with the Cardinal, and the Sacred Heart of Bleeding Jesus Order."

They decided to grab a late dinner. While driving over to grab sandwiches at Milly's Diner on Division Street, Fenwick was in full grumble. "Who of these people we've interviewed so far has the money to hire burly strangers with expensive town cars? Or maybe they just have friends who are burly and rich. Or maybe a burly guy who is now rich was molested as a kid, owns an expensive town car, and now has the wherewithal to get revenge. Maybe they all got together and pooled their money. How much does it cost to hire a burly guy with an expensive car? People who try to hire killers aren't usually sophisticated about it. They screw up more often than not."

"The church would be sophisticated enough or maybe they'd have enough contacts they wouldn't need to hire somebody. Or maybe the burly guy has nothing to do with the murder."

"You're the kind of cop who insists on a video of the murder with the killer smiling, waving, and confessing to us on the tape."

"Just the kind of guy I am."

"We're being fucked over."

"Can you say fucked over in a case about a dead bishop?"

"I don't see any lightning bolts shooting down from heaven."

"Lightning bolts in heavenly retribution aren't what they used to be, and yes, we're being fucked over."

Turner's cell phone rang. It was Ben. "Both the boys are fine. Nothing's happened to them. You need to get to Sisters of Mercy Hospital."

"What's wrong?"

"Brian's really upset. You know his friend, Shane, from the baseball team?"

"The one from Inauguration day? I remember him." Ben and Paul had been watching President Obama's inaugural address. As it was the Martin Luther King holiday, the boys had been home with knots of friends visiting both boys. Jeff's buddies had been in his room, Brian and his crowd in the basement. When the President mentioned Seneca Falls, Selma, and Stonewall as historical Civil Rights moments, the two men had reached out and held each other's hands. The moment had affected them deeply.

They'd looked up in time to see their older son's friend Shane in the doorway. While looking at them with their hands clasped, he'd whispered, "I want to have what you have some day, be like you." And then he'd disappeared. Neither man ever mentioned the moment to Brian. Paul had assumed the kid was gay, but that it wasn't his business. And if he and Ben were some kind of a role model for the kid, that was okay. Certainly Shane had never said anything to them or asked to talk with them, and if the kid wanted to bring it up, fine, but Paul wasn't going to.

"Yeah. He tried to commit suicide a couple of hours ago."

"No."

"Tried to hang himself in his backyard."

"How awful."

"Brian's the one who found him and saved him."

Paul gulped. "He's a hero."

"Not from the way he's acting. I've never seen him so down."

"How'd he happen to be there?"

"He was supposed to meet him to study. They still have a few finals this week."

"Did the kid plan it so Brian would save him?"

"Brian didn't say. He probably didn't know. I'm here with Brian at the hospital. Jeff is at Mrs. Talucci's."

"I'm on my way." He hung up.

"What's happened?" Fenwick asked.

"Sisters of Mercy Hospital. Brian saved a kid from committing suicide."

Fenwick turned the car around. Turner knew there were detectives who sacrificed their whole lives, family, kids, wives, to the pursuit of the killer, to bring the corpse closure and justice. Turner figured the corpse didn't care anymore. It was dead.

Paul Turner cared even less about bishops of the church, living or dead, than he did about his sons. It didn't take an instant to make the decision. He was going to be there for Brian at a moment like this. As a father with a child with spina bifida, this was not his first rush to a hospital. A few years back, Jeff's shunt had clogged requiring an emergency hospital visit. Paul knew well parental fears. In this case it wasn't directly his own child, but he was going to be on hand.

Fenwick yanked the rotating red light from under the seat, reached out the car window, jammed it on the roof, flipped the switch on their seldom-used siren. They rushed to the near west side hospital. They found Brian and Ben with a cluster of people on the fourth floor.

Brian stood up when he saw his dad. The boy looked crushed and worried. Besides Brian and Ben there were two other adults. Paul knew them as Shane's parents, Dave and Betty Swearingen.

Paul asked, "How's Shane?"

Betty Swearingen said, "He's going to live."

Dave Swearingen held out his hand to Paul and said, "Your son saved my boy's life. We can never thank him or you enough."

Paul looked at Brian, who didn't look up.

The parents praised and fussed for a few moments. The doctor came to speak to them. The parents gushed a few more words of thanks their way and then hurried into a nearby room with the doctor.

Paul walked over to Brian. "You okay?"

"I'm not sure."

"It must have been scary."

Brian looked up at him for the first time. There was little trace of the teenager in the anguished look his son gave him. "I'm still scared."

"Do you want to talk about what happened?" Paul asked.

Fenwick idled in the background out of hearing. Ben stood with his husband and son.

Brian said, "It might help." He pulled in great lungfuls of air, let them out. "We were supposed to have a study session at seven. I was late. His mom was supposed to be home from work, but she was late, too. I got there. He's got this basketball hoop set up in the backyard."

The doctor came out of Shane's room without the parents. He came over to Ben, Paul, and Brian. "Another couple of minutes and that teenager would have been dead. Your son's a hero."

They thanked him. He left.

Brian's phone buzzed. "Everybody wants to talk to me." He glanced at the readout, turned the phone off, then continued his story. "I always go around to the back door. So I went around. While I was walking along on the side of the house, I heard the basketball net kind of clink. He's got one of those outdoor, metal nets. I turned the corner of the house and saw him."

Brian breathed deeply for several moments, looked at his dads. "I don't remember thinking anything. I rushed up and grabbed his knees and sort of lifted him up. I held him like that and didn't know what to do. I could tell he was breathing. The rope was tied around his neck and connected to the backboard. I couldn't let go to try to find a knife to cut him down. I sort of leaned him against the basketball pole and held him up at the same time with my shoulders and arms. I yelled fire, like you always told us to do if you wanted people to come running. But I didn't hear anybody coming. I was desperate. So I kind of held him up with one hand, shoulder, and arm and braced him against the pole. I didn't know if I could hold him up with just one arm like that, but I managed. I had to be so careful. I was afraid if I moved wrong, he might slip and…" He gulped and drew several breaths. "Somehow, I managed to get my cell phone out and called 9-1-1." He was very pale. "I think I need to sit down."

They moved to a set of plastic chairs. Each dad held one of his hands. Brian had moved beyond the early teenage phase of having difficulty touching his dads.

"The paramedics showed up a few minutes later and got him down."

Brian trembled and pulled in more deep breaths. The men kept hold of his hands and put their other arms around him. They huddled close until Brian stopped trembling and his breathing eased.

Paul said, "You thought quickly. You did right. You were very brave."

"I was scared shitless. I still am a little bit." He pulled in deep breaths.

The Swearingens came out of Shane's room and walked up to Brian and his dads. Mrs. Swearingen had tears in her eyes. "Thank you, thank you, thank you for my boy." She hugged Brian. Mr. Swearingen shook his hand. Mrs. Swearingen unclinched and said to Brian, "He'd like to see you."

"Uh, sure."

"You want us to go with you?" Paul asked.

"Sure, it's okay."

Brian and the assembled parental units crowded into the hospital room. Shane saw Brian and got tears in his eyes. Brian stood by the bed. Shane clutched his hand. "Thanks, dude, you saved me."

"You okay?" Brian asked.

"Yeah."

A nurse came in and bustled them all out.

In the hall Paul said, "We'll go home and get settled."

Brian said, "You don't have to hover. You can go back to work."

"I think I should be with you."

"For what?" Brian asked.

"I'm concerned about you."

"I'm fine. Ben will be there."

Fenwick had waited quietly in the background the whole time. Now he joined them. "Fuck the case. I called the Commander. You want to stay? Or I can drive you back to the station and you can pick up your car. You do what you need to do."

Brian said, "There's nothing more to be done. He's saved. I'm fine. The emergency is over."

Paul said, "Buck, I can get a ride over in the morning so I don't need my car tonight. I'll go home, and we can get settled."

Fenwick said, "If you need anything, call me."

They got home. Brian turned his phone back on, examined the readout list of calls, then turned it back off. Jeff was falling asleep in his wheelchair.

After the boys were settled in their rooms, Paul and Ben sat at the kitchen table.

Ben said, "Could this have been another gay kid trying to commit suicide?"

"Could have been. Maybe we should have tried to talk to him after he saw us Inauguration day."

"It's so hard to know when to talk to a teenager or what to say."

Paul said, "So the boy was expecting someone to be home earlier or Brian to come over. He was hoping to be saved?"

"Or hoping to punish one of them."

"For what?" Paul asked.

"Brian may know or not. Shane may not have told anyone. Maybe Brian is feeling guilty for not recognizing the signs. Same for the mom and dad."

Paul said, "Shane was one of the kids who was going in their group with them to the prom."

"We'll get him through tonight and then figure out what to do next."

TWENTY-TWO

Sunday 11:00 P.M.

Paul and Ben stood on their front porch in the unusual mid-May warmth. The boys were settled. Paul wanted to take a breath of fresh air before heading up to bed.

Paul checked for any incongruities or oddities on the street, the way any cop always checks his surroundings no matter what situation he found himself in. It was an automatic reflex. No limos. No burly guys bigger than Fenwick. No bishops swinging a thurible on the end of a chain, incense smoke spilling from the holes in the top.

But a Lincoln Town Car idled across the street from Mrs. Talucci's. He could dimly see a skinny guy in wireframe glasses and a Roman collar in the driver's seat.

He noted Mrs. Talucci on her front porch in her rocker. Mrs. Talucci waved and stood up.

Paul said to Ben, "I'll be back in a minute." He strolled to the bottom of her front porch steps. Mrs. Talucci was in shadow. She wore a summer shawl over her shoulders and a faded yellow-flower print housedress.

She asked, "How is Brian?"

"Doing okay. Asleep, I hope."

"He's a good man, just like his dads."

"Thanks."

She spoke so her voice barely carried down to him those few feet away. "I have someone who wants to talk to you."

Paul wanted to get into his house, hug Ben, check on the boys, but Mrs. Talucci would not be mentioning someone wanting to talk to him if it wasn't important.

Paul climbed the steps. Mrs. Talucci patted his arm, smiled, and said, "Don't be gentle."

She led him into the house.

A dim pole lamp burned next to Mrs. Talucci's dark brown easy chair. The Cardinal Archbishop of Chicago, Albert Duggan, sat in the chair. A steaming cup of coffee and a plate of butter cookies sat on a small, round table next to him with a napkin and a doily in place for crumbs and aesthetics.

Mrs. Talucci said, "Al, this is my neighbor Paul. The detective on the Kappel case. You need to talk to him."

Turner wondered, Al?

The Cardinal remained seated. He held out his right hand an inch or two above his thigh, palm down, wrist bent, which caused his Cardinal's ring to flash in the light from the votive candle Mrs. Talucci had lit on the mantelpiece. It wasn't that Mrs. Talucci was religious. She liked the soft lighting as she listened to classical music using her headphones connected to her iPod. The bishop's hand remained extended as if waiting for Paul to kiss the ring. Paul reached and shook the hand.

After an instant's touch, the cardinal yanked his hand away, reacting as if he'd been stung. What, Turner thought, he'd never shaken hands before? The Cardinal's world was that insulated, he never soiled himself outside his own circle?

Mrs. Talucci noted the brief handshake and chuckled. "Give it a rest, Al, we're beyond all that here."

Again with this 'Al' shit. Mrs. Talucci indeed had connections.

Mrs. Talucci asked if Paul wanted coffee or another beverage. After he declined, she motioned for Paul to seat himself then settled herself onto a straight-back chair.

The detective sat on a dark brown settee that matched the chair the Cardinal was in.

The Cardinal's short, squat body filled the armchair. His body wiggled against the afghan that covered the back, seat, and arms. Perhaps the gold and yellow spread, knitted by Mrs. Talucci, had a large wrinkle and the man's ass hit it just wrong as he sat, or maybe the Cardinal had a hemorrhoid.

Turner wondered if cardinals got hemorrhoids. He figured they must. They were human. Presumably.

Mrs. Talucci prompted, "Paul, you had some questions."

"Where were you at the time Bishop Kappel was murdered?"

Cardinal Duggan gave a smirk the Republicans had perfected then added a sneer. "That's the best you can do?"

Turner said, "I'm tired. I suspect you're up to your eyeballs in murder. You and all of your ilk have not been helpful." His sharpness caused him to reflect that he sounded like Fenwick. He saw no harm in that approach at the moment. The evening had drained him emotionally. He didn't care if the Cardinal was offended in this world or any theological haven he constructed in his mind. The case was a mess. He wanted answers. If he channeled Fenwick for a few minutes, that was okay with him.

The Cardinal Archbishop tottered to his feet. "A Chicago detective can't talk to me that way."

Mrs. Talucci spoke, "But I can and I will. You will sit down and you will answer his questions."

The Cardinal glared at the diminutive woman sitting calmly across from him.

"Albert, sit down," she ordered.

Mrs. Talucci raised her cane in her right hand. Paul saw that it trembled, a sure sign she was tired.

Paul asked, "Do you need to rest?"

Instead of answering him, Mrs. Talucci gazed at the Cardinal. She shortened her command. "Sit." She thumped her cane on the rug.

The Cardinal sat.

What kind of hold did she have on him? Paul wasn't sure he wanted to know.

Mrs. Talucci held the prelate's eyes until he lowered his gaze.

She asked, "Do you want me to start telling stories?"

"That was a long time ago."

She said, "Some from not so long ago."

"How do you know things?" he asked.

"I listen. I learn. Same as you. I wait and think and imagine. You've got a dead bishop, Al, and you've got to help my friend here. He's a good man and a good detective. You will not abuse him in my presence here and now, and then you will cooperate fully between now and the moment you draw your last breath."

"You insult me."

"I know you."

"No one would believe your stories."

"What's been your motto for fifty years, Al?"

"Rose, do you want a creed?"

Mrs. Talucci laughed. "The most vital thing in your universe has been the repeated plea to 'not scandalize the faithful,' which has always meant that you want to save your butt, your cushy job, and your selfish ways. And don't try standing up again as if you were going to walk out. You and I both know your butt is going to stay in that chair, and you're going to talk to this detective, and if he or I are not satisfied with your answers, my next calls will begin an avalanche of humiliation that will bury you and scandalize, as you so quaintly put it, the faithful, the unfortunate few who still believe your bullshit. And you know I'm not bluffing, Al."

The Cardinal looked stubborn.

Mrs. Talucci said, "The name of your first boyfriend your second week in the seminary was…"

The Cardinal's gasp interrupted her. His whisper was bathed in fear. "You couldn't know that."

Mrs. Talucci raised her right eyebrow an eighth of an inch.

The Cardinal sat in stupefied silence. "How do you know these things?"

Mrs. Talucci smiled.

The Cardinal's fat seemed to melt as he sat in the chair. His shoulders slumped, he leaned heavily on one arm, he held his head in his hand. He nodded, "Fine," with a snarl in his voice that neither of Paul's sons would dare use to an adult.

Mrs. Talucci said, "Your cheerful acquiescence is not necessary, but your complete compliance is."

The Cardinal harrumphed and faced Turner and arched an eyebrow.

Turner asked, "Did you kill Bishop Kappel?"

Silence infested the room.

Finally Duggan spat out, "No."

"Did you ever visit the apartment they shared?"

"No." With a snarl and a sneer.

"That's kind of a stupid lie," Turner said. "You were recognized."

"Whoever saw me was mistaken."

Turner sighed. "Do you really think we haven't done our homework? You were recognized by more than one witness. You're a public figure. You really think you're anonymous?"

"I visited their apartment. So what?"

"You knew they were lovers."

"Again, so what? You're living with another man." He shot a spiteful look at Mrs. Talucci. "You're not the only one that can find things out."

Mrs. Talucci sat forward in her chair. Her voice was very soft as she asked, "Are you making a threat?"

"I'm just saying."

Mrs. Talucci held his eyes until the prelate looked down and mumbled, "No, no threat."

Mrs. Talucci sat back. "Good."

Turner asked, "Their relationship didn't bother you?"

"No."

Turner said, "We have information that Bishop Kappel was investigating the diocesan finances past and present. Among other things graft, nepotism, cronyism connected to awarding contracts at inflated prices, irregular purchasing procedures."

"Everything is under control."

"We need to see the diocesan financial records. We need to know what and who he was investigating. These could involve millions of dollars."

"That's not possible."

Mrs. Talucci cleared her throat.

Duggan glared at her. "Fine, I'll get you the damn records. If you bring scandal to Holy Mother Church, you will be sorry."

"Another threat?" Mrs. Talucci asked. "Really. Al, you know better."

"It's not a threat."

"Yes, it is," Mrs. Talucci said, "and I'm kind of tired of it." She stood up. "Look to tomorrow's headlines."

"Rose, please." He half stood up. "I'm sorry. It's a habit of a lifetime."

Feeling a bit like a debating Fenwick, Turner asked, "That's how you run things, by threat? Is that really a good way to run a multi-million dollar do-good organization?"

"It's worked for two millennia. Do you have a better suggestion?"

"Quite a few," Mrs. Talucci said. "And you don't believe all that malarkey any more than I do."

The Cardinal objected, "It's not malarkey, and I have faith."

Mrs. Talucci's eyes twinkled, and she got a mischievous glint in her eye. She asked, "Which of us has a PhD in the Philosophy of Religions and another in the Philosophy of Theology and which of us has more articles written and published about those subjects?"

Turner knew that after her husband died forty years ago, Mrs. Talucci had gone back to school. She had degrees from numerous universities in the area although she preferred the University of Chicago. She'd averaged a degree about once every five years. She said learning all the foreign languages slowed her down. He didn't remember all the areas she studied. She used the vellum diplomas to line her kitchen cabinets.

Duggan insisted, "We are doing good for the world. A lot of people think it's possible to just run around in sackcloth and ashes and preach peace, love, and joy. Well, detective, you're in a profession where you see the worst in people. I've listened to confessions. I know this world and how it works and how rotten we are to each other. Have we in the Church learned what it takes to run things? Yes. Do we try to influence the world, people and politicians? Of course."

Mrs. Talucci said, "So your goal is to get the government to enforce the laws of the church?"

"If that what's for the best."

"That's a theocracy," Mrs. Talucci said.

"We know best."

"Pah! You're a sad old man."

"Is that what you really came here to discuss?" Duggan asked.

Turner pulled himself up. That was a comment he'd have made to bring a halt to a Fenwick inspired debate.

"Who were Kappel's enemies?" Turner asked.

"Everyone in the Sacred Heart of Bleeding Jesus Order got along. We are a Christian community."

Turner said, "We've got reports of infighting in the organization going back years. We've got people talking about investigations."

"Any organization has internal politics. You know that. It's just typical, human interaction, nothing more. As for the investigations, really, the people involved care deeply about religion, but they are not murderers."

Turner pointed out, "Somebody is. You've got a dead bishop."

"Maybe it was a random killing."

"It looked pretty planned and organized to me. He was tortured before he died."

Duggan looked pained. "He was a good man."

"Where were you around midnight, Friday?"

"Asleep in bed."

"Do you know a big burly guy in a town car?"

"No. Who is he?"

"Someone who might be connected to the case."

"I know no such person."

"Do you know Vern Drake and Bishop Pelagius?"

"Of course."

"Did you talk with them before they came to meet with us?"

"When was this?"

"Late Saturday."

"No."

"Would Kappel's enemies try to kill you?"

Duggan looked thoughtful a moment then said, "I can't see a point. Killing a cardinal gets you what?"

"Killing a bishop must have gotten somebody something. Maybe it stopped an investigation."

"But the death of one cleric wouldn't be enough to stop the vast machinery of the Catholic Church. There's always another cleric. Why kill just one? You couldn't possibly even begin to kill enough clerics to halt the progress of the Church. If it's not an eternal organization, it's as close to one as mankind has come up with."

"Did you know Kappel was hiring call boys to service him?"

"That I don't believe."

"Can you help us get in to talk to Bishop Tresca?"

"I presume that's up to him."

"Abbot Bruchard wouldn't assist us."

"Tresca is an adult."

"We want to follow up in Kappel's room at the Abbey. We need to get into his computer as well."

"I'm sorry. I have no influence in getting you into the Abbey."

"You're the Cardinal Archbishop of Chicago."

"As you can see by my presence here, I am not all powerful."

"Did Kappel have an office in the chancery?"

"No."

If he knew more, it was not forthcoming. The Cardinal huffed and puffed as he squirmed up out of the chair. With a few words of thanks to Mrs. Talucci, he left.

Paul and Mrs. Talucci stood on her front porch.

Paul said, "After all this time, you have such control, influence. You don't even go to church on Sundays."

"Or any other day of the week, although the local priest told me I didn't have to because I'm so old."

Paul remembered the local parish priest, Father Damien, a short, rotund young man, one of the few Chicago area natives graduated from the seminary in the past decade. Paul asked, "Is that what the dustup was about at the Taylor Street Fair last summer?"

Mrs. Talucci laughed. "No, that was because he was an asshole. My granddaughter told me that dickless wonder had the nerve to tell her in the confessional that she was a slut for using contraception." After all these years, Paul didn't find it odd that, especially when tired or upset, Mrs. Talucci could sound like an angry stevedore.

"What did you say to him?"

"I told him if he ever chose to give anyone I knew marital advice again, I'd make it unnecessary for him to ever have to use contraception in or out of the priesthood for the rest of his life."

"Oh. What on Earth do you have on the Cardinal?"

"Do you really want to know?"

Paul paused, met those twinkling eyes, hung his head, muttered, "Yes."

She chuckled. "One for you for honesty. The strange thing is, a few of the biggest things aren't criminal, at least not in the arrest-and-go-to-jail way. He would certainly find them a scandal to the faithful. I'm afraid mostly the twenty-four hour news cycle would care for about half a day, but even a whisper of scandal, that would kill him."

"It must be powerful."

She smiled, took his arm. "It's two things, actually. Well, two major things. Remember, I know his mother from the neighborhood so I know him from when he was born. The thing he'd probably be most embarrassed about is the fact that he paid his way through college working in a drag show in Atlanta."

"He wasn't in the seminary in college?"

"No, dear. He didn't get religion until after he graduated from college."

"You have proof?"

"Well, this was in the time before everyone had a cell phone and everything got recorded, but I do believe there are some photos and at least one video. I'm told his Diana Ross number was the hit of the show."

"Diana Ross?"

"Who knows what crowds like?"

"The cardinal archbishop of Chicago was a drag queen?"

"Really, Paul, you see the way the Catholic prelates dress up for their rituals. You think Catholic drag is that different from the show at the Baton?"

"I never thought about it that way." The Baton was the most well-known drag bar in Chicago. Paul had enjoyed the show the few times he'd been.

"You've been to the Baton?" he asked.

She smiled. "I was at one of the first shows."

"Oh." He didn't think she would ever cease to amaze him. "How did you find out about the video, and even more intriguing, how did you get a copy of the video?"

"Actually, I have the original and copies are in the hands of my attorneys and other discreet, interested parties."

"It is provably him?"

She laughed briefly. "I never bluff."

She didn't add where she got it, and Paul didn't press. Obtained through mundane or Machiavellian schemes, he wasn't sure he wanted or needed to know. He switched topics, "Was he ever involved in the transferring of priests who molested kids?"

"I have nothing on that. He wasn't specifically in charge at the time. Others would be sued or blamed or defrocked long before him. He covered his tracks with that issue, or maybe he wasn't smack in the middle of screwing up other people's lives. He's done enough that isn't involved directly in harming children. If he was, his ass would have been gone long before this. I'd have done everything in my poor power to make that happen."

"What's the other main thing? Are there dead bodies in his background?"

"I wouldn't be surprised, but it's far more ordinary than that, but in my book, far worse and very sad."

Paul raised an eyebrow.

"His mother is in an extended care facility. She's a dear old friend of mine. I visit her once a week. Her mind isn't what it was." She sighed. "Whose is? He visits her two times a year, on Mother's Day and Christmas. That, my dear, is a crime. I don't care if his job was performing emergency surgery on widows and orphans from war-torn countries. You go visit your mother. She's not going to be around long. He's an irresponsible oaf. How can you not visit your mother? He should be deeply ashamed of his absence from her side." She sighed. "But he's the kind of man who would be in more of a panic having it known that he was a drag queen fifty years ago than that he doesn't visit his mother except twice a year. He should be ashamed of that, not of being a drag queen." She sighed. "He's from here, but he went to college in Atlanta. Like many kids, he wanted to get away."

"I wonder if he was ever arrested for it. Fifty years ago it could have been a huge problem in the South."

"That I don't know."

"It would be another level of fear for him."

"He's lived his whole life in fear."

"Of being found out?"

"Well, that, sure, but I was thinking of the most important doctrine of the Catholic Church."

"The Trinity?"

She patted his arm. "No, my dear, the most important tenet of the Catholic church is, as I pointed out to our dear Cardinal less than half an hour ago, 'don't scandalize the faithful.'"

"I don't remember that from catechism class."

Mrs. Talucci smiled. "It's in there. Believe me, it's in there."

"Is that much awful stuff really going on?"

"What do you think?"

"Unless they molest little boys, most often the Catholic church personnel do get away with most anything."

"It's a soft life they don't appreciate. It's what makes the clergy such good Republicans, especially all those above the level of monsignor." She shook her head. "The reality is almost as sad."

"What's that?"

"People knowing now that he was a drag queen then, he would find embarrassing. The poor man was living his life then and enjoying himself, I'd presume, and now he'd be ashamed of it. A lot of the fear is in his own head." She sighed. "But the poor thing would be laughed out of Chicago and the Curia. It is sad, and I'd feel sorry for him." She caught his eyes. "Well, okay, I'd feel sorry for him if he wasn't such a shit."

As he took the first step down off the front porch Mrs. Talucci said, "If you don't have the financial records on your desk when you walk in tomorrow, call me. I doubt if it will be necessary."

"Can I tell people I met the Cardinal?"

"I wouldn't call a press conference about it, but you wouldn't have done that anyway."

He thanked her and walked next door to his own house. The boys were both asleep. As he undressed, he told Ben about the meeting with the Cardinal.

He was tired. He crawled into bed and felt Ben's arms around him as he drifted off to sleep.

TWENTY-THREE

Monday 6:57 A.M.

Before going downstairs Paul tapped on Brian's bedroom door. He'd heard the boy's shower earlier.

"Yeah." Brian's voice sounded muffled.

Paul entered. Paul noticed the room had been cleaned. Everything was neat and in its place. There were no dirty clothes on the floor, dust on any surface, or crumbs piled in the corners. All clear indications that his son was very upset. His son wore silk boxers as he dried his hair with a large, fluffy beach towel.

Paul said, "You okay this morning? You don't have to go to school if you don't want."

"Thanks. I'll go."

His son wasn't meeting his eyes. After carefully folding the towel and placing it neatly on a chair, another unheard of activity, the boy pulled on jeans, socks, shoes, and a T-shirt.

"You need to talk about what happened?" Paul asked.

"I'm good."

"You're sure? You don't save someone's life every day."

"I kinda really don't want to talk about it. I did what anybody would have done. It's no big deal."

"Are you going to go see him or talk to him?"

"I don't know." Brian examined himself in the mirror above his dresser, nodded to himself as if he thought what he saw was satisfactory, said, "I gotta get moving." He grabbed two books from his desk. He glanced quickly at his dad then looked away.

They left the room. Paul noted that his son did not bound down the stairs as he usually did.

Paul was tired. Work had been many hours of overtime. That

plus the emotion of dealing with the attempted suicide and his son's continuing upset were taking a toll on him. Through the front window he saw that a light rain had begun to fall. The weather forecast predicted steady showers developing during the morning.

Ben was in the kitchen with Jeff. The younger boy was using his crutches to maneuver from refrigerator, to stove, to table.

As they did every weekday morning, the Turner household had breakfast together. Paul insisted on them having at least this one meal together every day. Each week one of them took turns cooking. Jeff was on duty this week as he would be for the next as well as part of his punishment for telling his older brother to go to hell. This morning he'd made reasonably simple French toast with strawberries.

Brian ate only a small bowl of strawberries and drank no odd concoctions, made no comments about his brother's cooking, and said little. All were odd. Usually they couldn't fill him up or shut him up. Today, he rarely met the eyes of other family members.

At one point Jeff said, "It's all over the Internet about you saving Shane." Jeff seemed to be bursting with pride.

Brian said, "Thanks." No teasing, no retorts, no details about the story.

Paul knew several things must be going on. Brian had to be still processing what happened. And what was proper teenage behavior the morning after you saved a friend's life? And the feeling that nagged at Paul was that he suspected he didn't have the full story.

After Jeff and his wheelchair were aboard his special needs bus, Paul returned to the house. Brian came down the stairs. They both stopped in the living room. Brian met and held Paul's gaze for the first time that morning.

Brian said, "Gotta go." But as he passed Paul, he grabbed his dad and flung his arms around him and held him tightly. As Paul returned the embrace, Brian whispered, "I love you, dad."

Paul hugged him and said, "I love you, son." His athletic son was now taller than he was. Visions of holding his boy when he was a baby sleeping in his arms flashed in Paul's mind. He wished he could always keep the boy as safe and secure as he had then. And then the hug was over and the boy was out of the house.

He found Ben in the kitchen and helped with the final tidying up. He told Ben about the embrace. Paul finished, "Something is still wrong. I'm afraid we don't have the full story."

"We'll just have to see. I wonder if their plans for the Prom have changed?"

"Maybe they haven't thought that far ahead. Shane might still be planning on going. We'll have to see what Brian says."

Ben headed for the shop. Paul often caught a few more hours of sleep on those mornings during the weeks when he worked the late shift. He was too restless today. He tidied up their bedroom, put in a load of laundry, tossed a pile of newspapers into the trash, spent an hour with bills and email. He emailed his parents in Florida several paragraphs of news about the boys and the neighborhood. He included a description of the events of the night before. His parents still had a lot of connections in the neighborhood and would find out about what happened. Better they hear it from him first.

He stopped at Rose Talucci's for a moment.

She asked, "Is Brian okay?"

"It's a lot for him to get used to."

"He did right without thinking. Like his dad."

Paul blushed at the complement. He said, "Thanks for your help with the Cardinal."

She gave him a grim smile. "Just let me know if he gives you the materials you wanted and if they help."

He thanked her again.

Before he left for Area Ten, he walked over to Ben's because he liked to see the man he loved before he left for work. Already by ten-thirty in the morning Ben smelled of grease and sweat.

Paul loved it, hugged and kissed him, and left for Area Ten headquarters. He was going in early because of all the pressure coming down on them because of the Kappel case. He also needed to use one of the loaner cars from the shop. Ben said he'd send one of his workers over to get Paul's car from the Area Ten parking lot and that Paul could use the loaner for as long as it took.

As he got in the car to head to work, his cell phone rang. It was Ian.

"You should get here."

"Where's here?" Turner asked.

"I'm at The Last Gasp and Gulp Coffee House next to the El at Ravenswood and Montrose. There are some people here who want to talk to you."

"Who?"

"I've got Graffius along with my buddy from the Order. Tresca is expected."

"I should call Fenwick."

"You can do that, but I wouldn't suggest bringing him. This is a skittish bunch. They're willing to talk, kind of sort of. You better hurry."

TWENTY-FOUR

Monday 10:59 A.M.

A harsh wind off the lake pushed the promised rain in sheets onto his windshield as Turner parked the car on Montrose near Ravenswood. People opened umbrellas as they rushed from the protection of the El station in the rain.

The Last Gasp and Gulp Coffee House was a mixed bag. Two items stood out. Paul loved their toasted four-cheese sandwiches. Fenwick thought they made the best peanut butter cookies in the city, but except for them he could pass on the rest of the offerings. Delicious aromas promised gustatory delights that the food, with the two exceptions, rarely delivered or matched.

It was in an old, brick, Queen Anne style building nestled flush against the El tracks. The original interior of the mansion had been restored. The dark hardwood floors gleamed, deep brown moldings ran along the floors and outlined the doorways. Oak paneling covered the walls half way up. The deli case to the left of the entrance ran the length of the room.

Prints of Parisian sights hung at tasteful intervals on the walls. Intermixed with these were photos from the early years of the last century along with ad signs from the same era. The chairs around the tables were an eclectic collection, from rocking chairs, to chaises, to straight back chairs, aluminum folding chairs printed with World War II army surplus on the back, and unmatched vinyl-padded flower-print kitchen chairs. Most looked like they'd been rescued from a garbage dump.

Fenwick's favorite waitress, Melanie, who looked like a graduate from the frump school in the movie *My Big Fat Greek Wedding*, was on duty. Tattoos ran up her arms to her shoulders revealed by a sleeveless top. She wore jeans or granny dresses on her nearly skeletal frame. Most of the places on her face that could be pierced, were pierced. Even some that Turner thought must have been very painful, especially the multiple bits of steel protruding from her eyelids. Her black stringy hair matched her ill-applied makeup. Fenwick always said, not in her hearing, that a mole on the side of her nose with a hair growing out of it would have been a great complement to her look. Turner reminded him at those moments that those of a heft such as Fenwick's should probably be loath to comment on the way others looked.

Paul told her he was looking for a group of friends. She took him to the room farthest in the back and pointed to a dark corner. Three pews from an old church formed a U around a deep brown scarred-oak topped table. He saw Ian, Graffius, and another man he didn't recognize.

Ian waved him over. When Paul got to the table, Ian said, "You look like hell."

"Thanks."

"How's Brian?"

"You heard?"

"It was on the Internet. I saw his name."

"He's okay, thanks."

Ian said, "This is Father Louis Demarco of the Sacred Heart of Bleeding Jesus Order. Louis is a friend of mine." They all stood up to shake hands then sat down and ordered coffee. Melanie departed.

Turner pointed at Demarco. "This is the guy you told me about that you dated."

"We're still good friends."

Turner didn't ask what that meant. Father Demarco was mostly tall and a lot of thin with high cheek bones and a heavy beard growth. He looked to be in his late thirties.

Ian began, "We wanted to meet to give you information about Bishop Kappel and the Sacred Heart of Bleeding Jesus Order."

"I appreciate it."

"Bishop Tresca is supposed to join us," Ian said.

"How'd you get him to agree?" Turner asked.

Graffius said, "I think he's afraid. If he's not, he should be." The older priest wore a black wool sweater and thick dark pants.

"Of whom or what?" Turner asked.

"All of his so-called friends."

Ian glanced at his watch. "Tresca is almost thirty minutes late."

"Does that worry you?" Turner asked.

Graffius said, "This whole situation should worry you and everyone involved." Graffius used his cell phone to call Tresca's number, but the call went straight to voice mail.

Turner noted that the old priest had placed his hands firmly on the table. His body still trembled but shook less than the other night.

Ian said, "I know what a goddamn stickler for rules you are. You'd never have snuck into the Abbey to hunt for evidence."

"Invalid search. Anything found would have been tossed out in court."

Ian snorted. "Details. So I figured I'd get in myself and snoop around. I called Louis here. You should tell him what you know."

Their coffee arrived. Melanie brought along sugar, diet sugar, cream, vanilla, and cinnamon. Graffius took his black as did Turner. Demarco added vanilla. Ian dumped in cream.

Demarco gave the few other patrons in the room wary looks. None made eye contact or seemed to be paying attention to them. Graffius looked grimly pleased. Turner had a lot of questions for both of them, but Ian had organized this party and he was willing to cut a whole lot of people slack, for a while at least.

Demarco leaned forward. "It's kind of complicated."

Turner sat back. The pew was as uncomfortable as any in the most cash-starved church. Demarco said, "I'm one of the youngest priests in this province, in this country, too, in the whole

Order for that matter." He sighed. "I get a lot of the shit jobs."

Ian interrupted. "He had to clean out Kappel's room."

"They came to me Sunday morning at three A.M., woke me up. I had to go right then. They wheeled an industrial strength shredder into the room. I was to destroy every piece of paper no matter what it was. They took the computer and any storage device connected with technology they could find. I was to bundle up the clothes and get them into the trash as soon as possible. I was still there at dawn."

"There were that many papers?" Turner asked.

"The older priests have suites. In the last major renovation, they took old rooms, single bare rooms, and converted them into two or three room suites with washrooms. They used to have only communal washrooms."

Ian interjected, "Which were great to keep the men together. Must have been a gay guy's dream."

"Or a nightmare," Graffius said. "Depending on how closeted or guilt ridden you were." He reached for his coffee. His hands shook and his head swayed a bit, but he took his time and smiled in satisfaction as he sipped.

"Even the Abbot had to share?" Turner asked.

"No," Graffius said. "The Abbot, Master of Novices, Formation Director, all that sort always had their own private rooms with accommodations. They mostly lived in the most ancient section. Even when the dorms were built, they did have private washrooms for the priests who had higher positions in the Order."

Demarco said, "One room in Kappel's suite had seven three-drawer file cabinets filled with papers. All neatly organized, labeled, color coded. A lot of it was pretty ordinary. A few gay porn magazines that I shredded. I took the sheets off the bed, checked under the mattress, examined the floor under the bed. I went through all the pockets in the clothes. I was told to bring anything I found in his pockets or that was hidden to the Abbot immediately." He placed the black briefcase on his lap and opened the lid. "I couldn't take very much stuff because I was afraid someone would see me. It was very early in the morning but a lot of the men keep irregular hours and they might be up and around and spot me."

Graffius interjected, "And they would tattle. They'd think it would get them in favor with the Abbot."

"How would a random priest know he was taking something he wasn't supposed to?"

Graffius shook his head. "Do not underestimate the prevalence of paranoia and back stabbing."

Demarco continued, "I saved a lot of what looked to me like personal things. Irreplaceable stuff, photos, letters from long ago, that kind of thing. Plus the papers that seemed most relevant to what he was doing nowadays, some big summary." He shoved the stuff across the scarred oak wooden table. "Here, keep it. The most interesting was in the top center drawer of an old oaken desk." He reached into the briefcase, pulled out a manila folder, opened it, and angled it so Turner could read the contents.

Turner realized he was looking at a sheaf of papers, about twenty-five of them. Each investigation was listed by organization. The first record dated back to the late eighties. Turner saw pages of small squares with dates, names, and larger squares with what seemed to be summaries. There were columns for date started, people involved, date ended, disposition.

"Does that help in the murder investigation?" Demarco asked.

"I'll have to go over it. This is real?" he asked. "He kept such a record?"

"Why not?" Demarco asked.

"Wouldn't his enemies kill to get this?" Turner asked.

"Only if what they were doing involved criminal activity."

Ian said, "If he kept notes on felonious behavior that would incriminate people, any one of those people might be willing to kill him to get them. Seems kind of a stupid thing to do."

Demarco objected. "Bishops don't make stupid decisions like

that."

"What makes bishops so special?" Ian asked. "They're not human?"

Turner interrupted. "But nobody broke into the Abbey. If these were all just sitting there, if the Abbot wanted to see them, he could get in any time. If he doesn't have a key, he's in charge of maintenance. He could just have a work crew break in."

"So Kappel wasn't a threat to the Abbot?" Ian asked.

Nobody knew the answer to that.

"Why did you choose to save anything?" Turner asked.

"Ian called."

Ian said, "Right after I spoke to you outside the station, I called him and filled him in."

Demarco shook his head. "After the call, I was eager to help with the murder investigation. When they picked me to be the cleanup guy, it made my life a lot easier. From what Ian said, I felt like I was helping the police. Maybe weeding some dead wood out of the Order."

Turner asked Demarco, "How well did you know Kappel?"

"I certainly knew of him, and I'd met him, but he never really spoke to me. He wasn't at the Abbey that often. He travelled and there was the condo with Tresca. I don't think he knew many of the younger priests."

Graffius' old voice cracked but he managed to imbue his tone with contempt and a snarl. "Because younger priests were of no use to either one of them."

Turner asked, "So you knew about the condo they shared?"

Demarco said, "We all did." Graffius nodded confirmation of this.

"How'd they get away with it?"

Graffius shrugged. Demarco said, "I have no idea."

Turner asked, "How did the older priests get along?"

"When I joined right out of college, the place was nuts. There were two factions. Still are. I learned the history from before I got there. Once they dumped poor Graffius here, it's always been Duggan versus the Abbot."

Graffius added, "I united them for a brief while. All the good it did them."

"Why do either of you stay in the priesthood?" Turner asked.

Graffius's hands shook. "I believe in my vows."

Demarco said, "I'm not sure any more, but that's not a decision for today."

Turner glanced at Ian then back to the priest. Demarco blushed. "I'm human. Or at least I'm aware of my flaws. Some call those needs."

Ian said, "I seduced him and led him into sin."

Turner said, "I know how that works."

"You were more than willing."

Turner sighed. "I'm aware of that." He remembered the frantic fumbling of his first time with Ian. His first time with a man. It had been exhilarating.

Graffius said, "I'm worried that Bishop Tresca is late. He should have been here more than forty-five minutes ago."

A distant thundering began. For a moment Turner thought perhaps the storms had intensified, but as a city person, he quickly recognized the rumble of an approaching El train. Within moments the rush of noise intensified to a deafening roar, far too loud for them to hear each other. The train paused in the station next to them. They waited. Moments later, the El roared away and conversation could resume.

Ian said, "As for Tresca, you know how traffic gets snarled when it rains in the city. Or maybe he was on the train that came in."

Graffius snorted. "A bishop on an El train? I think not." He shook his head. "I'm worried."

Demarco smiled. "You always worry."

Graffius said, "His lover is dead. He should be worried. We all should be worried."

Turner decided not to add to the worry by mentioning that he'd made the trip from the near southwest side of the city to the mid-north side of the city in the usual time frame in spite of the weather.

Demarco drank coffee then said, "I want the Order to be what it was. I want the Order to be true to itself. I want it back the way it should be. The old guard, both sides, needs to go. Right now it's a bunch of old men who have been involved in various sets of corruption, strains of corruption. Some of which go back centuries. It needs to stop."

"Centuries?"

"The secrecy, financial and political chicanery, their attempts to influence society when their doctrines, and threats, and fears of the hereafter don't work."

Graffius said, "And then there's the problem of gay priests."

"Is there any other kind?" Ian asked.

Demarco said, "It doesn't matter if we're gay or straight. Things have to change."

Ian said, "It matters a great deal to some people."

Demarco said, "I can only change the bit of the world that I'm a part of."

Ian said, "And take over the Order and run it the way it should be run with a hot stud by your side."

Demarco frowned. "Don't be mean. Your sarcasm will keep you from having a lasting relationship."

Ian laughed. "Who are you to judge?"

Demarco's lips set in a firm line. They both sat forward. This didn't sound like the first time they'd had this fight. Turner wasn't in the mood to be part of a lover's quarrel. He and Ian had nasty arguments when they dated. Ian could be a trial. Turner preferred him as a friend not a lover. Although sex with Ian had been the best up until Ben. He asked, "How did Kappel and Tresca get away with their relationship all those years?"

Graffius shrugged. "Power, money, influence, threats, deals, love, sex, any or all of the above and more, I suppose. I don't know the details."

Turner placed the briefcase between his chair and the wall. He looked at Demarco. "Thank you for all this."

"Just trying to help."

"When we were in the condo, Tresca got a call. He seemed willing to cooperate before the call, but afterward he hustled us out the door. He look frightened. Who would have that kind of effect on him? Who has that much power over him?"

Demarco said, "I don't know."

Graffius said, "The Cardinal, the Abbot, Bishop Pelagius, even Vern Drake? Someone with power he was afraid of. I don't know specifically."

TWENTY-FIVE

Monday 12:01 P.M.

A commotion at the entrance to the room drew their attention. As the noon hour had approached, the room had begun to fill. None of the new patrons had evinced an interest in them. Tresca, trailed by Melanie the waitress, rushed into the room. He dumped his rain slicker onto the end of the last empty booth on the far side of the room. Then he walked up to Turner and his group and pointed at the detective and said, "We need to talk." No explanation or apology for his late arrival, barely a glance at the others.

Tresca wore a black sweater vest over a gray long-sleeve shirt, and black jeans.

Graffius said, "Hello, Josh."

Tresca gave him a half-second nod then said, "I don't have much time." He turned to Melanie who had hovered. "Coffee. Black." He pointed to the booth where he'd thrown his slicker. "Over there." Without waiting to see if Turner followed, he marched to the booth.

"Charming as ever," Graffius said.

Turner stood up. "He was closest to the dead man."

He walked over. The booth was two high-backed old church pews, their short ends flush against the wall. This table top was stained Formica. The shaded lamp attached to the wall illumined a painting of a woodland waterfall. Turner tucked the newly acquired briefcase behind his legs under the pew.

Without preamble, Tresca began, "Those two are losers. Demarco won't be a priest in a year and Graffius will probably be dead in a year."

"That's harsh." Turner thought Tresca was talking unnaturally fast, but perhaps that was his way. He seemed hunched over enough to be thirty years older than he was. Every minute or so, a muscle under his left eye twitched. He thought the man might be ready for a breakdown.

The priest said, "I've faced a lot of realities in my life. That's just a minor couple of them."

Turner asked, "Who called you Saturday night at the condo?"

Melanie brought coffee and left. Tresca ignored his.

"Detective, how about for now you let me tell this my way."

Turner gave him a brief nod but thought, if I don't outright arrest your ass after this, you'll be lucky.

Tresca did a three hundred sixty degree turn around the café and eyed each of the patrons suspiciously. He hunched forward. Did he think the church had enough minions to spy on him in every café in the city? Was his paranoia justified? Would he really lose that much if the church found out what he was doing? Then again his lover was dead.

"The Cardinal and the Abbot. Both hated Timothy."

"I thought he worked for them."

"He did. And he had the goods on both of them."

"What kind of goods?"

"Well, the Sacred Heart of Bleeding Jesus Order is going broke. It's the Abbot's fault."

"How so?"

"He's been skimming. He's been getting them into bad investments. When the stock market crashed the Order lost even bigger."

"What's he got on the Cardinal?"

"The Cardinal was in deep with covering up molestations in his last diocese."

"We checked that. The cops said they had nothing on that."

"No, no. When he was a monsignor. He was the third in

command, but he was the one directly involved with accused priests. This was all before it made national headlines. He's the one who got them plane tickets out of town. He's the one who got them reassigned around this country or on continents overseas. It's a very big Order. There's lots of places to send people. You want a priest who's embarrassed the Order out of the way, send him to Mumbai where the Order has seventeen parishes, runs schools, and orphanages. He mostly got away with it because he was in the Order, not officially part of an archdiocese. It was a very clever cover-up scheme. Timothy found all the records of the priests and the victims."

"Why didn't they just transfer Timothy halfway around the planet?"

"They couldn't. He was controlling them. He was controlling any number of archdioceses and the Order. Timothy had real power, and they were afraid of him."

"Did he keep any kind of records on his investigations?"

"He said he did. I never saw any. I didn't have a key to his room at the Abbey. We kept our work lives separate."

"You were his lover, didn't he confide in you?"

Turner didn't tell him he may have the very records he was talking about. Nor that he found it suspicious that Tresca didn't know Kappel kept records.

"He never got transferred. He always got his way."

"Got his way about what?"

"We were living together."

"How'd you guys wind up in the condo?"

"That was Timothy again. He knew how to do deals. He knew the guys who lived there before us. He performed services for them."

"Priestly or sexual?"

"Does it matter? They're dead. They couldn't have killed him."

"Was the place where we found the body familiar to you or

your lover?"

Tresca looked away. Turner suspected a lie for sure was coming.

"Never been there."

"Had Timothy?"

"I don't know."

"He never mentioned it?"

"No."

"The church owns the land."

Tresca shrugged.

"Why didn't the powers that be stop him doing investigations?"

"They couldn't. Partly he was good. Partly he did help them out and got rid of thorns in their side. Partly he had the goods on them. He was a sort of out in the open double agent."

"A dangerous game."

"Up until this weekend he was winning."

"Besides the Abbot and the Cardinal, who would want to kill him?"

"I don't know enough about his investigations to say who would be angry enough to kill him."

"He called you several times that evening. The calls lasted only a minute. What were they about?"

"Just routine schedule checks." Tresca's eyes looked away. Turner wondered if the bishop knew he was such an incompetent liar.

"Did he sound worried?"

"No. You have the records from his phone?"

"Yes. Is that a problem?"

Tresca gulped coffee. "Uh... No."

"Why were you wearing your cassock Saturday night?"

"I'd just come from an official function. I'm stuck attending far more than I care to."

Turner wasn't sure he believed much of what he was being told. It just all seemed so smooth, so pat, almost rehearsed, certainly not spontaneous. He switched tacks. "We know he paid escorts. That can be dangerous."

Tresca turned very red. He hung his head and lowered his voice. "We loved each other for years. I wasn't perfect. Neither was he." He looked at Turner. "For however smart he was, Timothy could be stupid about things, maybe naïve is a better word."

"How so?"

"Say he'd be in a restaurant, and he thought the waiter was cute. He'd go back several times. Or he'd wait for an opening the first time, and he'd offer the guy money."

"He didn't visit web sites?"

"No. He liked the danger of personal contact. He said it gave him a rush to approach a stranger."

"Wasn't there a risk they might be hostile straight guys, or at the least that he'd get thrown out of a restaurant or attacked?"

"He never got thrown out, but there was one time at The Proletarian Workers Sandwich Works on Belmont. He gave a guy a hundred dollar tip and told him there was a lot more where that came from. Guy's name was Hal. He got really angry and tossed his money back at him. Timothy told me about it. He found it exciting. I thought it was embarrassing. It should have been embarrassing. I told him to be more careful. You have to be careful with straight guys. Even in this day and age, they can get very angry, very quickly." He smiled.

"What?" Turner asked.

"Have you met his brother, Terry?"

"No."

"Very straight, but back in the seminary he'd beat off for us guys. He'd never let us touch him. He just liked putting on a show. Very friendly, but kind of frigid."

"Did you ever meet any of the other members of his family?"

"No."

"Could one of the straight guys he tried to pick up have been angry enough to attack him?"

"I don't know."

He and Fenwick would have to visit Hal.

"But him using escorts didn't make you angry?"

"Why should it?"

"You were living together."

"We'd arranged things. He had different needs than I did."

Tresca hunched closer to his coffee cup, glanced at the other table with Turner's earlier companions. "You can't trust anybody." Tresca sipped his coffee.

"Why did he let himself be appointed to all these controversial positions?"

"He wanted to be. He loved being in the thick of intrigue and scandal. Timothy was the kind of man who loved to debate. He loved discussing obscure things such as Roman Canon Law in Reformation England. He could go on about the philosophical implications of liturgical movements and rulings from the fifteenth century."

"He would have been killed over canon law?" Turner asked.

"Wouldn't be the first time," Tresca said.

"Why are you telling me all this?" Turner asked.

"Because I loved him and somebody killed him. Whoever did it has to pay."

Turner was still having trouble believing the guy.

"Where were you at the time of the murder?"

A train rumbled into the station. The noise level silenced them. Tresca began to stand up.

"Who called you at the condo?"

"I must leave. Now. Find who killed my lover."

Turner could have physically stopped him, but to what purpose? Tresca had come without a lawyer, but had implicated other people. The cleric rushed out.

A moment later Melanie arrived with Tresca's bill. Turner handed her a five and told her to keep the change. He stopped at the table where the other three sat.

Ian raised an eyebrow. "Anything helpful?"

"Hard to tell."

Graffius slapped a hand onto the table. A bit of coffee sloshed out of his cup. His mashed a napkin in his trembling hand and tried to mop up the spill. Demarco took the napkin and wiped up.

"Thank you," Graffius said to the younger man. He began to rock in his chair and pointed a shaking finger at Turner. "Do not believe a thing that lying son of a bitch told you."

Demarco held the old priest's hand until the rocking and shaking stopped.

Turner said, "Father Graffius, I wish you well. If there is ever something I can do for you, call me." He took out his palm size notebook and wrote down his number and gave it to Graffius.

"Thank you, young man."

Turner reiterated how much he appreciated their help and left.

TWENTY-SIX

Monday 1:17 P.M.

The first thing Turner did at headquarters was walk over to Wilson and Roosevelt. They'd caught the case of Shane's attempted suicide.

"You got any details," he asked, "from that kid yesterday evening?"

Wilson said, "Your son saved him."

"Yeah," Paul said, "but what exactly happened?"

"All evidence at the scene points to attempted suicide," Wilson said. "Why, is there a problem?"

"No. My son's been involved in something life-changing. I just wanted to make sure I had as many facts as I could."

Wilson and Roosevelt outlined what they had. The kid had written a note saying he was sorry. No one had been blamed or accused.

Paul wished his son had talked some more. He didn't like the silence.

Twenty-seven

Monday 1:22 P.M.

Turner headed for his own desk. Smack in the middle was a box labeled "Office Paper". He plunked the briefcase he got from Demarco next to the new container, which was the size that would normally contain ten reams of paper. There were no other markings. Turner lifted the lid.

Fenwick lumbered up to their station. "How's Brian?" he asked.

"It'll take a while for him to process what happened."

"He's a great kid." Fenwick used his doughnut to point at the box on Turner's desk. "You got a gift?"

"I think so."

Turner peered inside. The top page on the left said, "Financial Statements Archdiocese of Chicago." He riffled through a number of them. Columns and columns of numbers.

"What is it?" Fenwick asked.

"The diocesan financial records."

Fenwick whistled and plopped into his chair. "How the hell did you get that?"

"Divine intervention."

"I've retired my goddess who was mostly a pain in the ass. You're not picking one up, are you?"

"I've got better than a goddess. I've got Mrs. Talucci."

As he unpacked the box and Fenwick munched his doughnut, Turner told him about his meeting with the Cardinal.

Fenwick said, "I can't wait to tell Carruthers."

"Tell him what?"

"That his beloved Cardinal is a drag queen."

"Carruthers is Catholic?"

"You didn't know?"

"I didn't care. I still don't." He pulled another fistful of papers out of the box. "Oh, and this noon I had a meeting with Bishop Tresca along with our buddy Graffius plus Ian and his buddy, a Father Demarco."

Fenwick dropped his doughnut onto the top of his desk. "More divine intervention?"

"Ian set it all up."

"See, you've got all these inside people. That's not fair. All without me, I'm beginning to get jealous."

"You want to grouse or you want to hear what they said?"

"Do I have a choice?"

When Turner finished narrating the stories from the meeting, he said, "I wish I wasn't so suspicious of all these people."

"How many suspects do we really believe?" Fenwick answered his own question. "Not many. Why the hell are these people telling us all this? And why now? Somebody grew a conscience?"

Turner shrugged. "In this bunch? Tresca I could sort of understand. His lover died and he wants revenge or at least answers. All I know is we have more stories to add, maybe a few facts. We've got to go through this financial crap and the papers that Demarco saved from Kappel's room."

"They must have been desperate to order his stuff shredded so quickly."

"Why didn't they shred it earlier?" Turner asked. "These people don't make sense to me. For example, say Kappel jets off to Rome. Why not just go into his room at the Abbey and destroy everything then?"

"These can't be the only records he kept. He must have backups to these. Everybody backs up things these days, don't they? I'm practically a Luddite, and I still know to back everything up."

Turner tossed a stack of papers from the briefcase on to his desk. "Could his enemies be sure they got everything? They'd fear his retribution when he found out, and where is all this back-up stuff?"

Fenwick sighed. "We won't know until we look."

"I don't have any proof anything said so far today was anything but bullshit."

"It's amazing how many other people Tresca managed to throw suspicion on. Turns him into a prime suspect in my book."

"And what better book could there be than yours," Turner said. "For a grieving husband, he didn't seem all that sad. I'm not sure I believe a word he said."

"This is kind of nuts. I got the same question about Tresca, the Cardinal, and all these people. Which one, if any of them, is telling the truth?"

"I listened to them all. I just don't have a good handle on them. If we want, we can doubt Demarco and Graffius. We have what Demarco took from the room. What did he bring and why did he bring it? Was he editing as he stole? Or were all of them standing there, the Abbot, the Cardinal, the whole crowd, picking and choosing and laughing at us?"

Fenwick grimaced. "Fuck-a-doodle-do."

Turner said, "I've got to write it all up. They certainly had a lot of information. The stuff from Tresca gives all kinds of other people motives for killing his lover."

"Which is good?"

"Which is suspicious, at least to me. Many of those people are really rotten, and yet, we've got Tresca, right there in the thick of all this, and we're supposed to believe he's lily pure? I think not. In fact what he said raised him to near the top of my list."

"Who's at the top?"

"The Cardinal Archbishop of Chicago and the Provincial

Abbot of the Sacred Heart of Bleeding Jesus Order, but Bishop Tresca is right there with them. I'd prefer physical evidence tying any one of the three of them, or anyone else for that matter to the killing."

"See, there you go again, wanting real evidence," Fenwick said.

"We've got this box of papers to go through." Turner tapped the top of the stack from the briefcase. "And all these papers."

"And nothing on who he got that call from when we met him in the condo?"

"He rushed out before I could press him on the issue."

Fenwick said, "We also need to find this Hal guy at The Proletarian Workers Sandwich Works."

"We better go through this stuff to see if there's anything we could use, but I bet it's all useless."

Turner wrote up reports on his conversations while Fenwick began on the financial forms. They'd start on the briefcase materials together.

A half hour into their work, Turner said, "I'm going to make a spreadsheet with all this information on it."

"Spreadsheet?"

"A huge chart with everybody he investigated, with everybody we've talked to, with everything that's connected to Chicago, with all the data we have from the Internet, names, dates, times, cross references. I'm going to start with what we've got on his credit card expenses."

"It'll take hours."

"I know, but sorting this crap is useless unless we have it organized. I've got to be able to see who is connected to who."

"To whom."

Turner ignored Fenwick's almost automatic grammatical correction.

Five minutes after he began setting up the spreadsheet on the computer, Commander Molton showed up. Barb Dams trailed him with a stack of the day's new memos. They asked after Brian. Turner told them what little he knew. Wilson and Roosevelt wandered over. Molton pointed at the materials on Turner's desk. He asked, "What is all that?"

"The Chicago archdiocese financial records."

"How the hell did you get those?"

He told the Commander the story.

When Turner finished, Molton said, "A drag queen?"

"Fenwick wants to tell Carruthers."

Molton laughed uproariously. "I'll be damned. We should put Mrs. Talucci on the payroll."

Turner said, "She'd solve too many crimes, and we'd all be out of jobs."

Fenwick said, "His new best friend is the Cardinal Archbishop of Chicago."

"Kind of trumps that goddess bullshit you were pushing," Molton said.

"Is anyone going to give that a rest?" Fenwick asked.

Dams, Molton, Wilson, Roosevelt, and Turner gave him a spontaneous chorus of loud nos.

Fenwick sighed. "I try to make your lives a little brighter."

"Ah," Wilson said. "You're right about that one little thing. You are trying. I can't tell you how trying you are. And do us all a favor, stop now."

Fenwick replied, "It's my version of torture. Be glad I don't tell St. Olaf stories."

Roosevelt said, "You started this goddess shit."

Fenwick stuck his tongue out at him.

The others left. Turner checked his email and found a preliminary report from the ME on the debris at the crime scene. He found page after page of single spaced details. Other than the smallest rocks, they seem to have taken everything from the scene and begun to examine it. Nothing Turner saw in the report gave him a hint about the killer.

When they finally got to the briefcase, after a cursory examination, Fenwick said, "Didn't we get most of this investigation stuff from the Internet already? We're being hosed. This is nonsense."

Turner thumped the stack he'd been working on. "The ones I've got are from around the world and years ago."

"Around the world?"

"Peru in the late eighties. It must have been one of his first investigations."

"Maybe there's a Peruvian mafia. Everybody else has a mafia, why can't they?"

"That investigation was to get evidence from and about," Turner peered at the report, "some bishop and his buddies looting antiquities from a mission that dated back to just after the Incas got wiped out."

"Might have been valuable."

"In the disposition section, it says they all went to jail."

"Maybe they all got out and came after him."

"You want to take a trip to Peru to find out?"

"Is Peru nice this time of year?"

"I have no idea."

Fenwick grumbled. "We don't even think about going unless all of this other shit turns up a bunch of nothing."

But that's what they mostly had after another hour. They searched the Internet. They made lists of those investigated in the Chicago area. Turner filled in the ever-expanding spreadsheet with relevant people, events, and details from all that they'd discovered. He cross-referenced the phone logs and credit card records they had from Fong. This way he had a summary of all their current information and thoughts in one spot. He made electronic copies, emailed a copy to himself, and printed out a copy. Turner always backed up everything three ways.

About five thirty he went down to Fong's lair. The lanky tech genius was switching between three screens at once. Turner said, "I'd like to borrow your biggest monitor. I've got a spreadsheet, and it's too big for my screen."

He and Fong lugged the giant thing up to the detectives' area on the second floor. On the first landing, Turner asked, "How did you get such an expensive thing on the police department budget?"

"I knew a guy who knew a guy who got me a deal."

As good an explanation as one was likely to get in the CPD.

They pulled two unused desks together and put two heavy straight back chairs on top of them. They rested the seventy-two inch screen on the desk top and leaned it against the chairs which stood at the far end of the desk against the wall. Fong set up the connection with his computer so Turner could work on both screens at once, or switch to doing one thing on his smaller screen, while saving what could be seen on the larger screen. Fong got ready to plug the screen in.

"This going to blow a fuse?" Turner asked.

"Maybe not."

Their doubts were eased as the screen came to life. Fong showed him where to push on his computer to switch from screen to screen, or see the same thing on both screens at once, or to have different things on both screens at once.

Fong left and Turner put what he had so far on the large screen. There were already columns and rows of dates, times, and people, and he still had stacks of documents to go through.

Fenwick walked up to what he had so far. He said, "Damn that's good."

"Yes, I know," Turner replied. "Now it just has to help us find a killer."

TWENTY-EIGHT

Monday 5:57 P.M.

Sanchez gave them a brief call reporting the absolute nothing he and the other beat cops had come up with on the canvass of the people on the boats that went by and the businesses in the neighborhood.

After more sorting and examining, Turner and Fenwick took what they had to make copies of all the originals. The stuff on the computer they had backed up, but they wanted multiple electronic and hard copies.

They had to spend half an hour with the copying machine with all the documents from the diocese and Demarco. Before they even pressed copy, they turned the machine on and off twice, opened and closed the top cover once, fanned the paper numerous times before putting it in the tray, and thumped the machine hard just past the eternally blinking needs toner display. The proper sequence of thumps and incantations was on a piece of paper taped above the printer. Fenwick would have willingly sacrificed several suspects on the altar of technological intransigence. Even after all that, it might have taken less time if the copier didn't tend to jam every twenty pages. As always at Area Ten nothing worked as it should.

Then they took a copy of the financial records to Jeanne D'Amato. She'd agreed to stay late to meet with them. Her office was on the top floor of the Algonquin Building, one of the earliest sky-scrapers in Chicago. It was now dwarfed by much newer buildings. Turner liked the wrought-iron stairs and faded tile.

They placed the financial documents on the accountant's desk. D'Amato and her agency had the most respected reputation in the city. She refused most governmental work, but did occasional favors for Molton's district.

Her secretary brought beverages as they exchanged pleasantries. For a minute or two D'Amato glanced inside the box at the mounds of papers then sipped from her tea. She put the cup into the saucer and said, "You're being lied to."

Fenwick said, "You've barely looked at them."

D'Amato gave him a pitying smile. "Think for a minute. The Chicago Archdiocese is a full-time, big time organization. Everything would be on spread sheets on computers. They gave you paper. It's useless." She pointed at the stacks. "You could get that all onto a four-bit jump drive. I'll have my best people look at what you have here, and I'll glance at it some more as well, but…" She shook her head. "Whatever you want is not going to be in there."

They left.

"Mrs. Talucci is going to be pissed," Fenwick said as they sat in their unmarked car on Dearborn Street. "I'm going to have to eat chocolate for days to get over it."

"We all know the Catholic church lies," Turner said. "Ask all the kids who've been molested about the clergy's level of honesty. Hell, ask all the lawyers and insurance companies in the past few years dealing with their deception."

Fenwick said, "The Cardinal would know we'd have them checked."

"Delay. Obfuscation. The church has been around a long time. They don't care how long it takes."

Twenty-nine

Monday 7:11 P.M.

They drove to The Proletarian Workers Sandwich Works on Belmont. The rain had let up to a light drizzle and the traffic was reasonably unsnarled.

As they pulled off the Drive and headed west, Fenwick said, "I hope this Hal guy is big and burly and goes to work in a big limousine."

"We don't get that lucky."

There were few sandwich shops in the city Fenwick hadn't eaten at. Fewer still that he'd only visited once. The Proletarian Workers Sandwich Works was one of these. The establishment's first sin was that they emphasized trendy, with it, vegetarian ingredients. Fenwick's main philosophy was that if the food at an establishment wasn't filled with artery clogging glop, what was the point? Pushing vegetarian glop, as far as he was concerned, was a mortal sin. He liked his glop pure, that is health-food free.

Second, he'd gotten violently ill after they'd eaten there that first and only time. Turner hadn't eaten the grilled cheese sandwich that was delivered burnt with a bowl of tomato soup that was cold and slimy. Fenwick had the All-Spicy-Turkey-bacon sandwich/salad combination.

But it was the third flaw that was the death knell in Fenwick's pantheon of culinary sins, the choices of chocolate confections were limited and those available days-old and hard as rocks.

The restaurant was in a two-story filth-encrusted, red-brick house just west of Southport on Belmont. The interior was lots of unvarnished wood including the walls, floors, and ceilings. Display cases ran along the wall on the left.

They had brands of soda of which Turner had never heard. Next to them were ready-made salads to go. Today, next to the salads was a half-gone chocolate cake dripping with raspberry sauce. Fenwick considered the addition of raspberry to chocolate, whether it be juice, sauce, berries, or a combination thereof, to be one of the greatest of gastronomic blasphemies. Turner guessed that if Fenwick ever found out the name of the cooking school that had perpetrated the raspberry mixed with chocolate trend, he would launch upon it a massive, destructive attack of shock and awe, little short of a nuclear strike. Certain things were sacred to Fenwick.

Turner tended to agree about the chocolate/raspberry issue but didn't find himself as fanatic about it as Fenwick. Instead of a nuclear strike, he might suggest a drone attack consisting of vanilla frosting.

The place seemed to attract a younger crowd from the nearby north side branch of Pope St. Agatho's University. As far as Turner could see, the main draw had to be that the prices were incredibly low. The food was served on mid-seventies floral serving trays. The tables were accented with painted flower salt and pepper shakers along with brown ceramic bread warmers that, as far as Turner could see, warmed no bread.

They showed ID and asked for Hal.

"You gotta talk to the manager," said an eighteen or nineteen-year-old man with serious acne covering most of his chin.

A few minutes later, a man with enormous ringlets of poofed-out black hair emerged from the back. His name was Stan Javley. His tight jeans and T-shirt covered a well-muscled frame. After introductions and the initial question about Hal, Javley said, "Hal Poutine? What's he done now?"

Turner said, "We just wanted to ask him a few questions about one of his customers."

"Who?"

Turner showed him the picture of Kappel on his phone.

"Never saw him," Javley said.

"We'd like to talk to Hal."

Hal was outside the back door of the restaurant under a small canopy out of the drizzle. He threw away a lit cigarette as the detectives came through the door. When they showed him ID, he said, "Come on, you're not going to bust me on that." He leaned his head toward the smoldering remnants of what he'd been smoking.

Fenwick said, "Not unless it starts the trash in the alley on fire."

Hal stamped it out with his foot.

"What do you want?" Hal asked. He was tall and lanky with straight, dirty blond hair that hung to his T-shirt collar.

Turner ignored the attitude and showed him the picture on his phone.

"Him." He snorted with contempt.

"He cause you problems?"

"He was an asshole."

"How so?"

"He offered me a hundred bucks to blow me. That's sick, man."

"It wasn't a hundred dollar tip?"

"That's what he called it initially. He said I could get a lot more if I would do a lot more."

"Did he give you his name?"

"Nope. I didn't want anything to do with him. I told him to get out of the restaurant. He looked kind of scared and took off. Then he came in again a couple weeks ago. He offered one of the other guys a thousand bucks to suck him off. I hadn't said anything to anyone. It was too strange, and the manager is kind of an asshole. He might have thought I was supposed to be nicer to a customer. I don't put up with that."

Fenwick said, "Were you pissed that he only offered you a hundred and the other guy a thousand?"

Hal looked confused. "No, dude."

Turner asked, "Who was the other guy?"

"Alfred. He's on duty now." They told Hal to wait.

The detectives found Alfred bussing tables. He had an enormous black eye. After ID showing, introductions, and picture displaying, Alfred said, "Yeah, I know the asshole. We chased him out of here."

"Who?"

"Me and Hal."

Hal was summoned.

Hal sulked. "Sure, yeah, I helped chase him out of here. So what? He was a shit."

Fenwick said, "His name was Timothy Kappel. He's dead. He was murdered. We're looking into his life. To those who might wish him harm."

Alfred said, "We just chased him."

"How'd you get the black eye?"

"That was last Thursday. I was coming off a late shift and some big, burly guy jumped me as I was walking home. He knocked me unconscious. Didn't rob me or anything, so it kind of didn't make sense."

Turner asked Hal, "Anything odd happen to you lately?"

"My apartment got broken into, but I don't live in a great neighborhood. My iPod and my computer got smashed, but they didn't take anything."

"You guys report this to the police?"

They both nodded yes.

"Anybody see anyone suspicious around your apartment?" Turner asked.

Hal shook his head. He left and went back to work.

Turner said, "Had you ever seen the big, burly guy before?"

"No."

"You look like you work out. He must be pretty strong."

"I keep myself in shape. I was in the marines. If he hadn't blindsided me, I'd have beat the crap out of him."

"He say anything?"

"Like what?"

Turner said, "We think there's a connection between the big burly guy, and the man whose picture we showed you."

Alfred busied himself chucking dirty dishes, napkins, flatware, and glasses into a large gray-plastic container. His level of upset seemed to have trumped his concern for chipping the serving paraphernalia. Alfred glanced over his shoulder.

"I got a shift to finish."

Fenwick was fed up. He glanced at all the mid-afternoon empty tables. "You got time, now."

Alfred leaned close. "I don't want no trouble."

Turner said, "We're interested in solving a murder not in bringing trouble to you."

"I'm not a whore."

Turner said, "This isn't the highest paying job in the city. You needed money. You put on a show for Hal of getting rid of the guy, but maybe you made a deal with the man whose picture we showed you."

Alfred glanced around. None of the other restaurant employees were nearby. He mumbled, "Yeah."

"What happened?" Turner asked.

Alfred wiped a table with a mid-size hand towel. Tossed it on top of the dirty dishes. He moved closer to the detectives. "Let's make this quick." He looked around again and spoke in a rushed whisper. "Okay. I needed money. I met him at a coffee shop. We made a deal." He hesitated.

"What happened?" Turner asked.

"Nothing. Well, nothing much. We went to my place. I let him do a little."

Turner said, "Somebody big and burly who knows our dead guy doesn't come beat up guys when nothing happened."

"Okay. Okay. Not much happened. I didn't even get off. Neither did he. I think he felt cheated. Maybe. I don't know. A few days later, I texted him. I needed more money. I'm broke. This job is for shit." More glances around the nearly empty establishment.

"How did you get his number?"

"When we set up the first meeting, we exchanged phone numbers. We texted back and forth. I offered to do more with him. I kept texting over and over. We finally met at my place. He told me to stop texting him. He said he found what we did for the amount he spent unsatisfactory and wasn't interested in meeting again. Maybe I got a little mad."

"You beat him up."

"I may have pushed him around a little."

Turner remembered the ME didn't report any older bruises or other signs that Kappel had been attacked recently.

Alfred said, "I didn't hurt him. He ran out. I texted him to apologize. I really needed money. I guess I was stupid. Then he blocked my number."

Turner said, "You threatened him with more than physical violence. You threatened to call the cops, tell people he tried to pay you for sex."

"Jesus, I'm not a bad guy. I just needed money."

"And you thought you'd make some, and that's why he came over to your place the second time to try to get you to back off."

Alfred gave another look around. "After he blocked my number there was nothing I could do. I didn't know his last name or where he lived." He leaned close. "Are you sure him and the burly guy are connected? Am I in danger?"

"When was all this?" Turner asked.

Alfred gave him the dates and his phone number. They would

check the phone log when they got back to the station.

As the detectives prepared to leave, Alfred said, "I'm not going to get in trouble, am I?"

Fenwick said, "If you're going to be a whore, seems like you learned an important lesson here. Don't cheat clients."

The detectives left.

They dashed through the now enhanced drizzle. In the car Fenwick said, "Hal is not a big, burly guy."

"Kind of skinny, and I bet he doesn't ride in a limo."

"But a big burly guy attacked two people who were not nice to Kappel?"

"Neither one of us believes in coincidences. Does this mean Kappel had his own enforcer? So the burly guy wasn't a threat to Kappel?"

"Then why was he banging on the door?"

"An emergency of some kind? If he was working for Kappel, it would explain him having a key for the underground garage."

Fenwick opined, "I didn't like those guys."

"Hal and Alfred? They were kind of skuzzy."

"It wasn't that. As you know I'm not prejudiced. I just don't see why Hal made a big deal out of what Kappel asked. Just give him a polite no. Maybe it's odd, maybe even weird, but what skin is it off his nose? A simple 'no' and the moment is over."

"I guess some people don't handle weird as well as you do."

"I'm good at weird. And catching criminals."

"So, Kappel had his own lethal minion," Turner said. "Maybe the minion turned on him."

"Kappel, a bishop of the church, turned a guy loose on someone who wouldn't stop texting him?"

"He was a bishop who got chased down the street. And my guess is Alfred's threats were out and out blackmail. I suspect he tried that on the wrong victim. Alfred didn't seem used to pulling off that kind of caper."

"Neither one of them knew he was a bishop. Didn't even know his last name."

"I guess this means that Kappel was not without resources and was capable of getting even on his own terms."

When they got to the car, Turner called Fong. "Are there any text messages between Kappel and…?"

Fong interrupted. "There are no text messages between Kappel and anybody. He, or someone, erased them all."

"Can you recover them?"

"I'll try."

He gave Fong Alfred's number. Fong came back on the line in a few moments. "Yep. He called that number, and it's on the blocked list. He blocked it last Tuesday."

"Thanks. Please check on recovering the messages."

"Sure thing."

Turner reported to Fenwick, who said, "So Alfred may have been telling the truth."

"Looks possible."

"We gotta find this big, burly guy."

"I am open to suggestions."

But Fenwick had none.

Turner leaned back as Fenwick drove. He closed his eyes and said, "I need more sleep."

Fenwick braked hard at the entrance to Lake Shore Drive as a delivery van made a sharp left in front of him onto the ramp. Turner took out his phone to check for messages. There were none. He called Ben. All was quiet on the home front.

THIRTY

Monday 8:04 P.M.

Back at the station, Molton said, "I've got a strange request here."

"Stranger than the time—" Fenwick began.

Molton cut him off. "Either of you heard of St. Raguel of Leon church?"

They shook their heads.

"It's on the near north side. Used to be a huge immigrant parish. Then when the neighborhood changed, it became an activist church for a lot of very good causes."

"What kind of good causes?" Fenwick asked.

"In the sixties it was Civil Rights, helping poor people, helping the community. They did some good. The same priest ran the parish for ages beyond ages."

"Isn't that against diocesan policy?" Fenwick asked.

"What do you know about diocesan policy?" Turner asked.

"I read the papers. Didn't that priest on the south side who did a lot of good stay on far beyond the term limits they have?"

"Diocesan churches do. I'm not sure churches run by religious orders do."

"Don't tell me," Fenwick said, "This was a church run by the Sacred Heart of Bleeding Jesus Order."

Turner said, "It was run by the Sacred Heart of Bleeding Jesus Order."

"How would you know that?" Fenwick asked. "And I said don't tell me."

"We're working this one case," Turner said. "Why else would

the Commander be bringing us this call?"

Fenwick snorted. "Show off."

Molton said, "Paul's right."

"What did the caller say?" Turner asked.

Molton said, "You can find information about the bishop's death if you call at the rectory."

THIRTY-ONE

Monday 8:22 P.M.

After he jammed on the brakes to avoid a bus at Congress and Dearborn Fenwick said, "You know what worries me?"

"That the brakes will fail?"

Fenwick snorted. "I don't expect physical danger from these desperately sad old men, but I get an uneasy feeling when I'm around them."

"They aren't that much older than we are."

"It's like Drake did all that fist smashing on Molton's desk, but the one I'd be worried about is Pelagius. Not a frontal assault, something sneaky, devious, and vicious." He shook his head as he maneuvered around the bus. "Graffius is pretty old, but I mean they seem that way. They talk and act like they're in their 90's and from medieval times."

"How did people talk in medieval times?" Turner asked.

"Like these guys."

"You really worried about danger from them?"

Fenwick said, "Somebody got violently murdered and there's all these pompous guys blubbering or blustering. You'd think they were Republicans. Anybody is capable of violence. One of them is a murderer. They could afford to hire minions. And Kappel seemed to have his own private minion."

"Like the Spanish Inquisition?"

Fenwick emitted a grumble and a fart at the same time, a sure sign to Turner, who was all too aware of his partner's peccadilloes, that Fenwick was upset. They took Wacker Drive to the Chicago River and crossed onto Orleans Street north toward the rectory.

Fenwick asked, "What real threat are these people to us or to each other?"

"Obviously someone was or there wouldn't be someone violently dead."

"No, I mean, sure you violate some ecclesiastical law, but who really cares?"

"Yeah, but we're getting more than hints of scandal and money. Anyone can screw up either to cause a problem or take advantage of it. Maybe both perpetrator and victim were trying to or needed to cover up something or get away with something. A whole lot of time, as we both know, we've found money as a motive. Or maybe Kappel asked a whole bunch of waiters and busboys and hired help for sex and finally some homophobe beat him to death. It happens."

"I know that."

"We're kind of testy with each other tonight."

"These shits are lying to us. They've spent their whole lives lying to themselves, each other, and the world at large. I've met liars, but these guys are pros. I'm feeling out of my league and out of sorts."

Fenwick turned left on Erie Street and pulled up to the rectory. A slight breeze off the lake annoyed the leaves in the gutters.

Fenwick adjusted his bulk in the seat and said, "At least I hope the lies we get from this guy are plausible."

"You know we were followed here."

Fenwick didn't even bother looking in the rearview mirror. "Black town car, picked us up a block from the station, license SHBJO1, didn't turn onto Erie Street with us? Didn't notice a thing."

Turner didn't need to key in the acronym to recognize it was from the Sacred Heart of Bleeding Jesus Order. "Makes no sense. If they wanted to lure cops to a secret rendezvous to do us harm, just make a bogus call. Or maybe this was a bogus call."

"Why follow a couple Chicago cops?" Fenwick answered his own question. "To see where we go. To set up a trap for us."

"Like to a secret meeting at an old rectory."

"Like that."

"But then half the planet knows where we were going."

"Setting up the guy at the rectory?"

"They think we're that stupid and wouldn't notice? It's full daylight in a big city. And they're tailing cops? Are they amateurs? They think there's a point to it? They think we're not on alert and being careful?"

"Never underestimate the stupidity of a criminal or the desperation of a killer."

The short street ended in a half block where part of the old public housing project had been torn down. The urban renewers hadn't rebuilt the area yet. Weeds and trash nestled comfortably in every leftover nook or cranny. The rectory was a two story Italianate villa, orange-stucco, red-tile roof edifice that would have been at home on a hillside in Tuscany.

A short man wearing a gray shirt with a Roman collar and black pants and black shoes answered the door. He held a drink in one hand. With the other he held onto the door. His bald head shown in a hall light.

Fenwick and Turner held out their IDs and introduced themselves.

"Ah gentlemen, do come in." He spoke in deep, soft, mellifluous tones. "You are so kind to have responded to my summons."

Turner said, "We were told you had information about Bishop Kappel." The wrinkles and mottled spots on the man's neck told Turner that the man might be in his eighties, possibly older.

The priest let go the door and held out his hand to them. "I'm Father Dere, please do come in."

He led them deeper into the house. The front hall had a hardwood floor, pictures of saints in the process of being martyred hung on the walls. The one pierced with arrows Turner thought might be St. Sebastian. A woman going up in flames had to be Joan of Arc. None of the others jogged his memory of religion classes years ago.

The room the priest took them to was furnished as a plush den in the most exquisite mansion on Lake Shore Drive, deep brown leather chairs, antique side tables, brass lamps, a gigantic oak desk stained deep brown, two walls of books, on the two others exquisite paintings bathed with muted light showing scenes of pastoral repose, muted colors with trees and fields and reclining animals.

He led them to a sitting area of three chairs nesting on a deep purple Persian carpet. He offered them drinks. Turner and Fenwick declined. He poured liquid from several bottles into a tall glass, stirred with a crystal swizzle stick, tasted the concoction, added an amber drop from one tall thin bottle, tasted again, smiled. Then the old man subsided into a chair. When they were all seated he said, "I have a story to tell."

Turner and Fenwick nodded.

"It goes back a long way."

Turner said, "Anything you can tell us will be a help."

Dere said, "At least you hope it will be." He smiled. "I shall begin at the beginning." He sipped from his drink and placed it on a lace doily worthy of Mrs. Talucci's living room. "Timothy Kappel and Joshua Tresca have been looking over their shoulders since they were in the seminary."

"Why?" Fenwick asked.

"Seminaries in general breed a culture of obedience and compliance. Those who sucked up and caused the least problems, tended to not get thrown out. You were evaluated constantly by everyone who was a priest and superior to you. If you asked questions, you came under suspicion. Compliance to authority and the goal of continuing the good thing they had were the most important things. Those in charge didn't want boat rockers. Better to always keep someone uncertain about their future. And that works all the way up to Pope. Someone is always your superior. Someone can always judge you and find you wanting.

Think of those modern contest shows in television."

Fenwick said, "I've never watched one."

Turner hadn't either.

"But you know the idea. A board of overseers made up of people of varying degrees of competence passes judgment on you. Some know you well, others don't."

"Hell of a way to live," Fenwick opined.

Dere shrugged. "It's worked for hundreds and hundreds of years. For how much longer, I'm not sure. There are so few young priests or seminarians." He covered his mouth and hacked as if both lungs were heavily congested. He wiped his mouth with a tissue he took from the end of his sleeve, took a sip from the tall glass he'd filled earlier, and resumed. "The important thing I have to tell you, and you must remember this and always keep it in mind, everything everyone has told you in this investigation up to this point is a lie."

"You know everyone we've talked to?" Fenwick asked. "I find that a little hard to believe. We don't make a list and publish it. Are you saying you have access to our squad room, our desks, our paperwork? You'd be noticed."

"You want my help or not?"

He wasn't used to being doubted.

"Why should we believe you instead of them?" Fenwick asked.

The priest smiled and kept silent.

Turner said, "We listen to a lot in investigations. Most of it is kind of useless and peripheral. Are you saying the facts we've gotten from people are wrong? Which facts? Which people?"

"Obviously you don't want my help."

This time it was Turner's turn to smile. "Why would you lie for these people? What hold do they have on you?"

The old priest snarled, "I'm not lying."

"Don't be absurd. You couldn't possibly know who we've

interviewed. You might know who some of the priests were in the Order who we talked to, but then are you saying there is a vast network following us around? Or all the priests connected with your Order have this vast network of interconnection? Or you're all madly twittering each other? Or have reported everything to the Abbot or the Cardinal? And then someone has a way of disseminating all that information instantaneously? And that someone is organizing all the lies and only you can stop them?"

"I'm trying to help." He hesitated, took a long gulp from his drink. "I wish I could help."

Turner asked, "What was your relationship with Kappel and Tresca all those years ago?"

The old priest smiled. "Forty years ago I was in charge of formation in the Chicago Province. I ran the seminary in the Chicago Province for many, many years."

"So you knew them well," Fenwick asked.

The old man's smile got wider. He sipped from his drink, licked his lips, coughed. He looked them both in the eye and said, "Yes, I recruited them to the order from our high school. The two of them were quite the pair. Lovers back then, of course, as they are now."

"You knew?" Fenwick asked.

Dere smiled. "I fucked both their tight little asses." He glanced from one to the other of the detectives. "I haven't shocked you?"

Turner said, "I think you might not have been able to inflict the injuries on Kappel that killed him. So I don't think you're a killer. Were they over eighteen?"

"Yes."

"How does what happened then connect to the murder and catching the killer?"

"Well, our relationship benefited both of them. When it came time to evaluate them, I was always one of their champions. Some of the other priests who championed them were probably being honest. Some of them were for them for the same reason I was. We got satisfaction. They got to stay in the Order."

Fenwick said, "Didn't openly gay guys get thrown out of seminaries then and now?"

"Oh, my, yes. They were smart back then, very smart. So was I."

Fenwick said, "You took advantage of them at a vulnerable time." Turner who understood his partner well, heard the beginning of an outraged outburst rumbling under the question.

Dere smiled. "This was a college program. If I was still interested in sex, the image of what they and I did together would be what would bring me to orgasm. They were athletic and beautiful. We'd wrestle and horseplay in the halls and have sex in private."

Fenwick snapped, "Are you bragging or complaining?"

The old man shook his head. "You may save your outrage. Back then if found out, I'd have been transferred so fast my head would have spun. But no one knew, or if they knew, they said nothing. The culture of silence and willful blindness, of protecting Holy Mother Church was paramount, is paramount, and will always be paramount. I tell you this gentlemen so you realize I'm not holding anything back. That I'm willing to be honest with you. No, there would be little loss to my old age. If there is a Maker, I shall meet him soon, and if there is hell to be paid, so to speak, I suppose I shall pay it."

Fenwick asked, "You don't believe?"

"You do?" the priest asked.

Fenwick said, "Not so much, but you're a priest."

"Which does not mean I am not human." Again he sipped from his drink, coughed, and wiped his mouth. He placed the tissue back in his sleeve and said, "But you are right. You gentlemen came here for information that I do have. Not a history of past indiscretions. Yes, Kappel and Tresca were both excessively narcissistic and had a penchant for sex long ago and might still have had."

"Who would want to kill him?" Turner asked.

"Bishop Kappel was the financial guy, investigation guy, the enforcer, the fixer, the time study engineer, the efficiency expert, and was an enemy to almost everyone."

"Why would he want to be cast as such an asshole?" Fenwick asked.

Dere shrugged. "Maybe he enjoyed it. He was a bishop. He could indulge his vicious streak. If there were financial irregularities that needed to be investigated in a diocese, he was your man. But who you knew was always far more important than what you'd done. The personal and political were more important than your sins. Kappel was very, very smart. He was the best at navigating the minefields in the Church. If there was a problem, you sent him."

"In the Order?" Turner asked.

"Bishop Kappel was trusted by the leaders of the Order in Rome and by the Vatican itself, by people very high up in the Vatican."

"But isn't Bruchard the head of the Order?"

"Well, yes, he is now. It's been years of complicated back and forth."

Turner said, "But we heard the Cardinal and the Abbot hated each other, but they both trusted Kappel?"

"Maybe he had the goods on both of them, on all of them."

"What goods?"

"Graft, corruption, lies."

"He had that kind of leverage even though he was living openly with another man?" Fenwick asked.

"Did they know he was gay? What difference would that make? Most of them are as well. He knew how to keep his sexuality quiet. The two of them never went out to dinner, rarely appeared in public together. They knew the rules."

"So who was Kappel investigating?"

He gave them the list of financial chicanery, investigations, and duplicity about the diocese and the Order that they'd already heard. He finished with, "We've got it good. We all have cooks in these rectories. We all get the best foods. And parties! Every feast is celebrated: the anniversary of the founding of the Order, St. Charles of Avignon's birthday, his feast day, the anniversary of his death, on and on. You saw that obscene picture of him which is replicated in rectories throughout the world. They pay for original copies painted by living artists. You see these decorations in here." He pointed to the paintings on the walls. "These are original oil paintings, magnificently framed. All of this is on the parishioner's dime." He laughed, drank, coughed, and moved to the edge of his chair.

Turner half rose. The priest held out a hand. "I'm fine. Thank you." He continued. "But that's not the actual money scandal. I know these men. I know this diocese. I know this religious Order. Things are not right." He sipped again from his drink, tipped the glass slightly toward them, and asked, "Are you sure you won't have one?"

The detectives shook their heads no. Turner asked, "Was there an actual source on the financial irregularities in the Order?"

"The Abbot's protégé. He thought the Abbot's enemies were trying to destroy him. The idiot, the protégé thought by releasing secret documents, he'd boost the Abbot's power. He almost destroyed it."

"What happened to him?"

"He's an assistant in a village outside of Palermo in Sicily. He hasn't been heard from in years."

Fenwick asked, "Why don't these guys just quit?"

Dere shrugged. "It's what they know."

Turner asked, "Did Kappel rein in the rebel priests?"

"I heard there had been meetings where angry words were exchanged. Tempers ran high. I think all those involved are dead now. We're an old bunch." He took a sip of his drink.

Dere gave a railing cough that brought him out of his chair and to his knees. Turner and Fenwick hurried to him. Turner put his arms around the old man's shoulders. "Should we call the paramedics?"

"No, no. I am dying of various kinds of cancer. It grows slowly at my age. No, this is not new. Sometimes I cough so hard I pass out." He drew deep breaths. "It passes quickly. I've been to the doctors. They don't believe me. They don't think I can cough hard enough to pass out. They told me I was having a heart attack until all their machines said my heart was fine. They don't know what's wrong. The passing out doesn't come from the cancer or a heart attack. It's not something they know, so they say it's all in my head."

Turner helped him sit back down in his chair. Dere took three sips in a row from his drink. "Thank you." He harrumphed. "Who you really should be afraid of is Bishop Pelagius. That man is frightening. Bad things happen when he's around."

"Like what?" Fenwick asked.

"He knows that Vern Drake. You know that politician who tied his fate to a condom?"

"Why should we be afraid of them?"

"I guess we've all learned to be frightened of them for so long. And no, we don't leave the priesthood. We're old. We have nowhere to go."

Fenwick said, "I asked this the other day. They can't excommunicate me or deny me communion. Even if I cared, I'm not Catholic. What am I supposed to be afraid of?" He snorted. "Haven't they learned that they can't cover up crimes here?"

"They have power within power, wheels within wheels. They will stop at nothing to destroy someone, including yourselves."

"Wouldn't you have to be a member of the church and at the same time take all this Roman power seriously? I repeat, I'm not a member of the church."

"Timothy Kappel is dead, and he died violently. And no, I

have no proof of who directly murdered him."

As they were preparing to leave, Turner asked, "Who told you to lie to us?"

"The number of possibilities, like your suspects, is finite."

"Why all the lies?" Fenwick asked.

"They're afraid, we're afraid of all that we've got being taken away. I told you about how the seminary works. All those fears never really go away, from any of us no matter how old we get."

In the car Fenwick reiterated, "Was he confessing or bragging about his relationship with two hot young guys?"

"Both? Or he was lying about that as well."

"Tresca and Kappel were sexual predators, stop the presses," Fenwick said, "and this guy was too. He got what he wanted. Is that how those two became priests? They had a protector because they were willing to let him screw them?"

"It sounds like they were more than willing."

"He was in a power position over them."

"I'm not disputing the wrongness of it. I'm saying while in the middle of it, both sides were using each other."

Fenwick grumbled. "I can actually understand Kappel and Tresca a little bit. They wanted to have sex whenever and with whomever they could. Sound like horny guys everywhere, straight or gay."

"Talking about yourself?"

"Madge would kill me. And I'm too fat, old, and going bald, to even fantasize anymore."

"Madge knows about your fantasies?"

"Madge knows all and sees all. It's depressing. If she caught me with a stray thought, she'd cut my balls off."

They were stopped on Orleans Street going south in heavy traffic snarled at the on and off ramps at Ohio and Ontario Streets ahead of them. Fenwick thumped the steering wheel. "I don't get that part where he said they were excessively narcissistic with a penchant for sex. It sounds like a simplistic diagnosis by a third-rate therapist. It makes no sense."

"Excessively narcissistic with a penchant for sex." Turner shrugged. "Maybe it means they liked to beat off a lot in front of a mirror."

Fenwick laughed so hard he had to pull over in the nearest bus stop. He didn't start moving again until an angry bus driver leaned on his horn to get them to move.

Fenwick wiped tears of mirth from his eyes. "That was good."

"Just trying to keep up with you." But he found Fenwick's laughter contagious and chuckled along with him.

A few minutes later, traffic unsnarling, and Fenwick reduced to occasional chortles as he drove, he glanced at Turner. "This guy didn't really tell us much new."

Fenwick said, "We're not being followed."

"Go two blocks east, one south, and come back around."

They were in the River North area. A trendy, with-it part of town where Turner went to eat once with Ben on their anniversary. They found the portions skimpy, and the food burnt. They were told later this was 'charred' and was very with it and in. Turner thought maybe the chefs of the world were trying to make a virtue of not having an oven timer.

A few minutes later they turned back onto Erie Street. A black town car was parked in front of the rectory. No one was sitting in it.

"Well, well, well," Fenwick said.

"Let's stop in." They got out of the car.

THIRTY-TWO

Monday 9:15 P.M.

It took some time for their ring to be answered. This time an elderly woman housekeeper answered the door. "The Fathers are not home."

"What's your name, ma'am?" Turner asked as he took out his ID and showed it to her.

"Agnes Drabble." She clutched onto the doorjamb and glanced over her shoulder.

Turner said, "Mrs. Drabble, we think Father Dere may need some help."

"I don't like those two. The one who calls himself Bishop Pelagius. He's not nice. I've seen the other one. That Vern Drake on television. He's too young and too pretty. I don't like him."

"We need to see them."

"Father Dere is very sick. You make them go away."

Turner reassured her. "We'll take care of everything."

She stepped aside.

The detectives stopped outside the open door of the same room they'd interviewed Dere in minutes before. They could see him in the chair he'd been in. He didn't turn to them. The other two must be in the chairs the detectives vacated minutes before. They listened to the three.

"What did you tell them?" Turner recognized Pelagius's slight accent.

"Truth, something you wouldn't know about."

Dere began to cough. He lurched forward and fell to his knees.

Turner took out his cell phone, moved down the hallway a

few steps, summoned paramedics, and backup.

When he returned, he heard Dere mutter, "I told them what you told me to tell them."

"And how can we be sure of that?" Drake was screaming at the old man.

Dere's railing cough echoed in the room.

"I've had enough," Turner said. He rushed into the room. Fenwick followed.

Dere was on the floor gasping. Drake was on his feet. Pelagius was sipping from a large drink.

Turner knelt next to Dere. "Are you all right?"

"I'm fine." He coughed a long, agonizing cough and passed out.

Drake screamed, "Get out."

Fenwick inserted himself between the priest and the commissioner.

Turner said, "Paramedics are on the way."

Pelagius looked at the priest on the floor as if he was a cockroach that might need to be stepped on. Drake waved his fist in Fenwick's face. From Turner's spot on the floor where he cradled the head of the still-breathing old priest, he could see Fenwick's implacable visage.

Drake got up to within three inches of Fenwick's nose and bellowed, "This is what I knew you would do."

Fenwick murmured, "Back up or I will arrest you right here and right now."

Vern Drake tried to shove himself forward.

In his calmest tone, Turner said, "Aren't you worried about Father Dere?"

Drake waved his fist and screamed at Turner, "You are a pawn of Satan." The commissioner turned back to Fenwick and waved a finger in his face. "You are also a pawn of Satan. You are doing the devil's work."

Fenwick said, "Someone has to."

Pelagius said, "None of this is very constructive. We should all calm down."

Turner could hear car doors slamming and moments later the doorbell rang. Seconds later paramedics and blue-clad beat cops entered the room.

The paramedics hurried to the recumbent priest and ministered to him.

Drake pointed to Pelagius. "We're leaving."

Fenwick stood in his way. His ocean of calm met Drake's volcano of anger. His voice was even softer than Turner's had been. "If you try to leave, I will arrest your ass."

Drake screamed, "You can't do this to us."

Several of the beat cops took up positions next to the commissioner and the bishop.

While the paramedics worked on the Fr. Dere, the others in the room remained silent. Mrs. Drabble rushed in and knelt next to the priest on the floor. In twelve minutes they left with him on a stretcher. Mrs. Drabble, the housekeeper, accompanied them out.

Molton strolled in a few moments after they left. He looked at his detectives and then Drake and Pelagius. He stood in front of his detectives and faced the interlopers. "Can I help you gentlemen?"

"We need to talk," Drake said.

"I'd love to," Molton said. "You can come with me to Area Ten headquarters, or we can arrest you."

Pelagius stood up. "We'd be happy to help any way we can."

"Excellent," Molton said. He motioned to several beat cops. "My men will help you along."

They left. Molton looked at Turner and Fenwick.

Fenwick said, "We got nothing."

"We can't arrest them?" Molton said.

"Not yet," Fenwick said.

"Pity." At the door Molton turned back. "I'll let you know all the nothing they don't tell me."

THIRTY-THREE

Monday 9:58 P.M.

In the car Fenwick said, "Which one of us is the pawn of Satan?"

"I'm the gay guy."

"I tell the worst jokes."

"Maybe Dante missed one of the circles of hell," Turner suggested.

"Which one?"

"The one where they have you on a loop telling the wrist joke. That would make you the pawn, king, and queen of Satan."

"Does being a pawn of Satan come with health benefits? Maybe if it had a dental plan, I'd sign up."

"You'll have to ask Drake, or I suppose you could Google pawn of Satan. Or maybe pawns of Satan have their own web site, pawnsofsatan.com."

"Everybody has a goddamn website. Do I get special powers being a pawn of Satan?"

"Depends on how much chocolate you eat that day."

"I can eat a lot of chocolate."

"You know," Turner said, "this whole pawn of Satan thing could become a recurring theme."

"Call it a motif," Fenwick said. "That sounds classier."

"It all sounds like crap."

"Does that mean our kids are spawn of Satan?" Fenwick asked.

Turner groaned.

Fenwick added, "I've never been a pawn of Satan."

"You've never been a pawn of anything. Except Madge."

"Madge is queen."

"Got that right."

They sat in their parked car for a few moments in silence, then Turner said, "Let's go to the crime scene."

"For what?"

"I want to see what they saw. I want to see what Kappel was looking at when he was walking to his date with death. I want to see the problems the killers faced or didn't face. I don't have enough of a sense of place."

They grabbed sandwiches at Millie's. It was nearly ten when they got to the scene. They sat in the car and finished eating.

After his last bite, Fenwick said, "None of the streetlights are working."

"Random chance or the bad guys put them out?"

Fenwick knew he wasn't really expecting an answer. They were speculating, sharing observations. At times, such moments led to insights that helped solve a case.

Fenwick slurped the last of his diet soda, wiped his hands on his pants, and got out of the car. Turner grabbed a couple of heavy duty Maglites from the trunk.

They removed the crime scene tape from the gate and entered the junkyard. They walked to the far end. Turner shut off his light. Fenwick followed suit with his.

The ambient light of the city did not give them enough light to see their way.

"They had flashlights," Turner said. "Something else to carry along with the baseball bat, and if they were carrying Kappel."

Fenwick nodded agreement. "Kind of clumsy, if you've got a finite amount of time, especially if Kappel was struggling."

"And the ME said he hadn't found drugs."

Still with flashlights off, they stepped into the undergrowth. A few feet in, Turner stopped, pulled out his phone. "Not enough light from this really to help them."

"A herd of bad guys with phones out, carrying a baseball bat, moving along in some way with a person they were going to kill?"

Turner switched his flashlight back on. The path was now clear. "Okay, it was dark. They either stumbled along or had some way of lighting the scene." Simple summary, but they were stuck with the basics, which often enough led to the obvious that solved a crime. Except when it didn't. The ground squished under their feet from the rain earlier in the day.

After about five steps, Turner stopped. "Who could see these lights? How did they know someone wouldn't see them and ask questions? Call the police?"

He had Fenwick stand where they were on the path with his light on and went back to the junkyard gate. From there he could see nothing. He walked slowly in. Once he passed the mass of junk, he began to see a glow. When he got next to Fenwick, he turned on his light, but aimed it toward the ground. Fenwick followed suit.

"Okay," Turner said, "if they were smart and careful, unless someone was watching, no one would notice anything."

Fenwick said, "If we presume they were professionals, they'd be smart enough not to be having a laser light show in here."

They found the scene of the crime. They stood next to where the body had been and turned off the Maglites. First they looked. The clouds had parted and the few stars you could see in the city made their feeble attempt to shed light. No outside light penetrated here. It wasn't absolute dark, nothing outdoors in a major city really could be pitch black, midnight dark.

Fenwick asked, "Was this enough light to kill him?" Another rhetorical observation.

Turner shut his eyes. He heard the soft lapping of the river, distant sounds of the city. The wind rustled the leaves in the trees and undergrowth. He heard a few drops of today's rain disturbed from their places on the leaves hit the ground.

He opened his eyes again. They tried using just one of the lights with the beam aimed to the ground. "It would be enough," Fenwick said.

"Yeah," Turner agreed. "They didn't need enough light for brain surgery, just enough to bash his head in." He put his still-on flashlight on the ground under the clump of densest vegetation about seven feet away. He aimed it back toward where they'd come. He stepped to the bank of the river. "They could aim it like that and no one would notice. No flashing lights. No dancing lights that might draw someone's attention." Looking across the river, neither of them saw any place lit up that would draw a person's eye.

Fenwick said, "No killers returning to the scene to recover an accidentally lost clue."

"We don't get enough of those."

"Have we ever had any?"

With their Maglites they examined the area around where the body had been. The examination in this light added nothing to what they'd learned in the daylight.

Fenwick said, "We could try frantically waving our lights around and see if anybody notices."

"Yeah, in this day and age, everything is caught on some kind of camera."

"No cameras here."

Turner shone his light onto the river water. Other than more dark black, he got nothing. They left.

At Area Ten, Turner found an email on his computer from Jeanne D'Amato confirming her earlier diagnosis that the documents they'd gotten from the Cardinal were useless.

He and Fenwick did some paperwork, updated the spreadsheet, and called it a night.

Thirty-four

Monday 11:30 P.M.

Mrs. Talucci was on her porch. Paul stopped and filled her in about the case. She laughed nearly as hard as Fenwick at the pawn of Satan and excessive narcissism cracks. Paul finished with, "I also have information about the financial records we got from the Cardinal." He told her about the data, and Jeanne D'Amato's initial opinion, and the confirmation that had come hours later.

Mrs. Talucci said, "I am pissed. That is not a good thing."

She rocked in silence. When she dropped a stitch, Paul knew she must be really angry. Finally Mrs. Talucci said, "I never bluff."

Paul crossed the lawn to his own home. He was tired. First, he stopped at Jeff's door and eased it open. As usual his son was asleep with the reading light on and a book open on his chest. Paul inserted a bookmark, shut the book, put it on a shelf, leaned down and kissed his son on the forehead, shut the light off. The boy stirred but did not waken. Paul left.

Upstairs, he noted that the light was still on in Brian's room. He didn't hear any noise, so he entered his and Ben's room. Ben was emptying his pockets onto the top of his dresser. Paul sat on the edge of the bed to take his shoes off.

"How's Brian?" Paul asked.

"Still not saying much. He went to his room early and hasn't been out."

Paul stood up and said, "I'll be back in a minute."

Moments later he knocked softly on Brian's door. He heard a faint, "Yeah."

He entered.

Brian had his eyes closed and his arms crossed on his forehead. He wore sweatpants and a baggy T-shirt.

When Paul sat on the edge of the bed, Brian opened his eyes.

"Are you okay?"

Brian gulped. "I'm not sure." But he said little more. The boy wasn't ready for revelations.

Paul went back to their room. "I'm still worried about him."

"Me too. It's gotta be something." But neither as yet had an answer. As they undressed, Paul filled him in on the case. Once again, he got laughter about the pawn of Satan and the excessive narcissism crack. It felt good to listen to laughter in his own home, in the room he shared with the man he loved. The world felt safe for at least a few moments.

After they crawled into bed, Ben reached for him and said, "Why don't we find out how our pawn of Satan is doing tonight? Or we could even be a little excessive ourselves for a little while."

It had been a long day, and he was tired, but Ben was smiling his most sexy smile, and his arms were around him, and they felt warm, and safe, and good. They pulled each other close.

THIRTY-FIVE

Tuesday 7:01 A.M.

Tired as he was, Paul got up Tuesday morning for breakfast with the family. Jeff was making vegetable-stuffed omelets. Paul didn't mind the vegetables as long as there was no asparagus or zucchini. Jeff made Paul's with onions, tomatoes, spinach, and potatoes.

After he finished making the last omelet, Jeff sat down to eat. He turned to Ben and asked, "How come you guys aren't effeminate, irresponsible, unfunny guys like the gay guys on television?"

"What do you mean?"

"I watch some of those shows with gay characters on television. There's always one really effeminate, totally unrealistic one. You guys aren't like that."

Ben said, "We're just ourselves. That's enough for us."

Paul said, "I know you know television isn't real."

Jeff gave a mild snort while he reached for ketchup to put on his omelet. He said, "Yeah, but it sure seems strange."

Both boys were a little quieter than usual. Paul decided to enjoy the calm.

THIRTY-SIX

Turner wanted to get back to the station early to continue getting their mass of data organized onto his spreadsheet. He spent an hour and a half collating work on it as well as organizing who they were going to interview for the day. When Fenwick appeared at the top of the stairs, he lumbered his bulk over to their desks.

Fenwick asked, "Did you see the morning news shows, the newspapers, and the Internet?"

"I haven't seen the TV, and I've only checked email on the Net. I didn't go to the news."

Barb Dams appeared at the top of the stairs and hurried over to their desks. She carried a laptop computer open to the Internet.

She showed Turner the headlines. "Drag Queen Cardinal."

"What the hell?" Turner asked.

Fenwick said, "Do not piss off Mrs. Talucci."

Dams set up the computer so all of them could see the screen. She called up a YouTube site. They watched a drag show. From the look of the audience members and the quality of the video, it looked like it might have come from the early seventies.

Dams pointed to an overweight dancer wearing a very short skirt and belting out *Where Did Our Love Go*. Dams said, "That's the Cardinal."

Fenwick said, "I don't recognize him without his red robe. How could anyone prove it was him?"

Dams said, "Look closely." She waited for several seconds, hit pause, then enlarged the portion of the screen that showed the dancer's legs. "See the tattoo on the singer's left ankle. It's reasonably unique, a silhouette of Diana Ross. The Cardinal has one just like it in exactly the same spot."

"How do we know that?" Fenwick asked.

"Pop culture," Dams said. "The Internet. During some innocuous interview he gave seven years ago, he mentioned he had a tattoo. In the interview he was trying to 'reach out' to young people. He thought revealing he had a tattoo would mean he could relate to them."

"You're joking?" Fenwick said.

"When I try to be funny," Dams said, "people actually laugh."

"I am wounded," Fenwick said.

Dams chortled. "I wish."

"It's really him?" Fenwick asked. "I'm not doubting," he rushed to add seeing D'Amato's sardonic look, "I'm just awed." He looked at Turner. "Did you know Mrs. Talucci had this?"

Turner smiled.

"Did she tell you she was going to do this?"

"Mrs. Talucci has never asked me for permission to do anything. She wouldn't telegraph this to me. She knows it's connected to my job."

"The Cardinal thought we were stupid," Fenwick said, "and he thought Mrs. Talucci was bluffing."

"She did say that," Turner admitted.

"That what?" Dams asked.

Turner smiled. "That she never bluffed."

Molton arrived at their desks. He and Dams walked over to the huge screen and the rows and columns of names, dates, numbers, explanations, and details.

Molton whistled, "Damn."

Fenwick said, "This is not going to be an excuse to add another layer of paperwork to each case."

Molton whistled again. He and Dams read and looked for a

few minutes. Molton turned to Turner. "I'm impressed."

Turner said, "I'd be more impressed if it led to an arrest and conviction."

Molton asked, "Where the hell did Fong get such a huge screen?"

Dams spoke another CPD truism. "Do we really want to know?"

Fenwick asked Molton, "Did you learn anything from Drake and Pelagius last night?"

"They were quite miffed. Which one of you is the pawn of Satan?"

Turner and Fenwick pointed at each other and said, "He is."

Molton and Dams laughed.

Molton said, "Drake was a fulminating fool, but that Pelagius, I don't trust him. He just kept that superior smirk on his face. As if he knew something or knows something."

Fenwick said, "They were threatening Dere last night."

After the detectives summed up what they'd learned the night before, Molton said, "I don't know if there's any truth to be had from any of them." The Commander chuckled. "I'm afraid Bishop Pelagius is not ever going to be your friend."

"How long did you talk?" Turner asked.

"I invited them to stay as long as they wanted, but they were quite angry. The main problem is, they have no one to listen to them. The head of the County Board has no real power in the city, at least not over the police. And no one likes Vern Drake in the mayor's office so he can't cause as many problems as he would like."

Turner said, "But they weren't confessing or adding any actual facts to the case."

Molton gave him a grim smile and held out his empty palm. "Here's all the real help they gave."

Turner said, "But they must know something. People this

concerned have got something to lose."

Fenwick said, "Gotta be covering up for the killer."

"But why?" Turner asked. "All these people are going to lie for each other? They don't seem to be close friends or lovers. Why lie? Why protect each other? For some esoteric notion of 'church'? None of them seems to really care. Who is so worth all this lying? They really think they're 'saving' the Catholic church by all this?"

Fenwick tapped the top of his desk. "They're saving their own asses. They've got it easy. They've had it easy for a very long time, and they're frightened. That much money is that scared?"

Molton said, "That much money is usually the most scared."

The four of them were silent and mulled this for a few moments.

Fenwick broke the silence. "He told you he called us pawns of Satan?"

"He is very not happy with you. Did you try to tell him the wrist joke?" The whole wrist joke shtick was known and feared throughout the station.

"No. You know that joke is on a "you asked, I told basis"."

Molton and Dams laughed and left.

Tuesday 2:02 P.M.

After finishing up more paperwork and doing collating and arranging more items on the spreadsheet, they decided to start with Fr. Howard Cehak, the parish priest who'd supposedly unearthed financial malfeasance.

At the rectory of St. Couffignals on the near north side, the door was answered by a florid-faced man wearing a Hawaiian flowered shirt and black pants.

He looked at their ID. He said, "I'm the old guy who has the goods on the Cardinal. Today's headlines aren't enough? I can add to his misery, if you guys are smart."

He led them to a kitchen table. Without asking, he filled three coffee cups, placed them on the table in front of the detectives, put artificial cream and diet sugar packets on the table, and sat down. He offered them each a dollop of whiskey for their coffee. They declined. He indulged then began, "I know everything. I have proof of everything. I have copies. They don't know I have copies. Thank God I knew enough to make copies. These people are ruthless. You'll never get to the truth. Even if the Cardinal is forced to resign because he was a drag queen." He chuckled for several moments. "A drag queen! That's great. Everybody thinks we're gay, but a drag queen. Ha! That's rich." He lost his smile. "But they're ruthless cheaters."

They let him rattle on for several more minutes, then Fenwick interrupted. "Exactly who was cheating, when, and on what?"

"Well, that is the question."

"How did all this start?" Fenwick asked.

"Fifty years ago I was a young assistant at a parish in Hegewisch, down on the southeast side. The church roof needed repair. I found a couple guys in the parish who were willing to do it for free. The pastor found out about it. He went nuts. He said we had to go through channels. Didn't matter that I could get it done for free. I got suspicious. It took a while, but I found out that it was all connected. That tiny little job! The local alderman and the financial office of the diocese got involved. I kept track of everything I could and kept records about those things that were supposed to be secret. I took note of anything and everything. And my young friends who'd been in the same seminary class as I was, when we'd talk, we'd go over stuff they noticed too. And they'd give me records. None of them was willing to stand up. Nobody in this organization really is. I found that out to my chagrin." He sipped coffee. The detectives had no intention of interrupting him. The man was on a roll.

"The second thing I found was just as simple. Most of them were, or they started that way. See, I was in charge of setting up the Christmas display in the church. It costs over a hundred thousand dollars."

Fenwick asked, "You spent a hundred thousand?"

"No, they did the year before. It took hours to set up all the lights on all the bushes, plaster and plastic animals on the roof of the church, just incredible stuff. The young guys from the parish who were helping me set it up blabbed. We were getting a beer afterward at a local pub. I didn't have my clerical stuff on. One guy blurted it out. It was a working class parish, and they spent this money. I found receipts later, but they were for less than ten thousand, but they'd paid for a hundred thousand." He pointed at the mass of papers next to him. "It's all in there. Even ten thousand I thought too much. I priced some of the items. They were way over priced for what they were worth. Somebody was getting a lot of money for Rudolf and his nose glowing on the roof. A hundred thousand all those years ago for Christmas?"

Cehak began detailing all the minutia he'd accumulated over the years. He said, "Finally fifteen years ago, I talked it over with a lawyer in the parish I was in. I was pastor by then. I thought I had some standing. The lawyer was real helpful. He said make copies of everything and hide them. Good thing I did. I went to the chancery office and laid out what I had. What a bombshell! What a failure!"

He paused and sipped more coffee, wiped his forehead, his hands moved restlessly, and his knee bounced continuously. From the man's red face and these personal tics, Turner suspected he had high blood pressure.

"What failed?" Turner asked.

"All of it. Every fucking thing. Excuse my language. It all came crashing down. They took my documents and then nothing happened. I had the sense not to tell them I had copies. Then the new cardinal came in, and I got a visit from Kappel. He had the sense to ask if I had copies. I had the sense to make another set of copies before I gave him what I had. And lie to him about having more copies."

"So Kappel knew all about it?"

"Yep. And nothing came of what I gave him."

Turner thought, Kappel either had another chance to cover up or a huge opportunity to have more leverage to get what he wanted. Turner just couldn't figure out what it was that he wanted.

"Did the malfeasance continue under the new cardinal?" Turner asked.

"I was out of the loop by then. I presume it did, but I have no proof it did."

"Can we get copies of what you've got?"

"And it will do what good?"

"We're not sure. We'll hope it will lead to a murderer."

"How?"

"We're not sure how," Turner said. "In a murder investigation we look into everything. Most things lead to nothing. A few things lead to a killer."

"A clue. You want a clue. And maybe I could give you a clue to Kappel's murderer."

"How did Kappel know to come talk to you?"

"They kept records in the chancery office. Complete records I'm sure. They know where everything is buried."

"How was he to deal with when you talked to him?"

"He seemed coldly efficient."

"Did you talk to him after he came here?"

"No. I figured nothing would get done."

"Why'd you even give him copies?"

He sighed. "Hope? I always start with hope. But he turned out to be like all the rest. Protect Holy Mother Church at all costs."

"When can we get copies?" Turner asked.

"Now. A few years ago, I took the time to have everything scanned." He pulled out a zip drive. "You got a zip drive? I can upload it onto any device that you've got, or I could email it."

"You have all this backed up, right?" Fenwick asked.

Cehak gave him a pitying look. "I've been dealing with this crap a long time. Of course, I do." He plugged his zip drive into a laptop computer and emailed everything to Turner. Turner opened his phone and saw that the attachment had arrived. He checked that it opened and he could read the documents. He could.

"Do you know Bishop Pelagius is in town?"

"The Papal Nuncio? No."

"You know a big, burly guy who drives around in a limousine who may or may not have worked for Kappel or the Sacred Heart of Bleeding Jesus Order?"

"Nope. Sorry. I know little about the Order itself. I'm a diocesan priest." As he led them to the door, he said, "It's you guys I'd be worried about."

"Why's that?" Fenwick asked.

"The church isn't going to let you besmirch them."

Fenwick said, "They can't stop a murder investigation."

"I pity you," Cehak said. "That's such a naïve, simple belief. I envy you your naiveté."

In the car Fenwick said, "Another old guy. Are these guys all alcoholics?"

Turner shrugged. "They don't confide in me much. I'm more interested in their insights on murder not if they belong to AA. Why wouldn't they kill Cehak instead of Kappel? This guy had damaging information."

"The murder wasn't about money?"

"Then what was it about?"

"If I knew that, we'd be home already."

Turner emailed his new attachment to Molton and to Jeanne D'Amato along with an explanatory note. D'Amato replied that she'd get right to it.

They got back to their desks and started hunting through what Cehak had given them and comparing it to the mass of documents they'd already accumulated. They continued to fill out their paperwork as they went through the information.

Turner added data he thought relevant to the spreadsheet he'd created of people and events, possible motives, and where who was when.

Thirty-eight

Tuesday 3:45 P.M.

Poindexter from the front desk came up the stairs and approached them with a tall, thin gentleman with gray hair. The man looked to be in his late sixties.

Poindexter pointed to the gentleman and said, "This is Terry Kappel, Bishops Kappel's older brother."

Turner said, "We're sorry for your loss."

"Thank you."

Poindexter left. The detectives grouped chairs to the side of Turner's desk.

"What happened to my brother?"

Turner said, "We're still in the middle of investigating. We're having trouble getting information about his life, about who would wish him harm."

Kappel sighed. "That whole crowd was nuts. Years ago I knew some of them personally."

"How so?" Turner asked.

"I was a week away from being ordained a priest in the Sacred Heart of Bleeding Jesus Order."

"What stopped you?"

"I got a girl pregnant."

"So they threw you out?"

"No. I never told them about her. Not before I left. I loved her. I was never going to be able to be celibate."

"What were the men in the Order like back then?"

"They fought. Intrigue abounded. I was there when the great coup happened to Father Graffius. He was a good man.

Dedicated to making himself a better person, making us better Christians, making the Abbey a better place to live."

"What happened?"

"The accident."

"He told us a little about a car accident."

"There's only the one. It caused a huge scandal in the Order at the time. Two people died in the crash. This was when the rival conservative versus liberal factions were going at each other like mad. Graffius wasn't driving the car. The priest who was and the seminarian in the front passenger seat died. The people in the back seat survived. Graffius was blamed because he organized the expedition and was in charge of it. His enemies were looking for an excuse to dump him from his position in the seminary and as Provincial of the Chicago province."

"What did your brother say about the Order these days?"

"Tim and I would talk sometimes. We were close back then, and we still were. He'd always come home for the holidays. He never said much about his investigations. We'd talk about some of the old guys who were priests or seminarians when I was in, but there were fewer and fewer of them as the years went by."

"You knew he and Tresca shared a condo, a bedroom?"

"Tim never discussed his sexuality with me, his living arrangements. He did often talk about the politics, here and in Rome. The whole Bruchard versus Duggan compromise was something else. I never did understand all of it. Tim claimed he had a hand in negotiating it."

"Your brother was that involved in making Cardinals?"

"He claimed he was. I never had reason to doubt him."

"Did he ever mention a Bishop Pelagius?"

"That old fraud! He and Tim were thick as thieves, plotted, planned together. Tim said he had the most fun working with Pelagius."

"Why do you call him a fraud?"

"Tim would laugh about their plotting and scheming. You know why Rome agreed to let Bruchard be in charge of the Order and not live in Italy?"

Head shakes.

"They wanted to keep Duggan and Bruchard out of Rome. The Sacred Heart of Bleeding Jesus Order is very powerful. They were allies of the last couple of Popes. Enemies of the current Pope wanted to create a distance supposedly so they couldn't have any undue influence."

"Pelagius is here."

"In Chicago?"

"Yeah. He couldn't have had something to do with Tim's murder?"

"No. They were friends. I can believe Bruchard or Duggan plotting against Tim."

"Why would they do that?"

"Tim never got real specific. He did so much investigating. He knew all the secrets about everybody, or so he said."

"How'd you and your brother get along?"

"Great. He was a good guy."

"Why'd he do all that investigating?"

"They picked him because he was honest and couldn't be corrupted." He leaned forward. "See, the thing is a lot of people thought he was this ruthless shit, but he wasn't. He really tried to help people through a lot of difficult, complicated issues, but also tough times in their lives. His job wasn't easy, and so much politics surrounded what he investigated, but he was always trying to do what was right."

Turner added him to the short list of people who had good things to say about Kappel.

"Did he have enemies among the priests?"

"That whole group was a mass of intrigue and jealousy. And that's when I was in the seminary."

"So you knew some of these people back then, the Cardinal, the Abbot, Graffius."

He smiled. "Old Graffius. He didn't look old and fragile back then. I used to love to debate theological questions with him far into the night. A bunch of us would gather in the common room and go over what we'd learned in whatever class we were in that day or that week or the latest book we'd read. One of us was a Joseph Campbell freak. Another read ancient mysticism from India. We'd compare and argue. You know the way college kids can go on and on about the ways of the world. And Graffius was always reminding us of a question we hadn't considered or a point of view that challenged us. He was a good guy."

"Any contact with members of the Order recently?"

"No. I haven't seen any of them in years, except Tim, of course."

"When's the last time you saw him?"

"Christmas. We emailed and talked on the phone about every other week."

"Did the last emails you got make it seem as if he were upset or concerned about anything?"

"They were a little more terse. He did say some investigations were finally winding down, but he didn't say which ones."

He knew no more. They gave him information about when the body might be released and he left.

They returned to the mass of paperwork, filling out forms, detailing conversations.

Thirty-nine

Tuesday 4:52 P.M.

Half an hour into his part of the Cehak file Turner was checking the list of companies Cehak claimed were involved in nefarious activities against information gleaned about those companies from the Internet. "Whoa."

Fenwick looked up from his writing. "What whoa?"

"Our beloved Vern Drake owned one of the companies Cehak says is in the middle of this whole financial chaos."

"He have proof?"

Turner examined what he had so far. "Proof? I'm not sure. Some of the contracts for spurious work went through Drake's company. I think it's enough to make the State's Attorney curious."

"It would have made Kappel curious. And he wouldn't need a subpoena."

Turner said, "Kappel made a lot of dangerous enemies." Turner hunted through several files. "Drake owns the company that leases that junkyard property on the river where the body was found."

Fenwick said, "I know a clue when I hear one."

Turner repeated their dictum, "Proximity is not proof."

An hour later, Jeanne D'Amato showed up with a minion in tow. She looked at the huge spreadsheet on the immense screen. She said, "Impressive and necessary."

She and the minion sat down with them for an hour and went over all the documents she had printed out from the Cehak data. Turner added more columns and rows on his spreadsheet for financial dealings.

When she was done and had left, Turner and Fenwick leaned against their desks and stared at the immense spreadsheet. Even the new screen wasn't large enough to contain the chart Turner had made. He scrolled to the end of the data, taking the time so they could each read every line. It took nearly half an hour as Turner made additions and corrections as the two detectives compared insights and notions.

When they were done, Fenwick said, "We know a lot of shit."

Turner sighed. "But not enough."

Fenwick asked, "Who among the people in the Sacred Heart of Bleeding Jesus Order have the knowledge, wherewithal, and power to hire minions to kill Kappel?"

"Bruchard or Duggan."

"Which one is more likely to do it?"

"Either one."

Fenwick shoved aside the mound of paperwork that was now this case. "Who are these people?" Fenwick asked.

"I'm not sure what you mean."

"We've got a raft of possible suspects. We've got people blabbing like mad."

"I thought we liked blabbing-like-mad people."

"Not so much in this case." He riffled the papers. "We've talked to how many people, ten, twenty, twenty-five? I can barely remember some of them."

"That's why they created paperwork." He pointed at the large monitor. "And now that thing."

Forty

Tuesday 6:45 P.M.

Turner called Ben, who reported that Brian spent the time after baseball practice reading a book and texting his friends. The eighteen-year-old had hovered around the kitchen and offered to oil Jeff's wheelchair. "No snark. He ate a slightly bigger than normal dinner, but he said he also worked out in the gym at school for an extra hour. I asked him if everything was okay. He said it was."

"Jeff?"

"Stopped burbling about having a hero for a brother when he saw that Brian wasn't responding. Brian wasn't mean, and you know how Jeff can be a little slow on picking up social cues, but he caught on to his brother's reluctance, and to his credit didn't press it. He spent the time after school improving, I think, a triple helix for that chess game he's been trying to create for months. At the moment, I think he and Ardis are on what might very loosely be defined as being on a date."

"A date?"

"They're playing chess in the living room."

Turner was never sure what got his younger son into trying to invent a new way to play chess, or a whole new game. Paul didn't think Jeff really knew which, but it took up hours of quiet work. Quiet work from kids was a good thing so he never pressed it. Since Jeff had been working on it, he had made no attempts to indulge in noisome, odiferous science experiments. It wasn't that Paul didn't appreciate his son's intellectual scientific pursuits, but he didn't want his kitchen destroyed in the likely pursuit of the impossible. He wondered if Jeff even considered what he and Ardis were doing as a date. Jeff could be as mercurial in his emotions an any teenager. Paul and his husband exchanged endearments and rang off.

FORTY-ONE

Tuesday 6:55 P.M.

Turner returned to entering Cehak's information by company, date, people involved, parish named, and cross referencing it. He was checking each company listed with the Internet, if it was still in operation, any news articles connected to it. As with most detective work, it was a lot of filling things in, doing basic work.

"I got another whoa on Vern Drake." He clicked at the keys. Fenwick walked over to the large screen monitor. Turner joined him. Fong had given them a wireless mouse. He used it to highlight several of the companies, then created a new column to the right of the one they were originally in, and moved these over to the new column.

Fenwick said, "I think a visit to old Vern would be in order. His businesses have come up any number of times in all these papers, including the items Jeanne D'Amato pointed out."

Turner printed only three of the cells they had on Drake. He had no intention of giving away the slightest bit of data even if Drake was the head of the Cook County Board.

They stopped in Molton's office and mentioned what they had and that they were on their way to see the commissioner. They weren't about to accost a high-ranking county official without mentioning it to the boss.

Molton smiled and said, "Only be gentle if you have to."

Vern Drake lived in a mansion in Evanston on the lakefront just north of the city and past the cemetery that formed a border along the lake between the two cities.

Vern Drake answered the door himself. He did not invite the detectives in.

Fenwick opened with, "Commissioner, we have evidence that

a business you own was involved in kick-back schemes with the diocese."

Drake tried to slam the door. Fenwick pushed his bulk into the opening.

Turner said, "Commissioner, we can be discreet about this here and now, or we can simply call the press."

"You can't do that."

"Can and will," Fenwick said.

Drake looked uncertain. It was the first time they'd met him without Pelagius in attendance. "What do you have?" he demanded.

Turner handed him the printout he'd made.

"What is this?"

"You can see dates, work orders, inflated prices."

"These are all legitimate." He threw the papers back at them and slammed the door.

Turner and Fenwick were back in the Loop by eight. The night was fine for early May with a full moon rising.

As they moved past Buckingham Fountain, Turner checked his notes. "We've got those old guard priests Garch mentioned Sunday we could stop and see."

"Let's do it."

On 47th Street just north and slightly west of Hyde Park, they entered the shabbiest rectory they'd been in yet. The originally tan brick work on the outside walls was rust-stained and crumbling. An ancient woman led them into a parlor with threadbare rugs, garage sale furniture, and a lone crucifix centered on otherwise barren walls.

Fathers McGinn and Wiltse swept into the room. Both were in their seventies. According to Garch, this was the heart of the old guard that Duggan had purged from the previous Cardinal's staff.

Turner said, "We're here about the Cardinal."

"Which one?" McGinn had a scraggly mustache. He brushed his left index finger across it.

"Both."

Wiltse had a full beard. He said, "Good. We can give you everything."

"You're willing to trust us so quickly?" Fenwick asked.

Wiltse rubbed his beard. "We know you're the detectives on the Kappel case. He worked for the Cardinal, and then poof, the Cardinal's life blows all to hell on the Internet. Who else can bring down a Cardinal except a couple of Chicago police detectives?"

Fenwick said, "He did the dancing all by himself. His choice."

Wiltse said, "It's glorious."

"Why's that?" Fenwick asked.

Wiltse grinned. His beard was white, the top of his head nearly bald. He said, "Even if the Cardinal stays in his position, his power and influence will be diminished. The position may be the same, but the perception will be far different. How can you sit there to discipline some priest when you know they're stifling gales of hysterical laughter at your expense right below the surface?"

McGinn went to a shabby desk that might have been used in a school seventy-five years ago. He unlocked a drawer with a simple key.

"We have this for you. This is all the information we have on the Cardinal."

Fenwick said, "And on what was wrong in the last administration?"

An hour later Turner and Fenwick sat in their car outside the rectory. They'd listened to the two priests spew venom and speculation. Fenwick thumped the folder with the new information. He sighed and belched. "More repetitious drivel."

"Yup."

"They didn't like Kappel or the Cardinal."

"Nope."

"They have alibis."

"Yup. You want dull and boring or you want mad shootouts while careening down the streets of Chicago?"

Fenwick scratched his ass and wiped his hand across his chin. Finally Fenwick said, "Which one of us would be driving?"

"Not you."

"Let me get back to you on that."

They both sighed. Nothing to be done. Repetitive and boring was a big part of a cop's job.

The detectives returned to the station. They spent several hours more cross-referencing all the new data from McGinn and Wiltse. At midnight, they gave up.

FORTY-TWO

Wednesday 12:35 AM

Brian sat on the top step of the front porch. Jeff's wheelchair ramp stretched to the right. The full moon rode high overhead. Brian sat in shadow. Paul was tired. He wanted to get in, grab a bite to eat, and go to bed.

He greeted his son.

Brian gave him barely a nod. Jeff might cause an uproar for attention, but Brian, since he was two or three years old, usually made barely a peep. Brian's cheerfulness, like his brother's, seemed endemic, and sometimes hid his deep emotions. Brian hadn't cried that Paul knew of since the time he and his first girlfriend broke up. He was in fourth grade when Mavis Lukachevsky had stolen his lunch.

The slumped shoulders and the silence raised Paul's level of concern. Brian wore jeans and a sweatshirt. The May evening had turned cool.

"It's late," Paul said. "It's a school night."

"I know."

Brian didn't really have much of a curfew as long as he was in at a reasonable hour, and that they had a notion of where he was, and who he was going there with.

"What's up?" Paul asked.

His older son sighed. "I was waiting for you. I think I screwed up."

Paul sat down next to his son. "It would be warmer inside."

"I'm okay here."

"What did you screw up?"

"I'm not sure."

"Not sure about what?"

Brian looked at him, looked down at the ground. It was a gesture both of his sons used.

Brian sighed deeply. He leaned back with his elbows on the top step and his butt on the bottom one. He gazed at the moon.

He said, "I'm not a mean person."

"I agree."

He looked at his dad and shook his head. "I was trying to do right."

Parental fears rushed through Paul's mind. Had the boy done something illegal? Got caught with drugs? Hurt his brother?"

"You know I went to Shane's birthday party ten days ago?"

"Yeah." He and Shane had been friends all through high school. Brian hesitated some more.

Paul prompted, "Something happened at the party."

"Afterwards."

Brian gulped, sat up, leaned forward, put his elbows on his knees, put his head in his hands.

Paul gave his son's shoulder a squeeze. "I can't help until you tell me what's happened."

Big gulp, big pause, then a whisper. "It's my fault Shane tried to commit suicide."

Paul swallowed his parental fears, wild concerns based on lack of knowledge. What was most important to him was his son and what was bothering him. "Why would you think that? His note didn't mention you. He thanked you at the hospital."

A desperate whisper. "It was me."

Paul said, "Tell me exactly what happened."

Brian stared into the neighborhood darkness, looked at his dad, then down. He whispered, "I didn't go there for a study session." Brian shifted uneasily. "He wrote me a love poem."

"I know what I think I mean by a love poem, but I'm not

sure what you or he means by a love poem. You mean like a Shakespeare love poem?"

"No, like a boy/girl love poem. He said he loved me, but it was all poetic and stuff."

"Okay, why would he write a love poem to you? Does he think you're in love with him?"

"Well, no. I'm not. It's just, well…"

Paul waited. Brian crossed his legs, uncrossed his legs, leaned back, leaned forward, stared at the night sky, stared at the ground. When he spoke his voice was barely above a whisper. "So at that party."

"Yeah."

"Well, afterwards. After everybody left." He rubbed his face with his hands, did some more body shifting. Paul thought if he kept at it much longer, the boy might wind up with his body twisted into a pretzel position. Brian looked agonized. He muttered, "I can't talk about this."

Fears and anxieties flooded Paul's mind. He wanted his boy safe. He was determined to help any way he could. He presumed whatever his son revealed, they would deal with. If the boy was this hesitant it must be pretty huge, or at least huge to his teenage mind. And he didn't get up and leave, and he'd been waiting here, which Paul thought all led to the logical conclusion, the boy wanted to talk and unburden himself.

"Would you prefer to talk to Ben?"

"No, it's not the person. It's what happened." Another big pause. "I don't know how to talk about this."

"Do the best you can, and we'll sort it out together like we always do."

"I guess." More pauses and gulps. Brian said, "You know Shane's gay?" Paul remembered the day of the Inauguration.

"Why is it important if he's gay?" Paul knew a love poem from a boy to a boy could be upsetting if one was gay and the other was straight. Or any love poem from someone who was smitten to someone who did not share the smitten ones feelings even if both were gay or both were straight.

Brian fell silent. The night noises of Chicago surrounded them: a far off car honked, tires swished on the pavement on Taylor Street half a block away, a distant stereo boomed from a car's speakers, an emergency vehicle, probably on Halsted Street, hurried by. All the sounds where muted here with the surrounding trees and houses.

Paul knew his son, he knew the ways of the world, and he was reasonably astute about teenagers. He guessed something physical had happened between the boys. A hug? Probably more. A kiss? Possibly. It was not unheard of in Paul's experience for gay men to offer straight guys physical pleasure with little expectation of reciprocation. Had an offer been made? Accepted? Even reciprocated? He didn't want to know. Certainly from the level of Brian's emotional reaction, it had been more than a hug.

The boy's emotional and maturity level had been or were being tested. His heroism in saving his friend had made the swirling feelings soar off the scale.

Finally Paul said, "And whatever it was that happened after the party and the love note are connected?"

"Right. Yeah."

"And now you think those two events and the attempted suicide are connected?"

Brian breathed a sigh of relief. His dad was filling in the blanks, and he didn't have to go into embarrassing details.

"I think so. I'm not sure. I'm afraid so, yeah."

"What did you do about the note?"

"That's the thing. I didn't do anything." Brian took several deep breaths. "All week he asked to talk to me. I didn't know what to do or say. It was a guy saying he loved me." He paused, gulped. "I ignored him and the note. I almost didn't go Sunday. We were supposed to talk. I didn't want to hurt his feelings, but I don't think of him that way. I don't want that kind of relationship with him. I didn't know what to say. That's why I was late that night. If I hadn't gone, I wouldn't have saved him." He wrung his hands. "I was almost too late."

Paul let the information sink in. He didn't want a clearer picture of what happened after the party, but he had a clear enough picture of the agony his son was in. He asked, "Do you love him?"

"No. I'm not gay. And I know it would be okay if I was, and I know it's okay that you guys are. I'm not prejudiced."

"I know."

"What should I have done?"

"What would you have done if it was a girl?"

"I guess talked to her."

"You know that's what we do in our family, talk to each other."

"That's partly why I feel so rotten. I know we talk. I was just too embarrassed. I didn't know what to say." He sighed. "I know, I should have. I was going to that night. I shouldn't have been late. I was delaying. If I'd got there on time." He held his arms out as if pleading. "Maybe if I would have talked to him before, like the day he sent me the note, right away, he wouldn't have… you know…tried to off himself."

"But you did get there in time."

"Barely."

"You are not responsible for his choices."

"But if I'd have done something, maybe he would have made different choices."

"You can't know that. No one can."

Paul wasn't sure what to say at such a primal and difficult moment. He wasn't sure how he felt about what he was being told. He knew for certain that he needed to concentrate on making sure he understood what his son was saying and feeling. He knew he had to take care of his son's needs and not concentrate on any reaction or discomfort he felt. Helping his son was the key. He just didn't know what to say or do.

Paul was not about to ask how his son knew how a girl felt doing whatever Shane or he and Shane had done. He wanted no details about his son's intimate attachments. First, he had to be clear about what his son was saying.

"You don't want a relationship with him?"

"He thought what happened meant I wanted a relationship. He'd been pestering me and pestering me, all week. He sent me flowers. And then he slipped that love note in my locker." He sighed and sat back again. "I ignored him. It's my fault."

"You're going to be on opposite sides of the country in a few months, right? He's going to USC?"

"Yeah, but he had all these ideas about us, having a long-distance relationship. He put it all in the note. About getting together. He wants to do…uhh…more intimate stuff. He's a nice guy. I thought he was, but I'm just not into him. Not that way. I just totally screwed up."

Paul said, "Let's take this a bit at a time."

"Okay."

"You guys did something you're uncomfortable with now?"

Brian nodded.

"Was it consensual? Nobody forced anybody, right?"

"No. I'm not that way. He's not."

"You were both consenting. You're both over eighteen. You didn't stop him. He didn't stop."

"No."

"Before it happened, did he ask you for a relationship?"

"Well, no."

"Beforehand, did he talk about a commitment?"

"No."

"So as far as you and he were concerned, as far as you know, it was just something happening for that moment?"

"Yeah."

"The problem then seems to be the different meanings you and he attached to it afterwards."

"Yeah."

Paul asked, "Did the suicide note he left say it was your fault?"

"No."

"And his parents read the note and they still called you a hero at the hospital?"

"Yeah."

"So as far as you know, the note said nothing about you. In the love note he sent you, did he threaten suicide if you didn't respond?"

"No, but I should have recognized something was wrong."

"Why? How? You got a note that made you uncomfortable. You weren't sure how to deal with a situation. You had a casual, fun moment and one of you took it for more of a commitment than it was. That happens to men and women, gay and straight. Your signals got crossed."

"I should have talked to him."

"There are a million things we should or could do in this world. If we lived by what we should have done, we'd probably be paralyzed. If we learn from what we wish we'd done, then maybe we're closer to being better adults. Did you tell any of your buddies about any of this?"

"No, it was embarrassing."

"So nobody could have teased him about being gay? About… aah…what happened after the party?"

"As far as I know, I'm the only one he offered to…do…what he did." He paused. "You know, he never actually said he was gay. I just kind of assumed it." He gave the briefest of smiles. "The notes and flowers afterwards were kind of a giveaway."

"More than a big hint."

The conversation paused as they both looked out at the night.

Brian asked, "Are you mad at me?"

"No."

"What did I do wrong?"

"I don't think this falls into easy right and wrong categories. You both made choices and assumptions. You both have feelings and personalities. It's something to think about and then decide if you want to make different choices in the future."

"I should have talked to him."

"Because of your actions, you still can."

"Should I go over there tomorrow?"

"I'd call ahead, but why not?"

"I guess so." Brian sighed. "I just didn't know what to do. It was so kind of flattering and sweet and kind. I just freaked and I should know better. He was paying me a compliment. If I wasn't into girls, I'd think about it, but that's how I feel today. I wish I'd have figured this out earlier."

"Because you're a good, brave, and honest man you can still talk to him."

They stood up.

Brian said, "Thanks, dad."

"I love you, son."

"Love you, too."

FORTY-THREE

Wednesday 1:16 AM

In their room as Paul undressed, Ben turned on his side and leaned on his elbow and rested his head in his hand. Paul told him what Brian had revealed.

"Poor Brian," Ben said when he finished. "I hope he's going to be okay."

"Well, the kid he saved is alive. I don't want Brian to be haunted by this for the rest of his life. He didn't do anything wrong or that can't be fixed."

"We'll love him like we always do, as much as we can, no matter how many health food drinks he guzzles."

Paul crawled into bed and leaned on his side and propped his head up the same as Ben.

Ben asked, "Anything special I need to do, we need to do?"

"I'm not sure. This is all new to me. I guess we watch and monitor and love him as best we can."

"We may have another problem."

Paul frowned.

"Our younger son may be in love. After Ardis and the gang left, he mooned around here. He barely actually got any work done on his chess helix."

Paul smiled. "True love." He clicked off the light on the bedside table, turned, and pulled Ben close.

FORTY-FOUR

Wednesday 4:17 A.M.

A crashing boom woke Turner out of a sound sleep. As he jumped out of bed he saw that it was four seventeen A.M. Ben was awake as well. They threw on jeans and rushed to the hall. There was another thunderous boom. Brian was out of his bedroom. The three of them hurried down the stairs, Paul in the lead. Jeff's light was on, but he was still in bed.

"What's going on, dad?"

"Don't know. Brian, stay with your brother."

Ben and Paul rushed outdoors. Porch lights were on throughout the neighborhood. People singly and in pairs emerged from homes.

The lights in Mrs. Talucci's home blazed. Her porch light flicked on and several younger women emerged from the house. Last came Mrs. Talucci bearing her shotgun. She leaned on her youngest niece.

Paul and Ben hurried over. Wisps of smoke eddied from the gun barrel.

The men met Mrs. Talucci on the top step.

"What happened?" Paul asked.

"Some big son of a bitch tried to break in the back door. I heard his footsteps on the porch. I was in my room reading. He must not have seen my light. I guess not sleeping much is a blessing in old age after all. I heard the noise. Took out my gun from under my bed and headed to the kitchen."

Paul remembered Mrs. Talucci's kitchen from the million times he'd been inside. The red gingham curtains, the copper bottomed pots and pans hanging from above the island, the gray, granite-covered counters.

"He was opening the back door when I flicked on the lights and let fly with a blast of buckshot. He was lucky I was aiming over his head. He was even more lucky he jumped back and that I waited a few seconds to fire the second blast. Aimed right at the son of a bitch."

Paul asked, "Did you recognize him?"

"Big, burly son of a bitch."

"Bigger than Fenwick?" Paul asked.

Ben said, "The Cardinal is getting even."

Mrs. Talucci harrumphed. "That's his third mistake." Mrs. Talucci did the ka-ching thing with the shotgun. "The first was screwing with you and the investigation. The second was thinking he could get even. The third was this attack."

Her niece asked, "Are you sure it was the Cardinal's order?"

Mrs. Talucci gave her a grim smile.

Turner examined the back porch and ordered a forensic team to examine it. He saw what looked like flecks of blood on the steps going down. Back in his house, he got the boys settled and sank into bed next to Ben.

FORTY-FIVE

Wednesday 6:53 A.M.

Before Brian came downstairs, Paul was helping Jeff make breakfast.

The youngster asked, "I heard you guys on the porch last night. Is Brian okay?"

"You were awake?"

"I heard you guys' voices, but I couldn't understand what you said. Is he okay?"

"Yes."

"What's wrong?"

"That's something for him to tell you if and when he's ready, and it is not something for you to pester him about. Now or ever."

Jeff looked at his dad. "It must be bad."

"Your brother is a good man. He's fine. I want you to drop it as of now. Okay?"

"Okay."

When Brian came downstairs, he no longer looked like he was carrying the weight of the world on his shoulders.

FORTY-SIX

Wednesday 10:35 A.M.

Turner checked the local news on CLTV before he left the house. The news showed a herd of reporters and cameramen outside a nursing home. He turned up the sound. The reporter was saying, "The Cardinal's mother is in a sub-standard nursing home. The word we have is he hasn't visited his mother in years. Added to the Cardinal's entertaining video from the other day, this news further tarnishes his reputation. His own mother…"

Turner smiled and turned off the television.

At Area Ten headquarters Fenwick greeted him with a grim smile. He'd seen the newscasts. "Do not fuck with Mrs. Talucci. I would not want to be Cardinal Duggan now and for the rest of his life."

First Turner called Bruno, Keerkins, and Bernard whom they interviewed on Sunday and who had all promised to attempt to find someone that might be willing to talk to the detectives. All three reported failure.

The detectives stood at the vast monitor with all of its well-filled-in boxes. They scrolled and enlarged and rearranged and added.

They got to a column on the town car found at the scene. Turner double checked, "The town car on the street was registered to the Order?"

"Right."

Turner scrolled to the finances and bills sections. "Yeah, well this says Kappel was paying the bills on a town car. Why is he paying for repairs on a car for the Order?"

"Why shouldn't he?"

"Nah, that can't be how it works. In any corporation the

corporate cars get paid for from corporate funds."

"Maybe he paid for it and was reimbursed."

Turner rechecked the now vast spreadsheet. He looked up the car found abandoned on the street and checked the details. "The VIN number on the town car we found on the street does not match the VIN number of the car he paid for repairs on."

"They keep VIN numbers on car repairs?"

"Ben does on all the cars he repairs. It's all on computer. He can look up a car by VIN number, customer name, maybe the phases of the moon for all I know. It all comes up the same, a screen with all the information ever connected to that car. Ben has to with those expensive foreign jobs. He compares them all to stolen car lists. When I take my car into the dealer for servicing, they have everything all on computer."

"So there's another town car?"

"Apparently."

"Where?"

They drove to the dealership where the repairs had taken place. They showed ID, explained what they needed, and gave the manager the VIN number. The records came up a few seconds later. "Problem with the car? It been stolen?"

"No," Turner said. "The owner died. Thanks for the information."

They headed for the address. On the way they talked about family and kids, this time mostly about Fenwick's oldest daughter who was dating a boy he didn't like, but about whom he was keeping his mouth shut. Fenwick explained, "As Madge put it, her dad hated me and look how well we turned out."

"Why'd he hate you?"

"He just did. Still does."

"Did you tell him the wrist joke?"

"No, I swear. Besides, he's not the wrist joke type."

"Would that were true of us all."

It was a fine pleasant early May afternoon. The address was in a distant suburb an hour south and west. They took the Dan Ryan to Interstate 57 and then west on Interstate 80 past Joliet to the Morris exit. Using their GPS they found a town car with the matching license plate sitting in a driveway a mile north of the Interstate. It was a farmhouse in the middle of newly planted fields. A barn and two silos stood beyond the back of the house, which was a one story, brick ranch built probably in the late fifties or early sixties.

A big, burly guy answered their knock. He gasped and burst out crying.

He was half again as big as Fenwick. He wore a tent-sized flannel shirt, and jeans that bagged over sockless feet. Turner reached for the screen door, found it unlocked, and pulled it open. The man turned and slouched into the house. The detectives followed warily. They entered a living room with deep cushy chairs and matching couch. He subsided onto the sofa, put his head in his hands, and sobbed.

Turner looked at a man with red, blotchy skin, brush-cut short hair, and well-chewed fingernails.

When he'd calmed and wiped his face with a large red bandana, Turner asked, "What's your name?"

He looked at them with deep gray eyes. "Joe Gorman."

Turner said, "Bishop Kappel paid for the repairs on the town car in your driveway."

"It's in my name, but he paid for it, pays for the repairs."

"Why's that?" Turner asked.

"We're lovers."

Turner avoided looking at Fenwick but his partner blurted the obvious question. "You don't strike me as his type."

Gorman said, "I'm not anybody's type, but we fell in love."

Turner said, "We're sorry for your loss."

"You know how hard it is to love somebody, and they die,

and they get murdered, and you can't find out anything about what happened, and you can't show anybody you've lost anyone because you're not supposed to say anything about your relationship? That's one of the reasons we had this house in the middle of nowhere. We had to hide. Him mostly." He gulped and a few new tears escaped down his red cheeks.

"It's difficult, not fair," Turner said.

Fenwick said, "He was living with Tresca."

"They were lovers years ago. They hadn't been in a while. Timothy was waiting for the right time to tell him to move out, that it was over."

"When was he going to do that?"

"I'm not sure."

If Tresca's love nest was going to be gone, that would give him motive for murder.

Gorman was continuing. "I can't even find out if there's going to be a service. I'd go. I wouldn't make a scene. None of those people would know who I was anyway. I could cry in the back and say goodbye. Thank God the last thing I said to him was "I love you"." More tears. The detectives waited for him to stop sobbing. What else was there to do? They weren't going to be able to stop him, and Turner, for one, didn't want to. The man was hurting, and he'd been unable to talk to anyone. Or so he claimed. Didn't he have family of his own?

When he was calmer, Turner asked, "When did you see him last?"

"We spent Thursday night here together. We made love. And no don't laugh. I know I'm a huge guy. He loved me. We made each other feel great. He was a great lover. Are you homophobic, prejudiced cops?"

Turner said, "We just want to find out who killed him. You know he hired call boys?"

"Yeah. Tim was human. I understood." He patted his belly. "I know I'm not the most fit guy. A few times we shared guys, here, but that was all. We made love every time we saw each other, but he had needs."

Turner asked, "Two guys at The Proletarian Workers Sandwich Works reported problems after Kappel had encounters with them."

Gorman turned red. "They were mean to him. I got even for him. Tim was a good man. He didn't deserve to be treated like they did him. I was supposed to protect him, and someone killed him. It's my fault he's dead." He wept anew.

When he was again under control, Turner asked, "If he told Tresca it was over, and he was throwing him out, maybe he got angry and wanted to kill Tim."

"Tresca doesn't have the balls."

"You know him?"

"Tim told me all about him. And all of them. Everything."

"Is this your house or his?"

"It's in my name. He'd give me money sometimes, always cash, for bills and things." He gave them a defiant look. "I wasn't a whore. He loved me."

"Who do you think killed him?" Turner asked.

"I'm betting it was all of them. Tim was afraid of Bruchard and Duggan. He had the goods on them. We used to laugh about it in bed. Sometime over the past weekend, he was supposed to meet with Duggan, Bruchard, and Tresca."

"For what?" Turner asked.

"I think a pretty normal planning session. Normal for them."

Turner wondered if that meeting had taken place and if so what the hell all these guys were up to.

"You were seen banging on the door of the condo last week."

"I had a key for the parking garage, but not an up to date one for the condo. Besides, I could never be there when he wasn't because Tresca might show up. I went that day because I was worried about him."

"Why?"

"I think he was in danger from these people. The lock is like one of those in hotels. He had it changed periodically. He hadn't gotten me my updated one by then."

Fenwick asked, "Did he leave records of his investigations here?"

"Yeah. He was always careful. He didn't trust those people. I never looked at the stuff, but I can show you." Gorman reached in his pocket, came out with a zip drive, and handed it to him. "He made a copy for me. He didn't trust Bruchard or Duggan. He was afraid of them. I warned him that those guys were dangerous. I tried to protect him." He shook his head, pointed to the zip drive. "I think it's all on there."

Along with the new data, they took him back to the station. On the way, Gorman kept repeating, "It's so good to finally have someone to talk to."

In a rare interval when Gorman was not dithering and babbling, Turner wondered if Kappel was maybe planning to break up with Gorman, not Tresca, or maybe both of them.

At the station Turner tried the zip drive on his computer. It was password protected. Gorman didn't know the password. Kappel had always told him, it was better he didn't know. Not telling him was designed as a protection for Gorman from the wrath of any clerics who thought he might know some of Kappel's secrets.

Fong worked his magic at Turner's desk for half an hour while Fenwick and Turner filled in Molton, then called for take-out for Gorman, Fong, and themselves.

When Fong broke the password, data flooded out. Some they had. Lots of it came from investigations from years and years before. Gorman could confirm only some of the more recent items. They spent hours with him, going over everything he could remember and all the records Kappel had left with him. They included more names, dates, times, details. On the spreadsheet columns and rows were added and cells expanded. Not only did they now have complete records of his investigations, and with the stuff from Gorman, even more of his personal records as well. At times they had to revise what they had or new information caused connections to be posited between events that hadn't been connected before.

At one point while Gorman was in the washroom, Fenwick said, "Kappel had over a million in investments and a million more in CDs in banks."

"Gives a new meaning to the word poverty."

"And he loved this big, heavy-set guy?"

"Madge loves you."

"Touché."

By six Molton brought the State's Attorney to look at their chart. He offered advice and suggestions.

Turner and Fenwick consulted with Molton before they let Gorman go. "He the killer?" Molton asked.

Turner said, "We've got no evidence, nothing to hold him on. He's been more cooperative than those religious men who were closest to Kappel. He said he was at the farm at the time of the murder."

Gorman was given a ride back to the farm by a uniformed cop.

The detectives spent two hours on the new information. When they were done with reports, forms, and adding everything to their chart, they gazed at the beautiful, well-ordered spreadsheet and their mound of paperwork.

Molton joined them in front of the large screen. "It's nigh onto perfect."

Fenwick groused. "Yeah, well, we ain't got a killer."

Turner said, "So Kappel had everything on all of them. All they'd done, all the financial chicanery, personal peccadilloes, and more. They were crooks on a large scale. Nothing says they were killers."

Fenwick said, "Too many suspects."

"We've got to talk to some of these people again."

In the next few hours, even with Molton's help, they were unable to get in touch with any of the principals in the case. A visit to the high rise and to the Abbey and the chancery didn't get them past any front doors.

Back at Area Ten around ten, they were all gathered at the huge monitor: Turner, Fenwick, Fong, Molton, Wilson, Roosevelt, and Rodriguez.

"This just looks so great," Fong said.

Fenwick repeated, "Yeah, but it hasn't gotten us a killer."

"Can't have everything," Fong said.

Wilson said, "But that nun Sister Eliade was right, on some of these Kappel was letting them go."

Roosevelt said, "Some maybe for kind, gentle reasons." He used the wireless mouse to point to several squares in the chart. "Some because he wanted to use the information."

"Complicated man," Molton said.

"Aren't we all?" Roosevelt asked.

Wilson said, "Except those of us who are complicated women."

Fenwick flopped into his chair. "Gazing at that thing doesn't get us closer to a killer. We already had enough motives for killing before we met Gorman. And we've got a lot more details on the lives of these people."

Everyone except Molton left their desk area. The Commander said, "I've been on the phone with the State's Attorney and various politicians. They may not have friends in high enough places, but the Church still has expensive lawyers and enough clout to put up a huge wall. I'll keep working on it."

Turner asked, "How long are they going to take for all these legal people to get these guys?"

Molton said, "I don't know. They probably don't know. With

the Feds involved, State of Illinois Attorney General's office, Cook County State's Attorney, half the damn planet. They may be arguing over who gets to do what for a long time before they get to who is going to arrest what powerful prelate for what insidious crime."

Turner asked, "I Googled cardinals in the US. I couldn't find a case of any of them being arrested."

Fenwick said, "Screw this financial stuff. We don't have a killer. Are they going to screw up our case?"

Molton said, "I wasn't aware we had a case against someone."

Fenwick swallowed a protest. This was the boss after all.

Molton said, "I'll let you know what the attorneys are up to. You've both got the day off tomorrow. Take it. You've been working twelve hour days. Do not come in tomorrow. The corpse won't care, and if one of these guys is the killer, he's not going to be able to leave town. Exhaustion on one case isn't going to help do justice to all the other criminals in the city."

Turner and Fenwick left.

FORTY-SEVEN

Wednesday 11:00 P.M.

Mrs. Talucci stood on her porch. One arm rested on the porch rail, the other clutched the top of her cane. She leaned forward and glared into the night.

As soon as Paul closed his car door, he heard her thump her cane onto the porch. She called, "Paul."

He walked over, climbed the porch, and looked down at her. She quivered with anger.

"Rose, what's wrong?"

"Did you hear?"

He offered his arm. "Do you want to sit down?"

"I'm going to stand here until I have a stroke or until the world responds to the way I expect it to work, and that better be pretty damn fast."

"What's happened?"

She looked up at him. Paul heard the screen door on his home slam shut. He saw Ben glance in their direction and hurry over. Up close, he could tell his husband was upset.

"What's wrong?" Paul asked.

Mrs. Talucci said, "You better tell him."

"Word flew through the school and the neighborhood about the latest news about Shane."

"Is he okay?"

Ben said, "Yeah. It's his baseball coach. That's why he tried to commit suicide. The coach found out he was gay and tried to get the university to drop the kid's scholarship."

"What the hell difference does it make to him?" Paul

demanded.

Mrs. Talucci said, "I don't know when I've been this angry. I'd best sit down."

They helped her to a porch chair. Paul assisted as she fussed with the summer shawl around her shoulders. Paul and Ben leaned their butts against the porch railing. Paul could feel Ben's arm touching his.

Ben said, "Brian confirmed the rumor to me earlier. He was really angry."

"Is he okay?"

"He wanted to go over to Shane's but it was late. They texted, and Brian said Shane was okay."

"What's Shane going to do?" Paul asked.

Mrs. Talucci snorted. "Hah!" She thumped her cane against the floor. She said, "I'm on the parish school committee. This will be settled by noon tomorrow."

She eased back in her chair and took up her knitting. She was making a shawl for her oldest great-granddaughter. In the silence Ben and Paul observed the street and listened to night noises.

FORTY-EIGHT

Wednesday 11:30 P.M.

Paul tapped on Brian's door. He heard the soft, "Yeah." Paul entered. Brian had the lights off and his window open to the soft night. Moonlight streamed into the room.

Paul asked, "You okay?"

"I had a chance to talk with Shane a little bit. I wished he'd have told me about the coach."

"It can be tough when it looks like all your dreams are being shattered."

"Yeah, I'd like to be at the first game of the first gay pro baseball player who comes out."

"Me, too," Paul said. "Mrs. Talucci promised to take care of the problem with Shane's coach."

Brian smiled. "I'd never cross her."

In their room, after he talked with Ben about Brian and Shane, his husband said, "There's other news. I think the course of true love has not run true for Jeff."

"What happened?"

"Yesterday's sort of, not really date?"

"Yeah."

"Well, he was moping around here before dinner. I asked what was wrong. He said he saw Ardis after school having ice-cream with Arvin."

"How does that mean they aren't dating?"

"Well, you know how it is in junior high. Jeff and Ardis weren't officially, really, committed to each other, exclusively dating, and I guess for whatever reason exclusively sharing ice cream after school, in their world, has become the definition of true love. So it's over."

"After one not really much of a date."

"I'm afraid so."

In bed as he pulled Ben into his arms, he said, "I love you so much."

Ben said, "I love you too."

Forty-nine

Thursday 7:02 A.M.

Paul was helping Jeff make Eggs Florentine the next morning. He said, "Ben told me things didn't go well with Ardis."

Jeff sliced an English muffin in half, placed both ends in the toaster slots, and shoved down the handle.

"She's not very good at chess," was the boy's only comment.

That evening was the prom. There was no school and all Brian's finals were over. The teen ran chores to pick up his tux and the corsage. He spent an inordinate amount of time texting. Paul didn't ask about what. He hadn't asked that question since the boy was in sixth grade. Paul managed to catch an hour's nap while the boy was out.

Molton called with the news around three that he'd made no progress getting through the Church walls. In the vernacular, they'd all lawyered up. Molton also reported, "A number of people have spent hours with that spreadsheet you've made. Especially the Cook County State's Attorney."

Turner took a guess. "He doesn't like Vern Drake."

"It seems that in the last election our Vern endorsed the current State's Attorney's opponent and was the biggest donor to that opponent's campaign. The current State's Attorney is not Vern Drake's best friend. He's had a team in here. The FBI's had a team in here. Hell, we even have a new copier."

"How'd that happen?"

"Everybody wants copies of everything, hard copies and electronic copies. They tried using our machine. Ha! Within half an hour they wheeled in a brand new one. I'm told we get to keep it."

"Maybe there are miracles. Are they going to arrest all these people?"

"Layers of lawyers on both sides. Remember, our guys are just getting all this information. Any number of people may be indicted in any number of jurisdictions. It's a mess, and the Church's lawyers have been in making demands."

Turner sighed. "But still no killer."

FIFTY

Thursday 6:00 P.M.

Brian was in his tux. Jeff was taking pictures. Because the number of venues were finite and the number of proms in the Chicago area were legion, proms quite often were on nights other than Friday or Saturday, especially if one wanted a particularly popular venue.

One of Jeff's sets of expertise was taking digital pictures. The first one he took that night when Brian came down the stairs in his tux was one of the teenager between his two dads. They got one of Jeff on his crutches with Brian, and then Jeff set up the camera with a timer and got all four of them.

Paul watched the limousine with Brian move off down the street. He and Ben held hands. Jeff took a picture of that as well. Paul felt his eyes get misty. Jeff swung around on his crutches. "I wonder who I'll take to the prom." He moved off to his room.

Paul and Ben stood on the porch, and watched the limousine glide onto Taylor Street.

After a few minutes of companionable silence, Ben asked about the case. They sat in the swing on the porch in the soft light of evening and Paul filled him in.

When he finished, Ben said, "I think the situation is sad. Their world is crumbling, and it's going to die, and there's little they can do or are willing to do to stop it. That must be very frustrating. It may not be a relevant world, and it may be and is mean spirited and cruel in many ways, but it's all they've known."

"Except when they molest little kids."

"I'm not talking about the criminal parts. Of course, that's awful. I'm talking about those who genuinely believe in a gentle Jesus, and those who care for and try to help those that they serve. Their world is going to be gone too."

"Maybe some bits will be saved."

"It'll all come crashing down, the good with the bad," Ben said. "What I don't get, is what do they get for all this?"

"What do you mean?"

"Well, they run around like mad things, plotting and conniving, and evening the score, and investigating, but what do they get?"

Paul said, "Kappel got a fancy condo."

"Which he had to share in secret with a man he sort of loved."

"Maybe there wasn't enough ever for them to have. Maybe they just fed the acquisitive impulse. Maybe feeding it was what they needed. It was the feeding, not the fullness."

"That sounds more plausible than I'd care to believe."

Mrs. Talucci came out on her porch and waved them over.

"Did you hear?" she asked. "Brian and Shane's baseball coach quit."

"What happened?"

Mrs. Talucci shrugged. "I asked to meet with him. Here, for a cup of tea."

"What happened at the meeting?"

"Nothing. He never showed up. I got word a few minutes ago that he quit his coaching job and his teaching job."

Turner knew real power when he heard it. It was always best when a person complied without any threat. Next best was making the threat but never having to carry it out. But if you were afraid to go to a meeting at which a threat could possibly be made, the person calling the meeting had real power. That's what Mrs. Talucci had.

Paul said, "I wonder if a coach and a college team will be any less homophobic."

Mrs. Talucci shrugged. "Alas, over that I have no control. The scholarship is safe, after that, with luck, Shane's success will depend on his ability and nothing else."

He filled her in on the case.

All she said about it was, "They are sad people. As human as the rest of us. It's such a shame so many of them don't understand that."

Back in his house, Paul thought of turning on the television, but all that were on were crime shows or contestant shows that he either laughed at or found boring. He thought he might pick up a book when his cell phone rang. The ID said it was Ian.

"They're all here," Ian said.

"All who where?"

"I'm upstairs at the Abbey. The newly disgraced Cardinal, the desperate Abbot, the vicious bishop Pelagius, the unbelievable prick Drake, and the pathetic Tresca."

"Why would I care?"

"They're fighting. They're guilty."

"They invited you in?"

"I'm with Demarco. We're hidden."

"What good will it do me to be there?"

"You don't want to talk to them?"

"Very much."

"Well, here they all are."

"I'll call Fenwick. This is different from the coffee house the other day. This is going to be an official visit." After calling Fenwick, he let Molton know what was going on. The Commander told him to keep him updated.

FIFTY-ONE

Thursday 7:35 P.M.

Fenwick parked in a tow zone on North Avenue. Ian and Demarco met them at the far corner of the property at the small park at the corner of North and Milwaukee.

"What are they doing?" Turner asked.

"Arguing," Demarco said."

"About what?"

"Everything," Ian responded.

"They'll still be there when we get in?"

Ian shrugged. "We won't find out until we get there."

Demarco said, "I can get you a seat where you can see and hear everything, but we'll be hidden."

They followed Ian and Demarco through the grounds. Turner walked next to Ian. The detective said, "You know your way through here."

"When you're diddling with a semi-closeted priest, you do all kinds of things you didn't think you'd ever do again."

Turner said, "You're in love."

Demarco whispered back at them, "Hush."

They walked around the rear of the buildings. The path here was crushed stone. Few lights shone in the downstairs of the Abbey dormitory. They came to an entrance in the section that connected the dorm to the immense medieval-looking sections of the complex.

Once inside in a small hall, Demarco said, "They're in the nave." He led them up several flights of stairs.

Demarco brought them to the choir loft in the rear of the

church. They crouched down and peered over the railing. Ian was on Turner's right, Fenwick and Demarco to his left. The five men they were observing were grouped near the center aisle, halfway between the altar and their perch. Pelagius and Duggan sat next to each other on the left. Bruchard sat across from them. Tresca paced on the altar side of them and Drake leaned against the pillar on the side nearest to the choir loft.

Ian put one hand over his mouth and whispered, "Well, well, well, a gaggle of horsemen with their own special apocalypse." Demarco put a hand out and leaned down near the ground and turned his head slightly in their direction. "Be careful. The sound carries."

Turner found Demarco was right about the acoustics. They could hear every word. Turner saw Ian take out his smart phone. Ian always had the most up-to-date technological marvel with him. He set it between two pillars of the choir railing and pressed record. Turner heard him mutter, "Eat your heart out, Mitt Romney."

Cardinal Duggan was saying, "Those detectives are relentless. I don't like them. We can't get at them."

Bruchard sat forward. "I thought you had power in this town."

Duggan shot back. "You always claimed you were the big shot."

Bruchard spat back. "Now that you're a drag queen, you're nobody."

"As always," Duggan said, "you bring up examples that have no logical connection to reason or the topic." He pointed an accusatory finger at Bruchard. "You're the one who bankrupted the Order. Kappel had proof."

"And you were going to use it against me? To do what?"

The two men were on their feet. Bruchard screamed, "You had him killed, you son of a bitch."

Duggan bellowed right back. "He was a good man, you fucker. You knew he was on to you. He knew you were going down."

Bruchard now waved his fist in the Cardinal's face. "Like all the times you went down on him?"

"No less the number of times you grabbed your ankles and turned your butt up to him."

Bruchard lowered his voice. "He had everything on you, you son of a bitch. He knew what you'd been doing with the finances. You really didn't think anyone would catch on after that cemetery fiasco?"

"You want a list of what you did?" Duggan asked.

"Where are all these lists?" Drake said. "They've got stuff on me too."

"They've got a huge chart in their squad room," Duggan said.

"How do you know that?"

"Some idiot named Carruthers is a good Catholic although not a very good source."

"Did your source make copies?"

"I don't know how competent he is. He feels guilt, but he's not too bright."

Turner knew that a reckoning with Carruthers about this would be in order on a day and a time in the very near future.

Tresca stopped pacing and spoke. "I knew he was going to dump me so I did what you wanted. I got the information that he had. You made promises to me. I expect them to be fulfilled."

Pelagius snorted. "Don't be absurd. Everybody seems to have all the information now. All promises are irrelevant in light of the murder. Did you kill him?"

"Now who's being absurd? I loved him."

"The question is," Pelagius asked, "can we limit the damage?"

They all looked at him.

"You have all screwed up. Rome is not pleased."

Duggan gave him a shrewd look. "You were here before Kappel died. You came with that message. You and Kappel have been conspiring all this time."

Pelagius cleared his throat. "Be thankful Bishop Kappel existed." He pointed at Duggan. "He got you your job as Cardinal." He swung his finger toward Bruchard. "And you your job as Abbot."

Bruchard said, "There was an election. The Order voted for me."

Pelagius chuckled and waved an effeminate hand. "You don't think we know how to rig the Italian vote? There are still more Italians in the Order than from any other country. We could have out-voted you. And you did get to be in charge and live here. Now there's a concession. The first head of the Order in seven hundred years who wasn't an Italian. You think that's an accident? It was all planned and orchestrated."

"Ha!" Duggan snorted.

Pelagius turned on him. "Just like your Cardinalate was part of the plan."

"What plan?"

"Kappel wanted to be a Cardinal in Rome. He's been monitoring the Order and the Catholic Church in America for years. How do you think he got appointed to all those investigations? Trust me, it is not because of the influence and charm of you two incompetent fools."

Bruchard snapped. "I wasn't afraid of an old woman with a video."

"I'm not afraid," Duggan said.

"That's right," Bruchard said, "the worst about you is known. You only have to attempt to clean up a mess before they transfer you to some quiet job in the third sub-basement of the Vatican. You're an embarrassment."

Drake waved his arms. "Forget the rest of this bullshit. Who is this new guy they found? The burly guy who lived out in Morris, Gorman. Did he have copies?"

Pelagius said, "I think so. My source was not available today."

Turner wondered if Carruthers had switched sides, gotten a conscience, realized whose side he was supposed to be on.

Bruchard turned on Tresca. "Why didn't we know about him?"

"How the hell should I know?"

Now Drake was pacing. "I don't want anything to do with you people. I'm not involved in murder. I think I better call my lawyer." He took out a cell phone.

Pelagius said, "If you want us to help save your career, you'd better listen for a while."

Drake hesitated.

"Listen to what?" Tresca asked. "Are you taking us all to Rome tonight in a private jet?"

"That could be arranged, I suppose, but we shouldn't need anything that dramatic, but it would help to know which of you ordered him murdered." His voice was calm as his eyes flitted from Bruchard to Duggan.

The church officials pointed at each other.

Pelagius said, "Who did you order to take care of it?"

Both clerics looked at Tresca.

The bishop began backing away. "You are not going to pin this on me. I just did what you told me to do."

Pelagius smiled. "So you both wanted to eliminate him. Well, well, well."

Drake whispered, "Are you guys all nuts?"

Turner thought this was an excellent question.

Fenwick whispered to him, "Do you smell smoke?"

Turner moved his head slightly in Fenwick's direction. He drew in a breath. "Not re…" He looked up, nudged Fenwick's arm, pointed up. "Is that smoke?"

Fire alarms began to clang and whine.

FIFTY-TWO

Thursday 8:46 P.M.

Ian grabbed his phone. The four of them scrambled out of the choir loft and down the stairs. Turner saw flames in the direction from which they'd entered. They hurried in the opposite direction toward the transept. They ran into the others in the nave.

"Not that way," Fenwick yelled. "There's fire back there."

They ran toward the altar. Flames and smoke filled the exit they used to go to Bruchard's office Saturday night.

Pelagius yelled, "We're all going to die." The chance of dying was what it took to move the prelate from his pseudo-suave manner.

Demarco said, "This way."

He led them to a confessional booth, opened the central door, and slipped inside. "Through here," he called back.

Most of them had to turn sideways to get through. The detectives let the civilians slip into the narrow opening.

Duggan turned at the entrance. "We should save the paintings!"

"Screw the paintings." Bruchard tried to shove him forward. "They aren't your personal property. Besides, they're all fake. And they're insured."

"That's insurance fraud."

Bruchard grinned. "Yes, I know."

"You set the fire?" Duggan yelled.

"Are you mad? I've been with you."

"You could have ordered it."

"Not while I'm inside, you moron. Get moving." He shoved him again.

Duggan stumbled and fell. Bruchard stepped on him in his rush to get out, but his ankle twisted and he fell on top of the prelate.

Turner and Fenwick untangled them, helped them up. When everyone else was out of the transept, Fenwick started through. Turner looked back. Flames had caught on the pews and were licking up some of the wooden trusses.

Demarco was on the other side. He pointed the way to go. In moments they were outside.

In the courtyard, fire trucks and lights filled the lawn and parking lot. An odd scene played out as Turner stumbled through the door. Ian was on top of Tresca. The bishop was squirming and struggling. Duggan and Bruchard were trying to rip Ian off of Tresca. Pelagius slapped at the mêlée ineffectually. Prelates went flying as Fenwick waded in. Demarco stood aside. The other religious leaders' screams were lost in the cacophony of the building conflagration and the accumulating apparatus to fight it.

"What the hell is going on?" Fenwick demanded. Ian had Tresca's right wrist up against the middle of his back. Every time Tresca attempted to struggle, he twisted the wrist and tried to yank it higher on his back. Tresca gave up trying to get free and began shouting to be let go.

Fenwick had his arms wide holding back any intervention by the angry prelates.

Turner saw that Ian had blood on his lip. Red oozed from Tresca's nose.

Breathing heavily, Ian responded to Fenwick's question. "He tried to run. I tackled him. He seemed to think making a mad dash away from us was a good idea. I felt like stopping him. I decided not to be gentle."

Duggan said, "He gang-tackled him. Let him go."

Fenwick ignored him. Fire personnel swirled around them,

directing their group away from the buildings. When they got to the street, Fenwick found a group of uniformed officers. He pointed to Tresca. "Cuff him. Take him to the back of a squad car."

Fenwick ignored all the prelates' protests.

Turner told the next few uniformed cops, two of whom were Sanchez and Deveneaux, "Keep these guys in one place." He indicated Pelagius, Drake, Bruchard, and Duggan. "Don't let them leave."

Fenwick added, "If they try anything, cuff them too."

Pelagius got in Fenwick's face. "I have diplomatic immunity."

Fenwick asked, "Do I look like the kind of guy who gives a shit about that right now?"

A group of priests, Turner presumed from the Abbey, stood half a block away inside the police perimeter but outside the walls of the grounds. They gesticulated and pointed towards their high ranking colleagues, but none of them moved closer.

The uniformed cops got Tresca into the back of a cop car. They surrounded the remaining clerics and Drake with a cordon of officers. They put Sanchez in charge.

They left the bellyaching clerics and headed back toward the burning Abbey. Turner noted the representatives of the church avoided getting near any of the crush of television vehicles and reporters standing half a block away behind the police line.

As Turner, Fenwick, and Ian walked toward the fire, the reporter dabbed at his still-oozing lip.

FIFTY-THREE

Thursday 9:15 P.M.

North Avenue was completely blocked off. They joined the battalion chief twenty feet up the Abbey driveway. Three huge Halogen lights from the fire vehicles lit the building. Turner, Fenwick, and Ian stood to the side of a fire engine out of the way of the firemen.

A line led from one hydrant up the front steps and through the front door. Several trucks were clustered near the chapel.

Moments later, the lights inside the Abbey went dark. A second later emergency lights dimly shone. They were dwarfed by the glow from the fire department apparatus. Turner asked one of the lesser chiefs standing with them, "Did everyone get out safely?"

The incident chief, a short squat guy said, "We managed to do a primary search of the dorms. They're not on fire, but they've been evacuated. The fire must have started in this medieval section. It's caught good. We couldn't get far in."

Seconds later, Ian pointed and shouted, "There's some poor son of a bitch on that second story balcony."

Everyone looked. Fully lit by the encroaching flames one level above the gothic entrance, a man stood with his arms outstretched. He was on the mansion tower.

The battalion chief issued commands. "Get a ladder over there." Men were already moving. It took thirty to forty-five seconds for a ladder to be placed up against the building.

The ladders against the building only reached to the second story. The person on the balcony watched the activity for a moment then reached over to the side of the balcony and began to climb higher.

The battalion chief shouted, "Get a truck ladder over there. What the fuck is he doing?"

"Is it too hot?" Ian asked. "Maybe he's trying to climb to safety."

"Another few seconds and we'd have had him from that balcony."

Turner said, "It's Graffius."

Fenwick peered intently. "Yeah." He shaded his eyes to try and get a better look. "How's the old guy climbing?" The incident commander who stood with them said, "I did the inspection on this place. That tower he's on? I checked it inside and out." He jabbed a finger at where, with obvious difficulty, the old man swung a foot onto a third floor balcony and eased himself onto it. For now there was no fire in the windows behind him. "See those iron things protruding out?"

Turner had seen Graffius's hands clutching onto them as he climbed. "Those things were put in when the place was built. The original owner was worried about fire in the tower. Those things are in there solid. They knew how to build back then. Even the doors and the floors between them are "fire rated." The fire's caught good, but it will take a little while to get that high in the tower. We should have time to get to the guy."

Turner remembered Graffius's mention of welcoming death. Maybe the old guy wanted to die. Maybe he even set the fire.

"Why don't the firemen use those handholds?" Ian asked.

"Can't get to them. The whole ground level is on fire."

None of the fire trucks were parked next to the building. Turner knew this was because they didn't know if the walls would collapse, or if in collapsing if the concrete would fall inward or outward. The ladder truck was not closest to the tower so it took several minutes for other vehicles to be moved so it could be maneuvered into position.

Pads swung out from the truck so it would be stabilized when the ladder began to rise. All of this took more precious seconds.

Now Turner could see flames in the room behind Graffius's third floor perch.

Finally, the longer ladder began to be deployed. Outriggers anchored it to ground, pads two feet by two feet. Graffius saw this ladder and climbed higher.

The fire alarms inside cut off as did the emergency lights. Turner knew a main line or main switch must have been destroyed by the rapidly moving fire. With all that aged wood, he presumed the whole place would go.

Minutes later the longer ladder was in position. The old man managed to move to the balcony next to the one he was on and then to the next higher floor.

Turner said, "He wants to die."

"He set the fire?"

"A fairly sane guess at this moment."

In the midst of the noise from the crackling flames, the shooting water, the firemen's cries, and the rumble of the diesel engines of the trucks, they could hear a faint voice.

"Is he calling for help?" Fenwick asked.

Graffius was shouting and gesticulating, but it was difficult to make out the words.

Fenwick asked, "What's he saying?"

Graffius had his hands up and was staring at the distant stars. They could hear a faint chant. "It's Latin," Turner said. "I think maybe Salve Regina."

Fenwick said, "Reminds me of Urfried the Hag in *Ivanhoe*."

Ian snapped, "Her name was Ulrica."

Fenwick snapped back. "It's Urfried when she sets fire to the castle of those who have kept her captive to destroy them all. She was chanting some ancient Celtic song as the flames took her."

"You cannot know that," Ian snarled. "Besides, it was a Latin chant."

"You can quote the first line Bette Davis said in every one of her movies, but I can't know a literary reference?"

"Yours is more obscure than mine."

Fenwick muttered, "Yeah, well, mine's bigger than yours."

Ian's gaze swung from Graffius to Fenwick. "How the hell do you know such a literary reference? Or are you making that up?"

"I'm not just a poet. I read Classic Comic books as a kid. I always thought that was a cool scene, a great way to get even."

"Good to know you're up on all this revenge shit."

"From Shakespeare to the morning news."

Turner didn't take his eyes away as the ladder approached Graffius, but the priest began to climb again. Maybe when he reached the top, they could get to him. He said, "That man wants to die. Poor old thing." He sighed. "And it was an ancient Scandinavian scald not in Latin or ancient Anglo-Saxon, and she was introduced in chapter 24 as Urfried, but is Ulrica as the castle burns."

Fenwick and Ian gaped at their friend.

Again, the firemen began to move the ladder toward where they presumed Graffius would be on the fourth balcony. Several firemen were on the roof and were, perhaps, waiting for the old priest to climb that high.

A young fireman rushed up to the battalion chief, who immediately yelled, "Get those men off the roof. The whole thing is going to collapse." A second ladder truck was maneuvered next to the first. This took less time as ladders had been presumed to be needed. The ladder headed straight to the roof.

Fenwick asked, "How the hell do you know that, or are you making it up?"

Turner said, "The world is burning down and crashing around these people, and only you two get to know obscure literary references? Besides, I had to read the damn book in eighth grade as a punishment. It was a true punishment, but I read the damn thing."

"What on earth were you in trouble for?" Ian asked.

"I'd turned in the same book report on the same book for five straight months. We owed the teacher one a month. She hadn't noticed my deception. I think she was embarrassed she missed what I'd done. She may have been as pissed at herself as at me. She never told my parents, but she got even. I had to stay after school for weeks and read *Ivanhoe*, the whole thing. I couldn't go home until I summarized everything I'd read that day. So at least I've got an excuse for knowing that nonsense."

They watched the fire department ladder as it neared the fourth balcony. As the aged priest saw it approach, he stopped chanting and began climbing toward the fifth floor. Flames were coming out of the windows above and below him.

Turner saw and heard firemen shouting up to him to hold on. Other shouts were for the firemen on the roof to get down now. The old man planted his feet on the balcony he'd reached and began pointing and shrieking.

Turner caught only occasional words. It wasn't Latin or anything else. He heard, "Traitors. Cowards." And little else. The glass behind Graffius burst outward. The flames took hold on his cassock. His shouting turned into a shriek, but he gripped the side of the end of the wall where it met the balcony, and he did not let go. Moments later, with a last horrific cry, flames engulfed him.

The firemen on the roof climbed down the ladder that had reached them. After another fifteen seconds, the roof collapsed with a roar.

FIFTY-FOUR

Thursday 11:35 P.M.

At Area Ten headquarters two hours later the assembled prelates had clots of lawyers with them. A representative of the Mayor's office stood with Molton. Those two drank coffee and chuckled.

Turner and Fenwick wrote reports, added bits to their spreadsheet.

Cardinal Duggan and Abbot Bruchard sat in separate interview rooms of the station. Turner eyed them both through the one-way mirrors. Duggan looked like he'd been rode hard and put away wet. He made demands and was ignored. For a prelate to be in a common police station must have been driving him just about nuts. Bruchard stood and stormed and stammered. Pelagius sat with his hands folded over his substantial stomach. A smile occasionally played across his face. Any time any person he did not know got into his presence, he began murmuring about diplomatic immunity.

They and their lawyers demanded to leave.

Drake and his cell phone seemed wedded to each other until his attorney showed up. They talked together at a furious pace.

Tresca sat alone in another interview room. He had his head down, his elbows on his knees, his hands gripped together. Other than his breathing, Turner didn't think he moved more than an inch. Early on, Turner commented to Molton, "Tresca needs to be on a suicide watch." The Commander had agreed.

Around eleven thirty, Ian called from outside. With the swarm of reporters around the front of the station, they met in their usual quiet spot in the Area Ten parking lot. As promised, Ian had a copy of his recording from the Abbey. Turner met him outside, took the copy and said, "Thanks for your help." He handed Ian a zip drive, which contained a copy of their spreadsheet.

"What's this?" Ian asked.

"You might want to get together with your friend, Tyrone Bruno. I emailed him so he expects a call. You'll want to share what's on that. It'll keep his paper in headlines for a long time. It should give you a few as well, although I'm not sure there's a major gay angle to this."

"Ah. And I didn't get this from you?"

"I've never seen you before in my life."

"That would be your loss, I think." Ian smiled. "Just to let you know, within a very short time, that tape is going to be on the Internet, and, I believe, CNN."

Turner smiled then returned to the station. He and Fenwick played the recording for Molton first. Molton said, "This was taped by one of the people involved in the conversation, but with the consent of people involved?"

"It wasn't taped by the people in the conversation."

"They're going to want to know who taped it."

"Ian."

Molton knew Ian. Didn't like him but thought he was a good reporter. Turner said, "I think what it will do is give us leverage here tonight. In court? I'm not sure."

Turner asked, "The whole question of admissibility will be kind of moot in a very short while."

Molton guessed. "Ian's going to blast it to the rest of the universe."

Turner nodded.

Then they played it for a crowd of representatives from the offices of the FBI, Homeland Security, and the State's Attorney.

Several people asked, "Is it admissible? Who did the taping?"

Molton repeated Turner's notion. "At the very least, it's leverage."

Turner and Fenwick entered the interview room with Tresca in it. A representative from the State's Attorney's office, Jane Folbe, accompanied them. She stood to the side.

The priest's lawyer, Judson Giles, was an old man in his seventies. The others all had teams of helpers, Tresca just the one.

"We should talk," Fenwick said.

"I have advised my client to remain silent."

Fenwick said, "You may want to rethink that. You might get a deal tonight you wouldn't get tomorrow."

The lawyer sneered. "I doubt that."

Turner placed his laptop on the table. Fong had already made digital duplicates of the recording. Turner let the computer play.

"This was obtained illegally," were the attorney's first words when it was done.

Folbe outlined the deal they would offer Tresca for his testimony against Duggan and Bruchard, along with anything else he knew.

Giles said, "I recommend against it."

Tresca muttered, "What kind of lies do you think it's going to take to keep me from going to jail? I've lived a life of lies. This needs to end."

They left Tresca and his lawyer alone to discuss the possible deal.

At their desks, Molton joined them with Barb Dams fifteen minutes later. They had a laptop with them set to the live CNN feed.

Turner, Fenwick, and the State's Attorney interrupted Tresca and his lawyer to show it to them. Tresca started to cry.

They left attorney and client to talk. A half an hour later his attorney joined them in the hall. "You've got a deal."

They reassembled in the room.

Tresca spoke mostly to the table top. "I didn't mean for things to get so out of hand. Nothing bad was supposed to happen."

Turner knew exactly what Fenwick would say at this point if they didn't have a cooperating, confessing killer. His bulky buddy would say, "You asshole, you brought a baseball bat and planned to kill him. This is bullshit."

Both detectives knew that with someone in the emotional state Tresca must be in, it was most important that the deal didn't fall apart and that the confession be admissible.

Turner asked, "How did this all start?"

"Timothy was going to break up with me. He was going to throw me out of the condo. He fell for that fat freak." Turner glanced at his over-weight partner. Fenwick didn't bat an eye. He knew when a killer was confessing, it was time to swallow all comments.

"You knew about the other man?"

"I knew of him. I didn't know his name. Timothy would never tell me." Tresca drew ragged breaths as he talked, frequently pausing as if the emotions might be overwhelming him. Turner thought that perhaps they should have some EMTs on call.

"I was desperate. I had to do something. I knew Timothy had been doing all those investigations all those years, of course. I suspected he'd been cheating all those years, making money where he could. He also had his income from his books. I had nothing. He paid for guys. I couldn't afford them. We'd go to Key West every winter. He'd go for four weeks. He let me come for two. Sometimes he'd invite me to join him with a cute guy or two."

Fenwick said, "It wasn't like the old days when you were younger."

Tresca glanced at him briefly. "We were cute, hot, and discreet." He actually smiled for a second. "I was happy then." He sighed. "We'd get together and mock the others in the seminary, vicious drag queens arming themselves in cassocks and Christ to fuck with you, but we'd screw them, and they liked it."

Turner was annoyed with his friend for getting Tresca off track. He asked, "How'd it all come to a head?"

"Timothy and I had some terrible fights. He said he'd moved on. He didn't care that I'd have nothing. It wasn't like we could get a divorce, and I'd get spousal support or alimony. It was all his money. I'd be stuck in that Abbey with all the other losers." He pulled in several ragged breaths.

Giles, his lawyer, said, "Can we get him something to drink?"

Bottled water was provided. Tresca continued, "Both the Cardinal and the Abbot felt threatened. They came to me separately."

"Neither one knew about the other?" Turner asked.

"No. I thought of a plan how I could use them both. I wanted recognition. I wanted my place. Bishop wasn't good enough. Timothy was moving up. Pelagius promised him possibilities of the Curia in Rome. The Cardinal and the Abbot hate each other." He glanced up. "I guess you probably figured that out. They wanted all of Timothy's records on them. I would have what they had. I'd get what they wanted. They were frightened. I could use their fear. They wanted him out of the way."

"What did he have on each of them?"

"For sure financial information. I think other things as well. The Abbot has bankrupted the Order. The Cardinal was involved in huge financial dealings in the diocese. Timothy had documents proving everything."

Turner didn't let on that they had all this information from Gorman.

"How did you wind up murdering him?"

"Duggan, Bruchard, and I met. They wanted him out of the way. I was losing everything. I didn't see any other way out. I asked to meet him by the river. It's where we had all kinds of assignations in the past. We knew how to get in. He came, expecting what I'm not sure. A resolution? A final fight? I told him I wanted us to part friends."

"You acted alone?" Turner asked.

"I wanted him to suffer. I wanted him to pay for making me miserable, for forcing me to take such drastic action."

Turner kept his sigh to himself. The self-justifying killer, bishop or pawn, the tune didn't change much.

Tresca looked up at the ceiling. "That night, I got there early. Duggan, Bruchard, and I hid. Timothy was late. He was always late. As if he was the most important one to a meeting. I got angrier and angrier. His being late always pissed me off. Here it was again, and all that he was doing to me just built."

Tresca's breathing was becoming labored. His lawyer leaned close, put a hand on his shoulder. "Do you want to stop? Take a break?"

Turner wanted to scream, "Shut up, you asshole," but he remained silent.

Tresca shook his head. His breathing came under more control but wasn't close to normal, but he continued, "It's always dark there. My eyes got used to it. I saw him. He didn't know we were there. I swung at him. I used every ounce of strength I had. He screamed and fell. He tried to get up. He couldn't. I taxed him with all he'd done. He begged. He pleaded. I smashed the same knee. I shoved my hanky in his mouth to shut him up, but I knew it was a place where sound didn't carry, where people weren't around to hear. It never was."

Turner thought, you were lucky no one else decided to use that as a trysting place that night. He reflected, sometimes killers did have a sort of luck.

Tresca continued. "He was squirming and gagging. I taped his arms and ankles. I'd brought tape. I wanted to make him listen to me, to all the things he'd done wrong. I gave him chapter and verse. He got quiet. I took the gag out. I told him if he screamed, I'd kill him. He didn't scream. He begged." His breathing became so ragged, this time Turner thought he might stop him, but Tresca held up a hand. "I let him beg. And I put the hanky back in his mouth. Then I smashed his other knee. The light was dim, but I could see enough to watch the fear in his eyes. And I hit him." Thirty seconds of panting later, Tresca said, "I hit him again and again."

"What were Duggan and Bruchard doing all this time?" Turner asked.

"They encouraged me as I hit him."

"Did you bring the bat with you?"

"No, I planted it and the duct tape earlier."

"What did you do with it?"

"Threw it in the river. It was covered in…" He hung his head for several minutes.

Turner asked, "Did they hold him down?"

"We duct taped his arms to keep him from thrashing around, but after the first blow, he wasn't going anywhere. The first blow was a surprise attack. We tried to get him to give us more information. We didn't know what he had or who he told or who he was planning to tell." He sighed. "I think he was in it with Pelagius. That's why the Nuncio was in town. I think their plans were ripe to destroy Bruchard or Duggan or both. I would have helped him, but he cut me out." A few tears fell. "I would have helped."

Turner felt no sympathy for the tears. Plus with the tape and this confession, they now had the Cardinal and the Abbot on either conspiracy or accessory to murder or both.

Fenwick asked, "Why'd you faint when we told you about his death at the condo?"

"I saw my world ending. I thought you were there to arrest me. I didn't know what to do. I panicked."

Fenwick asked, "Who was that phone call from?"

"The Abbot. He told me I was a stupid fool to have opened my mouth. He told me to get you both out of there and to get over to the Abbey before you could arrest me."

Fifty-five

Friday 2:06 A.M.

They took a short break and came back and got final details from Tresca. His visit to The Last Gasp and Gulp Coffee Shop had been to give the police all kinds of other suspects to look into. He'd been the one to plan and carry out the attack on Mrs. Talucci. Tresca had said, "I knew she was the one scaring all the other people. Everybody was looking for a big, bulky guy. It was dark. I wore a heavy coat and a big hat."

Fenwick hadn't been able to control himself at that point. He'd sneered. "Getting even with a ninety-year-old woman. How brave and tough you are, you son-of-a-bitch."

Tresca had replied, "She was the one with the shotgun."

By the time they were done with Tresca, bedlam reigned inside and out of Area Ten. The chaos inside was well-ordered with lawyers in suits with desperate clerics and a politician whose career was in as many ashes as the Abbey.

Desperate deals were being attempted among numerous parties. The police personnel spent another couple hours playing the tape for the Cardinal, the Abbot, and the Papal Nuncio and their attorneys who wrangled, fought, and argued. The detectives took statements. Attorneys negotiated and offered deals.

Turner could feel the adrenalin of satisfaction of very, very rotten people taking the fall they so richly deserved. Precisely who was going to jail for how long wouldn't be worked out for a while. Turner didn't care. Down was down. He knew once you won, there was no need for a victory dance in the perpetrators face. He'd celebrate wildly if he thought the arrest of this group of fools wouldn't be replaced by another group of fools when they came into the station for their next shift.

After they'd sat at their desk writing for half an hour, Fenwick asked, "Who are these people? None of these guys strikes me as very spiritual. Guys filled with hate and pettiness, worried about job protection. They throw around words like Holy Mother Church, but they don't strike me as holy. But they are all kinds of mother-fucking assholes."

Turner said, "They may be all that. I also think this has to do with their being sad, limited, short-sighted human beings, as are we all, at least some of the time."

"He was a triple fuck asshole murderer."

"That too."

Turner said, "I feel sorry for Graffius."

Fenwick nodded. "He got his wish and perhaps some measure of revenge."

Near the end of wrapping up the paperwork, and as dawn was breaking, Fenwick tried to get Molton to agree to a perp walk with all the assembled prelates and Drake. Molton vetoed this. He thought perp walks for the press's benefit were stupid showboating. The Commander said, "They're all going to jail, or at the least, they're all going to lose everything they ever had. Their lawyers may save them, although Kappel had everything on them, and if not everything, a whole lot, and he's dead. It'll take a lot of legal time to sort everything out, but we have the murderer. We've got a solution. That's enough for me."

As Turner drove away from Area Ten, he saw the television lights out front as reporters made their remote broadcasts to all the early newscasts.

Paul parked the car and grabbed his stuff. He saw Mrs. Talucci approaching down the sidewalk. She supported herself with her cane in one hand and held a wrapped gift box in the other. He got out of the car and went to her. When he got close, he could smell the contents of the box.

Mrs. Talucci said, "I thought I'd make chocolate chip cookies for my own personal pawn of Satan."

"Fenwick will feel bad for not getting any."

She smiled. "I made another batch for him. You can pick it up for the station later. I saw on television you solved the case. Your tape was more criminal than mine, although, I'm not sure, mine might have been more fun."

FIFTY-SIX

Friday 6:12 A.M.

Paul decided to have a cookie and some milk. He headed to the kitchen. The house was quiet. He'd taken his first bite of Mrs. Talucci's confections and a sip of milk when he heard a car park in the alley. He recognized the rumble of Brian's 1965 Nash Rambler. Dawn was breaking as Brian, in his disheveled tuxedo, shirt untucked, bow tie askew, slipped in the back door.

Paul asked, "How was the Prom?"

"You're up," Brian said.

"I just got in a little while ago myself."

Brian sat at the table and looked up at his dad. "It was great."

"How was Shane?"

"We talked before the dance. We had time in the limo because we were the first two to be picked up. I arranged it that way so we could talk."

"How'd that go?"

"Good. He knows I don't want a relationship, and he knows I'm straight. It was really kind of flattering." He got up, took a bottle of yellow goo out of the fridge, and sipped. He made a face. "He thinks you guys are cool."

"How so?"

Brian sipped again. "That's not the first word that comes to mind when I think of you guys, cool."

"What's the first word?"

Brian didn't hesitate. "Dad."

Paul smiled. He offered Brian one of Mrs. Talucci's cookies. The boy wolfed it down, swallowed some more juice, then said, "He asked me if I'd dance one slow dance with him."

"What'd you say?"

"He said it would be the highlight of the night if I'd do that." He sipped again. "So I did."

"How was it?"

"A little odd."

"That was a kind thing to do. I'm proud of you. Did the other kids make fun?"

"No. It's not like it was the first high school dance with two guys dancing. We're both pretty big and athletic. The people I care about know I'm straight. The people I don't know, I don't care about. And I'll be gone in a few months anyway." He stood up and put the half-filled container of yellow goo back in the refrigerator. "I gotta get changed and get my stuff for the Dunes."

Paul asked, "You heard your baseball coach quit?"

"Yeah, that was a shitty thing to do to Shane. I heard the coach was supposed to meet with Mrs. Talucci, but quit first." The boy smiled. "She's a marvel."

Brian hesitated in the kitchen doorway.

"You and Ben knew something was wrong, didn't you?"

"Ben and I suspected."

"How?"

"I've known you eighteen years. I must have learned something. You weren't yourself. You were doing things you do when you're down. And we know about your stash in the garage under your sports equipment."

"You know about the candy bars?"

"We found it by accident. Just because you don't clean your room, doesn't mean we don't clean the garage."

"You guys never said anything."

"It's best not to let you discover all of our parental secrets. The key is you're okay. The prom was good. You've got a scholarship to college. And I love you."

In two strides Brian was on him and giving him a huge bear hug. "Thanks, Dad." He grabbed a couple more of Mrs. Talucci's cookies and strolled out the door.

Mark Zubro is the author of twenty-three mystery novels and five short stories. His book *A Simple Suburban Murder* won the Lambda Literary Award for Best Gay Men's mystery. He also wrote a thriller, *Foolproof*, with two other mystery writers, Jeanne Dams and Barb D'Amato. He taught eighth graders English and reading for thirty-four years. He was president of the teachers' union in his district from 1985 until 2006. He retired from teaching in 2006 and now spends his time reading, writing, napping, and eating chocolate. His newest book *Another Dead Republican*, is his thirteenth in the Tom and Scott series. One of the keys in Zubro's mysteries is you do not want to be a person who is racist, sexist, homophobic, or a school administrator. If you are any of those, it is likely you are the corpse, or, at the least, it can be fairly well guaranteed that bad things will happen to you by the end. And if in Zubro's books you happen to be a Republican and/or against workers' rights, it would be far better if you did not make a habit of broadcasting this. If you did, you're quite likely to be a suspect, or worse.

TRADEMARKS ACKNOWLEDGMENT

The author acknowledges the trademark status and trademark owners of the following wordmarks mentioned in this work of fiction:

Amazon.com – Amazon.com, Inc.

Burma-Shave – American Safety Razor Company

Chicago Bears – Chicago Bears

Chicago Cubs – Chicago Cubs

CNN – Cable News Network

Dell – Dell, Inc.

DePaul University – DePaul University

Facebook – Facebook

Google – Google Inc.

Grande Hotel – Sferra Linens

iPod – Apple Inc.

Loyola University – Loyola University Chicago

MacBook Pro – Apple Inc.

Maglite – Mag Instrument Inc.

Mercedes – Daimler AG

Monty Python – New Media Broadcasting Company Inc.

New York Times – The New York Times Company

Opus Dei – Opus Dei Information Office

Oreos – Mondelēz International.

Parnian – Parnian

Speedos – Speedo International

The Salvation Army – The Salvation Army

YouTube – YouTube, LLC

CPSIA information can be obtained at www.ICGtesting.com
Printed in the USA
BVOW08s1024201113

336821BV00001B/7/P